TRAIN ROBBERS!

Just as Cole's eyes fixed on her, the rear door burst open. Two men with dusty bandannas over their noses charged down the aisle, their pistols drawn at all the passengers. "This is a robbery!"

A shriek from the side brought all attention to a lone woman. Her black hair reminded Cole of another beauty he'd met in Colorado. The black-shirted bandit yanked at her hand. "Give us the ring."

"Oh, please, no," the woman pleaded. "It's my wedding band."

"Give it to me," said the robber, reaching into his pocket and drawing a knife. "Or I'll cut it off."

She yanked but couldn't free her hand from his firm grip. Cole sat and watched, as if he had escaped the robbers' attention. The more the tugging went on, the bigger the fire inside him rose. He was not one to volunteer to get in others' squabbles, but he couldn't help getting riled over the robber's manhandling the young lady. With the robber's back to him while the other paraded in the front of the car wagging his pistol, Cole saw his chance. He took a quick breath. The move would have to be swift and without hesitation.

He stood and took one step. Swiping his coat to the side, he drew the Colt. . . .

OUTCASTS

TIM McGUIRE

LEISURE BOOKS NEW YORK CITY

For my mom, Jeanne;
no greater lover of westerns ever lived.
I'll miss you the rest of my life.
"Sons are raised by their mothers."

A LEISURE BOOK®

November 2001

Published by

Dorchester Publishing Co., Inc.
276 Fifth Avenue
New York, NY 10001

ISBN 0-8439-4882-5

The name "Leisure Books" and the stylized "L" with design are trademarks of Dorchester Publishing Co., Inc.

Printed in the United States of America.

Visit us on the web at www.dorchesterpub.com.

Thanks to the Nez Perce Tribe Cultural Resource Center for their assistance with my words. *Danke Schon* to Hanna Webster for a few choice ones. As always, much appreciation to the readers of these stories who have contacted me with their inspiring comments. And to the *DFW Writers' Workshop*. Though I've been absent from their fold, their spirit is in every word.

OUTCASTS

$5000 REWARD

WANTED

for the assault and wounding of federal troops in Platte Falls, Colorado, on August 7, 1879; a man known as:

THE RAINMAKER

Also wanted in the shooting of a town marshal near the town of Nobility, New Mexico, on October 16, 1879. Other crimes include complicity with renegade Sioux and Cheyenne Indians leading to treason in the massacre of companies of the Seventh Cavalry led by Lt. Col. George A. Custer at the Little Big Horn River in Montana Territory June 25, 1876.

Description: Stands over six foot tall; brown hair; blue eyes; two-inch scar over right eye. Known to wear wide brim black hat and tanned hide leggings. Favors U.S. Army Colt forty-five fired with the right hand. Seen last with a Bowie knife strapped to the belt. Believed to be in Texas or Indian Territory.

Reward to be paid upon capture and delivery to the Pinkerton Detective Agency under the order of the Hon. Joshua A. Blackman, Federal Judge of Western Territories, issued this day, September 1, 1881.

Chapter One

Cackling geese flew above. Although at a clumsy angle, the birds remained consistent in their flight south. Clay Cole reined in his palomino to pause his trek through the Arbuckle forest, watched the flock, and reflected on why he was headed in the other direction.

The call of the birds faded. His eyes sagged to sight a lone juniper he had just ridden past but hardly noticed.

Simpler times came to mind. Once, when he was only a boy on a farm, life didn't seem to go by fast enough. Kansas sat on the edge of what was known. He was eager to see what folks talked about beyond the tops of the tall grass, but daily chores of slopping hogs and toting water to the house didn't leave any time to find out. The need to fend for a mother with

11

an increasing cough of the consumption and a father battling the border war made for little chance to venture more than a few steps from the fence.

Still, the dreams filling his ten-year-old head, fueled by the flickering luminance of campfires of passing Texas drovers, made him creep barefoot from the house just to lie in the grass to watch and wonder what stories were being told. He snickered at the recollection of when his ma would roust him from the covers with muddy feet and glance at the clean soles of his shoes. Without a word said, he was made aware that she knew where he had been, but left it to him to realize that his place wasn't chasing off after cattle. She could always make more of a point with a single glare than most preachers could with a morning-filling sermon.

A brown leaf falling from a cottonwood brought another memory.

The snicker was lost when he thought about how those few happy times ended with his mother's final cough. The sight of her in a pine box had come at the same time the South declared itself separate from the North. Since he didn't have any kin to take him in, the army took charge and sent him to be with his pa, who had joined the call to arms.

The dream of traveling was bittersweet. Leaving behind the single person he had shared his life with meant going to another whom he hardly knew. Captain Robert Cole was more comfortable as an officer to soldiers than as a parent to a son. Once young Clay arrived along the encampment on the banks of the Mississippi, his father's advice was to stay well behind the lines, grieve quickly, and forget he ever had a mother.

War chased the child from him. Watching the lines' daily drills made his attention lag, until a stray ball ended the life of a scraggly bearded drummer and gave Clay the chance to be in the fight. Pounding out the step allowed him the feel of battle all through the time when whiskers sprinkled his own cheeks.

Just as the experience of witnessing men collapse from the fire of shot and shell aged him, it spawned the yearning to pick up a musket and point it at another man. He was first given the chance on the last day of the war.

On a cloudy spring afternoon, surrounded by rebels and the Texas salt grass, he pulled the trigger. In that moment, his life changed forever. The panicked attempt to end an enemy's life in the name of glory only drew return fire just as his own troops waved the flag of surrender. The final shot found the chest of his father. The next two days, he watched his pa die.

Recalling that day when he became an orphan, he blinked twice and peered ahead to the barren oak before him.

Six years as a trooper taught him the ways and land of the West. However, the fond dreams he once held had only turned to the realized hardship. Friendships didn't last long, mostly due to struggles brought about by white men's claims to the long-held homelands of the redman. When words became hollow, bullets argued the outcome. Those not as lucky fell in a bloody mess to the dirt where they would be buried. Their fate taught him not to become fond of too many people. It was a lesson he practiced to this very day.

Sickened by the misery he had caused others, he tore the blue uniform from his body, never to wear the symbol of death again. Fate proved an unkind companion the many years on his own. Like a catfish chasing a hooked worm, the only way to pay for his keep was to lead the bluecoats to western prairies he had come to know so well, only to hunt those who lived there and pen them inside a faraway land where the government said they must stay.

He had been content to do as he was told, until a fateful day five years before that now had branded him an outcast. In an attempt to stop bloodshed, his actions were blamed as the cause of the worst loss of white blood in the Indian campaigns. An unwanted reputation had chased him since that day.

He sucked in a long breath and thought about his years on the run, and his decision to finally face the charges against him he had dodged for so long. The only way to clear his name was to travel to the North, where he could tell his side of the story.

The brief rest over, he took the reins and huddled his shoulders to adjust the wool-lined collar of the coat to cover his neck. Nudging the palomino, he resumed his ride. The crackle of a single gunshot made him jerk the reins. The echo circled the dense woods. Another shot focused his attention to the east. A quick grip had the Colt drawn with his thumb on the hammer. A third shot convinced him its source wasn't careless hunters, but rather the clear sign of someone in trouble. He kicked his horse's flanks and steered him through the maze of the forest.

The crowd of trees didn't allow him to get to a gallop, but the sound held him to a steady course toward where he was sure the shots had come from. Old branches snapped clear as newer sprouts whipped at his hat. The palomino leapt over a rotted log, but the speed and a sturdy limb to the chest swiped Cole off the saddle.

As he crashed to the ground, his head smacked against the hardened dirt. In a daze, he shook his head to clear his mind. Another shot rang out just above him. He rose to a crouch and chased it up a hill. Yells and screams now filled his ears as the roof of a shack over a small hill edged into view. Unsure if he would be the next target as an unwelcome intruder, he peeked to find the solitary shack tucked into the tall woods. The single window showed the unlit interior. His first guess was that it was an old miner's quarters. The squabble likely was over who owned the most ore, a common wedge that often led to a parting of the partnership. Feeling a bit foolish for following the shots that weren't his business, he looked behind to search for his fallen hat.

A woman's shriek jerked his head about. The window now showed two dark figures in a mortal embrace. The shorter of the two had hair combed back in a tail and was desperately holding the arms of the long-haired other, struggling to hold off the deathblow of the shiny blade poised above. The attacker had a ragged shirt, and a band tied around the head.

The savage was about to strike. A moment's hesitation would see the woman killed. Cole cocked the pistol, aimed at the back of the renegade, and squeezed the trigger. The blast shattered the window into falling shards. When the smoke drifted away, both figures had dropped from view.

Before he could be fired on, he charged the shack with the Colt firmly pointed in front and the hammer back. At a full gait, he slammed his boot heel against the door, crumbling the weak wood to fling it open. He swept the muzzle from left to right. On the floor lay a hefty gray-bearded man with his hair cinched in a tail, his trousers twisted around his knees. The old man coughed as his hands covered the bloody slashes in his shirt. A six-gun wisped smoke by the old man's side. Cole scanned the room. Three holes in the far wall shone beams of outside light.

To the right lay a smaller body curled on the wood. Still clutching the knife, a long-haired squaw, her long skirt ripped from the hem to the middle of the thigh, winced in pain from the bullet hole in her back.

"Oh, no," he muttered. He knelt and gently rolled her to her side. She panted like a snared wild animal. Grunting, she raised the knife, but Cole grabbed her arm to stop any thrust. Her resistance was weak, and he delicately pushed her hand back to the floor. He shook his head in an effort to show he meant no further harm, reminding himself it was his shot that had put her down. Pressing his palm against her wound brought an agonized wail. He surveyed the ramshackle room in search of any medical supplies, but all that resembled a bandage was the tattered sheet on the single cot.

He lunged to yank the sheet. Taking the knife from his belt, he sliced a strip of the cloth, then tore it the rest of the length. With one end over her ribs, he stretched the remainder around her body, slightly lifting her from the floor to encircle her body. She squealed.

"I know, I know. Be still as you can." His whisper did little to comfort her.

The loud hacking cough from the old man interrupted Cole's concentration. "Help, help me" was the ached plea. A glance at the old-timer showed there was little that could be done for him, even if Cole had a mind to help.

"You bastard. What did you do to her?"

"She's a dirty redskin" was the huffed answer. "I took her in. Her and the other one. Took her in from the cold. This is how she repays me."

Cole resumed wrapping the cloth around the squaw. "And when your idea of keeping warm didn't suit her, you started shooting, thinking that would change her mind?"

A wheezed gurgle came from the wounded man. "Hell, it weren't that way. Besides, she ain't no kid." The remark made Cole observe closer. The old man was wrong. This girl didn't look much over fifteen. Another hacked convulsion came from the old man. "Damn you, mister, help me. I'm dying. You got to help your own kind first."

"Shut up," Cole snapped. As he glanced over his shoulder at the wounded man, blood dripped from the man's mouth into a pool on the planks. Returning to see the squaw's strained breathing, he knew there was little he could do for either one. "It looks like she's killed you," he mumbled. "And I've done the same to her."

"Damn—" the old man wheezed. A bellowed cough ended with a long gush of air. Cole needed only a glimpse to notice the graybeard's body slump. A life tending to gunshot wounds told him it would be a short time before the same would happen to the Indian girl.

He looked into her glassy eyes. "Be easy now. Be still. I'll get you out of this," he said, teasing his own mind. "I'm so sorry. I'm so sorry to have done this to you. If I'd just known it was someone like him doing it to someone like you." He cradled her body and wiped the tears from her cheeks. It wouldn't be long. It was the least he could do to keep her warm. Her mumbled chants were likely her form of prayer, and it wouldn't be right for him to fill her ears with his regrets.

She dropped the knife. Slowly she raised her hand to touch his face. Her fingers probed his nose, brow, and mouth. What he first thought were her chokes and swallows of blood seemed to take shape as words. Her wavering finger pointed to the corner. A blanket slumped in a bundle lay propped against the wall. Her concern for it confused him, and he ignored her action as a sign of pained delirium. She persisted, grabbing his nose and pulling his face toward the blanket. The notion that some portion of her religion was contained in the blanket convinced him to let her go, easing her to the floor so he could retrieve the bundle.

His grip of the cloth convinced him that something sizable was inside. He unfurled the end to see an infant's face. Its eyes were closed, and he feared he had found another body. However, spotting the small nostrils flaring on an inhale of air, he exhaled a breath of relief. Like a kick from a mule, he realized all at once what she was trying to tell him. This was her young. This is what the old man meant when he said "the other one."

"Oh no," he groaned. "Don't let this be true." In one arm he lifted the blanket-wrapped baby and brought it to the squaw. With a single embrace he joined mother and child. A cracked grin of joy came over the Indian girl.

"Haatya pik'uunpa."

He leaned closer to her, not understanding what she said. His jostling awoke the slumbering baby to a protesting cry. The mother raised her trembling hand to touch her child's mouth and prodded a finger inside. With the child suckling to the mother's touch, the crying ceased. The squaw's eyes became wide and turned to Cole. He recognized the sign. Every moment would be a fight from here on in, but he didn't know what to do for her next.

Her mouth fell open. She gasped for breath. Her eyes welled with tears, leaving only a glassy stare. She could only muster a whimper, and as he clutched her closer, he felt her body soften. Her resistance was gone. With her lips to his ear, she made a last breathy utterance.

"Haatya pik'uunpa."

19

Chapter Two

The morning overcast had given way to clear sky. Having finally tethered the Indian child to the saddle horn by rope, Cole steered the palomino through the forest. Once on level ground he continued north, and with nothing in his way but prairie grass, he tried to reconcile his nagging conscience.

Although there was little choice in the rocky woods, he wasn't happy that the two graves were dug so close together. The idea that they lay in common ground gnawed at him, but it was not nearly as bad as when he had to pull the bawling child away from the mother he had killed.

The mistake was an easy one to make. He harbored no natural dislike for the Indian kind. Perhaps due to a daze caused by being thrown from the saddle, he had rashly drawn iron and fired. His intent was to save an innocent life, not take one. Yet the action had ended the breath of the young mother and orphaned the scrawny waif now slumped against his belly.

There was no place for a young one of any skin color on this trip. To turn this one loose on its own would be a bigger sin than that of the mother's killing. As the sun passed by, the monotony of hill after hill with brown grass tipping in waves from the wind kept his mind mulling over the dilemma.

Upon reaching the crest of a hill, he saw the dark figure of a structure sitting atop a distant rise. It had too large a frame to be a farmhouse, and it appeared he had come across the keepers of the Indian kind. He dipped his eyes to the black hair of the slumbering child. If he risked returning this one to its people, it could cost him his own freedom.

With one arm on the polished bar, Maud Price eyed Kate Schultz happily astride the lone customer's knee. His long hair held stringy ends draping his collar, which matched his equally droopy and untrimmed beard. His dirty chaps left little doubt that he was a cowhand.

As one of two whores in the Colossus, Maud was more than enough to satisfy the demand of the four-table cardhouse. Business had been hard to come by in a former cowtown without any rails. With only three men in the room, her rival had struck a claim to being the only one with enough youth to consummate a successful sale. Amongst the trade, interlopers weren't welcome. However, just like a buzzard, she waited for a momentary distraction to snatch away the chance to earn the bounty lying in the pockets of the young man's britches. As Kate gently stroked the cowboy's chest, whispering her jagged German words into the mark's ear, Maud's opportunity presented itself with the entrance of another outsider.

Through the doors walked a man slight in stature. Under a pale brown hat, he wore a thick brown mustache and better than a week's worth of stubble. A large red neckerchief bandanna jutted from under his chin as if it were a bib. His white shirtsleeves were rolled to the elbow, and suspenders hung from his slumped shoulders. A vest of cloth with a carpet pattern had all six buttons fastened. His gray dungarees were hemmed over the top of his muddy boots but held no chaps. A plain belt surrounded the waist where a holstered six-gun sat high on his hip.

When the stranger lighted at the bar, Maud saw her chance to go to work. By the time she casually drifted next to him, his order of a whiskey shot had already arrived. "Better drink fast before the law comes. Passed a law against spirits this year. We're still selling what we got stocked. Buy a lady one?" she asked while dipping her finger into the liquor with a ticklish swirl, then suckled the digit in her mouth and slowly drew it out. He gave the act only a glance, and she realized her ploy to advertise her wares had fallen on uninterested ears. It wasn't something she was used to, and she even felt insulted by his reaction. "What's the matter," she said in a firmer tone, "ain't you looking for a good time?"

He eyed her from head to toe, making her uneasy

when his eyes passed by her more-than-slim hips, but her confidence returned when he came to her matching bosom. A previous late night with Norman Yater, the undertaker and one of the few men in town with cash money, and the early opportunity with the drover meant she hadn't washed her face, having had only enough time to recoat her cheekbones with rouge. Her uneasiness returned when his eyes seemed to pause at her brown hair pinned in a roll. The black dye had long since faded, and she was sure brown hair gave her a plain look—not one men wanted when ready to spend money.

"I don't need you," replied the stranger.

Maud glimpsed the door. "I don't see a parade of women following you. What's the matter, honey? You married? Have a sweetheart at home? That's okay. She's probably got—"

"I said I didn't need you," he answered, pushing her shoulder with slight but firm pressure. Maud knew to take the hint. She turned, ready to resume her buzzard's perch, when his hand clutched her wrist. She twisted about, first wondering why, and next to slap his face. However, he held her hand to her side with just his eyes. There was something to his manner that told her not to strike. With a subtle tug, she was drawn to him. Thinking she had made a sale, she rubbed her shoulder to his.

"Change your mind?"

"In some ways. I figured you're a gal who sells her service. Am I right?"

She was confused by the question, seeing as she was dressed in only a thin chemise and pantaloons

23

under her nominal skirt. She had sold just about every service she knew for the last eight years. "What did you have in mind?"

"You see that fellow over there?" he whispered, nodding his head at the cowboy. Maud darted her eyes to see Kate still on the cowboy's knee, then looked at the stranger. "I'll pay you five dollars if you keep his eyes off me."

The offer didn't seem fair, but what roused her curiosity was the purpose. "Five dollars?" she asked, trying to ferret out what the stranger really wanted. "Normally a girl gets ten for her attention."

"I ain't going to dicker. I'm wanting no poke at you. Only for you to keep his hand off his side arm." Maud asked why with a curled eyebrow. "Pay no mind to that." He drew a silver dollar and slipped it into her hand. "Just do as I ask and I'll fill this with four more."

This being a slow time of year, five dollars wasn't an unreasonable sum for a job that allowed her to leave her clothes on. She turned back to the pair sitting like two starry lovers. Kate continued to rub the cowboy's chest, her hand's circle ever widening. Maud knew that Kate's hand would soon travel farther south and the chance to earn those four extra dollars would be lost. There was only one thing for a workingwoman to do.

Unsure exactly as to her tactic, she strode to the cowboy and Kate. Standing above the couple, Maud stared at her rival. Kate noticed the distraction in the cowboy's eyes, then turned her attention to Maud.

"What you want? Go away," Kate chopped out,

then sank her hand to the cowboy's crotch and resumed her insincere gaze on her mark. "This my man."

"Oh yeah," Maud replied, accepting the challenge to earn a share of the prize. She plopped down on the vacant knee. The jolt unsettled Kate's balance and spilled her to the floor. "Oh, I'm sorry, honey," Maud apologized with equal insincerity, then began stroking the cowboy's snarled whiskers. "But I'm sure your man wouldn't mind double the pleasure."

Kate scrambled to her feet, her face glowing as red as her hair. Taking only a moment to build a head of steam, Kate shoved Maud's shoulder, but the meager push didn't dislodge the larger woman. "He's mine. Find you one yourself." Returning to her previous position, Kate stuck her hands between the man's buttons. Her fingers groping his chest under the cloth shirt resembled a gopher digging a new den. The cowboy's face reflected his delight with both women vying for his attention.

Maud peeked at the stranger at the bar. His back was still turned. She was failing in her mission. She thought a bolder attempt was needed. While keeping one hand around his shoulder, Maud slid her other hand from the cowboy's face down over Kate's tunneling hand and onto the buckle of his gunbelt. Kate's giggle meant she wanted to seal the deal, and she nuzzled her nose against the cowboy's, then slurped her mouth over his. While his mind was on other matters, Maud seized the chance and nimbly plucked the leather belt through the buckle and popped the latch free. The weight of the pistol pulled the belt from his waist.

"Hey. What the hell are you doing?"

The cowboy's surprise drew Kate's attention. With Maud's hand on the buttoned fly, the German red-head's face flushed red again; she obviously assumed Maud had invaded her private territory. Another peek at the stranger still showed his back, and Maud didn't know what she was to do next, but Kate's hand snatching her hair became the primary matter on her mind.

With a growl the German girl leapt onto Maud, slamming them both to the wooden plank floor. With her brown roots screaming from the yank, Maud returned the favor, filling her hands with the red hair. Kate let out a wail and released her grip, only to drag her nails across Maud's face. The one act a second-story sister never did was scratch another's face. All thoughts of four extra dollars left Maud's mind. This was now war.

With superior strength and weight, Maud rolled Kate to the floor. A trickle of blood seeped into her lips. A fury engulfed her. She pinned Kate's shoulders with her palms. Maud prepared her own claws to leave her mark on the young German girl. Kate's face showed her fear, and a quick jab into Maud's left eye stunned the larger woman. With her own wail, Maud fell off the redhead. Kate rose to her knees, but Maud didn't want to lose the high ground. A chance glance with her right eye caught her prey's puny bust. She latched on to the top of Kate's bodice, and as the

German girl lost her balance backward, one by one each button popped from the fabric.

Too slim to need a corset, Kate's top had no support to keep from shredding. The shock of being disrobed and the cowboy's hoot at the sight of her breasts showing in the light of day only fueled her rage. Exposing another's goods was the last act of warfare. With another growl, Kate got to her feet, her reddened face showing not only her embarrassment but also her intent on revenge. Without regard for pride, she stood with her tattered bodice hanging from her shoulders and dove on Maud.

The throbbing in her left eye robbed Maud of strength to repel the younger girl. A quick grasp of the chemise with both hands, and Kate had avenged the humiliation. Maud shoved the German girl off to the side and peeked at her dangling orbs, bare for all the world to see. The stakes had just gone up. Pain or no pain, she meant to strip the little tramp of every stitch.

In a rage, she pounced on Kate's waist and combatted the girl's flailing defense enough to grip and rip every seam she could get her hands on. First to fly was what was left of the bodice. With bare shoulders, Kate finally showed her vanity by crossing her arms over her revealed tidbits. Without hesitation, Maud continued to shred the girl's skirt. Kate cried for mercy while grappling with the remnants of the skirt to cover her bare thighs, but Maud was bent on a complete victory.

As she took a grasp of the skirt's waistband, confident one firm yank would end the battle with unconditional surrender, an arm wrapped around Maud's chest and dragged her from atop the German girl. She peeked around to see the stranger pulling her back toward the bar. He stepped around her to stand next to the seated cowboy.

"Hell, mister. What did you do that for? It was just about to be good. It ain't sporting to break up a cat-fight before one gets stripped naked."

"I thought I'd better do something before someone got hurt," replied the stranger, who then drew his pistol and clubbed the cowboy in the forehead. Blood spurted on impact. The cowboy slumped in the chair and slid to the floor. Kate quickly picked up her ragged bodice to shield her bare bosom and scurried up the stairs.

Maud squinted her left eye open to view the prone cowboy. "Just who the hell are you? And who the hell is he?"

"His name is Curtis Marlowe. Wanted for rustling in Texas and Louisiana. There's probably papers on him in other places, but in Texas he's worth a thousand dollars."

A shiver came over Maud. "Are you some kind of lawman?"

The stranger shook his head. "Gave that up years ago. That star only made for a target." He knelt and rolled the cowboy over to take the revolver, then tucked it into his own gunbelt. "I found a better line."

"Bounty hunter," muttered Maud.

His nod confirmed the suspicion. He rolled the cowboy back over and drew a short rope from his back pocket. "I've been chasing this fellow for thirty days.

Came up through Indian territory. I figured he and his partner knew the law would catch him in Texas," he said, flipping both of Marlowe's wrists to the small of his back. "So they came here, where they wouldn't think anyone was looking for them." With a quick twist, he knotted the strand around the wrists. "Probably thought they'd snatch a few cows while they was up here. Maybe drive them over to Abilene and sell them for a quick profit. A lot easier than driving them out of Texas."

Maud pressed her palm against her swollen left eye. "You said there was a partner."

"Yeah. Only two hundred for him. Older fellow. George Gross is his name. I ain't found him yet. I thought it best to go after the bigger fish in the pond."

"And where is old George?"

"Nearest I can figure, he's hid out in Indian territory. Shouldn't be too hard to find. Got a set of gray whiskers all over his face. Unless he's shaved them off. I'll catch him on the way back."

As the stranger gripped Marlowe's collar, a shout came from upstairs: "Let go."

At the top step, Kate held a double-barreled shotgun aimed at the bounty hunter. The bartender hurried around the bar and with the two old drunks ran out of the batwing doors, leaving Maud alone with a known cattle rustler, an unknown bounty hunter, and a frenzied German whore with only those barrels to cover her front.

"Take it easy, missy," the stranger calmly said.

"*Und dien* gun. You drop it."

Complying with the order, he slowly took the pistol

from the holster and tossed it to the side. A groggy moan erupted from the cowboy Marlowe. Kate took two steps down. "Get from him." The stranger stood and took a step back, but she waved the barrels his way. "His hands," she shouted. "Let them go."

Dipping his right hand into his pocket, he slowly pulled out a knife and unfolded the blade. He bent and sliced through the rope. As soon as Marlowe's hands were free, he rubbed his bleeding head.

"Curtis," Kate called. "Curtis. I am over here."

Maud thought about standing or even hiding behind the bar, but a mere motion from her finger might draw fire her way. "Why are you doing this, girl?" she asked.

"You shut up, you fat pig." The German girl's eyes were wide open and darted from the bounty hunter to Maud and back. "He is taking me from here. I be rid of you." Another step down and she was halfway to the floor.

"Be careful with that scattergun, missy. Now, this man here is a thief. Can't trust nothing he says. He was probably saying things to you just to get you upstairs and lower the price some while he was lowering his drawers."

"Stop talking, you," Kate said as she swung the gun barrels at the stranger.

"He's right, Kate," Maud added, hoping to talk sense into the young girl. She realized she had to be careful herself, considering that moments before she was about to do deadly harm to the young German.

With cautious steps, Kate came off the stairs, wagging the shotgun from side to side like a careless maid sweeping a broom. Marlowe's loud moans attracted more of her concern as she neared. "Curtis, you all right?"

"He'll live as long as you're easy with them triggers." Kate sneered at the bounty hunter, bringing her aim in line with his head. "Ought not do that, missy."

"Honey," Maud blurted. "Don't do nothing that you'd be sorry for." Kate's attention brought the gun her way.

"Be quiet! I know what I'm doing. I am an actress. I am a singer. I came here, this country, to be on the stage. To go to San Francisco, let the people hear my voice," announced Kate, her eyes slightly welling with tears. Her fingers released the triggers for a moment to point to her bare chest. "Not show them these!"

The bounty hunter lunged to grab the double barrels and yank them from her grasp. Kate shrieked at his sudden move, and once he held the gun firmly in one hand, he slapped her with the force of a punch. The little German girl collapsed. Maud saw Marlowe get to his knees and grip the bounty hunter's pistol from the floor.

"He's got the gun!"

The bounty hunter turned, his hands on the barrels, not the trigger. Marlowe cocked the pistol and pointed it at him. A loud blast rippled through the saloon, only it seemed to come from behind Maud. Marlowe fell facefirst as he had before, but this time blood spurted from his mouth. When he hit the wooden planks, more blood bubbled from the back of his head. Maud twisted about to see a tall man standing in the batwing doorway. Smoke drifted from the muzzle of his revolver.

Slowly, he came into the room. As he passed into the sunlight from the window, she saw his dark skin, but his face didn't have the features of a colored. His sharp nose was preceded only by his long jaw. A buckskin shirt covered his wide chest and shoulders, which were shaded by a large brown hat with a skin of snake as a band. As he came to stand next to the dwarfed bounty hunter, he tucked the revolver in a holster drooping from his right hip.

"He's mine," he wheezed.

"What are you talking about?"

The dark man needed only to grip the butt of his gun to get the bounty hunter to concede the prize. As he knelt to flip Marlowe over, he clutched the dead cowboy's jaw. "That's him." He grabbed Marlowe's collar and dragged the corpse across the floor, leaving a smear of blood on the planks.

"Now, hold on," the bounty hunter said, holding out his hand. "Let's talk about this. I've been trailing him near a month. He's worth a thousand dollars in Tarrant County, Texas, to stand trial for rustling."

The large dark man was still headed for the door. "He's worth five hundred in Abilene just like he is."

The bounty hunter swung the shotgun at the large man's back. "Stop right there."

The dark one stopped with the command. Slowly he faced about, but there was no fear in his face. He released the collar and let the body slam to the floor, to be ready to draw his pistol. The reaction was reflected on the bounty hunter's face.

"I know you. You're the one they call Choate."

Maud hadn't heard the name before: "Showed? Showed what?"

Her words drew the large man's grimace. His stare brought a cold chill into the stuffy room, enough for her to feel his eyes and remind her of her exposed front. She wasn't shy, but still she quickly draped the chemise across her bosom.

"Not *showed*," replied the bounty hunter. "Choate. One of them Frenchy names." He raised the muzzle of the shotgun and extended his right hand as he walked across the room. "The name's Bill Wheeler."

Having stopped in front of the dark man, Wheeler stood with his hand unaccepted. "Okay," he said, nodding his head. "I don't need to be friendly either. But I am a businessman. What do you say we sit a spell. I may have an offer that will interest you." The two eyed each other for a moment, then glanced at the body.

"I said he's mine," grumbled Choate.

"Yeah, I know you said it. But I still think I might have partial claim to the bounty. I have a way to settle it."

Choate moved across the room and pushed the batwings apart. "Nothing to settle." He slid Marlowe's body under the doors. Wheeler's voice could be heard as the doors slapped together.

"Five thousand dollars."

Several moments passed. Wheeler stood in the doorway. The echo of his voice faded just as the doors came to a stop. Maud rose to her feet and stretched the chemise over her chest enough to fasten two buttons. When it seemed all the excitement was over, she surveyed the aftermath. Kate still lay crumpled in a pile. A trail of blood led to the door and outside.

A huff of a chortle drew her attention back to Wheeler. An instant later, the big dark man slowly stepped through the batwings. "I thought you'd be interested," said Wheeler. He turned to Maud. "Get some glasses and a bottle, woman."

It was then Maud realized that the entire liquid assets of the Colossus were unguarded. She walked around the bar to grip the throat of a whiskey bottle and fingered three shot glasses together. As she came around the bar's corner, she saw that the two men had uprighted chairs around the nearest table. She placed the bottle in the center of the table, put a glass in front of the men, and pulled up a chair.

Wheeler filled Choate's glass first, then his own, and set the bottle back in place. Maud waited only a moment before giving up any notion that there were any gentlemen in the room, and poured herself a drink. She gulped it down, eyes closed, and wheezed the burn from her throat. When she opened them, both men glared at her manner. She didn't feel embarrassed—she needed the drink to calm her nerves. She poured another shot.

"Like I was saying," Wheeler started as he picked up his drink. "There is a bigger pot out there." Choate leaned back in his chair, keeping unimpressed eyes on Wheeler. "When I was coming up through Fort Worth, I came across something I thought about pursuing." He reached inside his carpet-patterned vest. The sudden move made Choate move his shoulder and Maud stop in midswig. Wheeler opened the other palm. "No need to fret," he said as he drew a paper folded into a square. He unwrapped it and handed the sheet to Choate. The black man looked at it but didn't raise a hand. Wheeler sipped from his glass, then retracted the paper. "Can't read? No matter."

Curiosity overcame Maud. She snatched the paper and eyed the big bold print. Eagerness made her mumble the words aloud. " 'Five-thousand-dollar reward. Man known as the Rainmaker. For the assault and wounding of federal troops in Platte Falls, Colorado.' " She silently read to herself. "Who is he?"

"One tough hombre," Wheeler said as he drained the glass. "Or so they say. Killed over thirty men is the legend. Quick to draw a gun and ain't afraid to use it, neither. He shoots men in the back, too."

"It says here he was at the Little Bighorn?" Maud said.

Wheeler nodded. "Yup. Word is he scouted for Custer. Conspired with Injuns to wipe out the regiment. Probably paid him with some fool talk of gold hid in the hills up there. He's a mean fellow. I hear the judge wants him alive, but will take him dead just the same."

Choate remained in his chair. Wheeler took a minute before refilling his glass. Maud still had to fend for herself, and did.

"What did you want with me?"

Wheeler smirked at Choate's question. "Gave thought of going after this fellow myself. But I thought better when I heard what kind of man this was. I ain't anxious to catch a bullet with my back. Two men can flank him, keep him off one another." The old bounty hunter leaned over the table with a little sparkle in his eye. "The paper says he's left Texas and is probably heading this way. The both of us can take him. What do you say?"

With an arched thumb, Choate pointed to the door. "What about him?"

"Well, if you accept, that would make us partners. We split everything right down the middle."

Wheeler's offer hung in the air. During the silence, Maud slipped the glass between her lips. She didn't want to miss a thing, and the first two slugs had already given a fuzz to her mind. Finally, she heard the groan of chair legs scuffing the planks, followed by Choate rising.

"No." He left the table with his glass still full. He didn't turn his back as he strode to the door.

"It ain't fair," Wheeler argued, his smirk blown away like the light of a candle. "I should get a share. You wouldn't know about the Rainmaker, wasn't for me." His voice grew louder the farther away Choate walked. Once the large dark man passed through the batwings, and they had swung long enough to hang still, the shouting stopped.

Maud sipped the liquor as she watched Wheeler's eyes turn to her. His grimace made her hand shake. There was one whore slumped on the floor. If she wasn't cautious with her action, there could be two. Slowly, she put the shot glass back on the table. "What are you going to do now, Bill?"

Wheeler leaned back in his chair. He let out a

breath of frustration and rubbed the stubble on his chin. "I think I made a fool's play. No point in closing the pen if the coyotes already have the chickens by the neck." He picked up his glass and threw the liquor down his throat. Gritting his teeth, he rose from his chair. "No time to waste."

"Where are you going, Bill?" Maud asked while he stepped for the door.

"I'm going to get my chickens back."

Maud surveyed the room. Kate lay motionless next to the pool of blood left from Marlowe's head. The sun's beams had climbed from the floor to the middle of the walls. Soon, she would own the room. Being left alone didn't scare her, but it did make her consider what was next for her. It brought about her need for the future and what she was owed. "Hey," she said, and he pushed one of the batwings wide. "What about those four other dollars?" When he stopped, she gave quick thought to enhancing her reward. "I'll give you a quick poke to tide you to the next town for an even ten?"

Without even as much as a grin, Wheeler drew four coins from his pocket and flung them her way. Before they wobbled to lie flat on the wooden planks, he was gone from the doorway. By herself, with the only other breathing thing in the room a slapped-out German whore not even twenty or with natural red hair, Maud let out her long-held breath.

It was time for her to gauge what was next for her. She bent over to retrieve one of the silver dollars, and with a quick clench of her teeth on the edge, made sure of its true value. She rose and picked up her fallen shawl, then wiped the smudged rouge on her cheeks. After one step toward the stairs to get the rest of her few possessions, she stopped, twisted about, and grabbed the shot glass left by Choate. A single gulp and the liquor was down her throat. From now on, she had to take advantage of every opportunity.

Chapter Three

The flag snapped at the top of the pole. The northern breeze stretched it to the end of the halyard. As Cole passed the gate, his eyes shot to the stockade. The army jail appeared vacant. Any careless word or movement would have him as its lone resident. He turned his eyes ahead, not wanting to draw any further attention to his interest in the wooden prison. By the time he neared the post headquarters, he felt all eyes on his back. He reined to a stop at the front awning. A young officer wearing a slouch hat and dressed in a uniform that appeared ready for parade duty stepped from the porch.

"What's your business?" Although the question was aimed at Cole, the soldier's eyes were fixed on the child at the front of the saddle.

"I come to bring this one back to his own."

"Where did you find it?"

Cole paused, trying to remember the story he had practiced. "I come across a cabin in the woods up in the hills. A squaw and an old miner had it out." Cole nodded to the child. "This one was left in a blanket."

"You should take it back where you found it. This isn't an orphanage." The curt reply surprised Cole. He peered from side to side to see the same attitude etched on the faces of enlisted men who had slackened their duty to surround the palomino and gawk.

"Wouldn't last a day on its own," Cole remarked as the officer turned to step back onto the porch.

"Just as well." The young officer stopped when he hit the first step. With a snap to attention, he saluted a figure emerging from the shaded door. A moment later, another officer dressed in Sunday blue came into the sunlight and propped a black-banded straw hat on his head.

"What is this, Lieutenant Miller?" the commander casually inquired.

"Sir, this man brought the Indian child here, saying it was an orphan left in a cabin. I told him we had no reason to keep it here, sir," Miller announced as he whisked his right hand to his side. The commander turned his attention to Cole.

"I'm Colonel Grimes. What is your name, sir?"

He needed another breath to pause. With his own known by more soldiers than he had ever met, Cole knew of only one name that had served him well to keep his past unknown. "Hayes. My name's Clay Hayes."

The colonel eyed Cole in a curious manner. "Have we met before?"

Not remembering the man, any admission of his days with the cavalry could spark a fire. "Don't think so," he answered without a hint to continue any friendly banter.

"Well, then," Grimes said, putting on his riding gloves. "What do you expect us to do with this child?"

"I thought it was your job to keep them here."

Grimes's head shot up. Cole's honest answer to the question appeared to have hit a raw nerve. "My job, as you put it, Mr. Hayes, is not to keep wayward orphans." The Colonel took a breath, as if to allow the raw nerve to ease. "I am a soldier assigned as the provost marshal of this reservation. My duty is to assure the peace of this region and to see to the needs of these Indians and this outpost."

"But you ain't got room for this one."

Grimes peered up at Cole, as if ready for another surly reply, but his eyes softened slightly and he took another breath. "I have something to show you, Mr. Hayes." He turned to the junior officer. "Lieutenant Miller, see to our guests' refreshments."

It was more than a polite invitation. Cole dismounted and untethered his sleeping cargo. He held the child to his chest. Quickly, it sought secure places for its tiny hands around his neck. Cole followed the Colonel up the steps and inside the headquarters. Shades covered the windows. A fire barely glimmered in the dark. A squaw dressed in a white woman's collared blouse and long shirt shuffled through papers at a desk.

41

Tim McGuire

The colonel removed his gloves and hat. "Rebecca, could you see to this child while I have a talk with our guest?" Her eyes didn't show any delight in the assignment, which Cole had expected. Once she took the child, Cole turned to follow the colonel through an open door into a private office at the far end of the building. "Have a seat, Mr. Hayes. You can take off your hat." Unsure if the colonel's gesture was meant as an offer or an order, Cole brushed the dust from the brim and sat in the single chair across from the desk. "So I understand you found this baby in a cabin in the hills."

"Yup," he answered, hoping to end the inquiry.

"The mother, she was living with a miner? As his wife?"

"I wouldn't say that. It didn't appear that way to me when I found them." The scene with both of them sprawled on the floor shot through his mind. "I'd say they hadn't been together long."

Grimes took the pen from the inkwell and began scribbling on a paper while he spoke. "What would you say happened to them?"

Another breath was needed to calm his pounding chest and recall what he had better say. "When I come up on them, I heard shots. I followed them up a hill. I spotted a shack about a hundred feet away and saw through the window the two was fighting." He paused, thinking he was a moth getting too close to a flame.

"Yes. Go on."

"Like I said, there were shots, so when I saw the two was fighting, I decided if I could help her out.

When I came through the door, they both were on the floor. The squaw was shot and the miner had so many knife cuts in his chest, he was bleeding too bad for me to do anything for him."

The scribbling stopped. "That sounds a little dangerous, don't you think? Entering someone's home during a fight. Especially when gunshots had been fired. Didn't you think you could have been shot at?"

The question made sense. All there was to say was an answer that didn't. "Like I said, I thought the woman needed help."

"But a squaw? I must say, Mr. Hayes, I do believe you must be one ready to act recklessly. What if it were the miner that needed help? What if the squaw would have shot you?"

"I didn't see it that way."

With a small smirk, Grimes leaned back in his chair. "Pity you couldn't have helped her more."

The simple remark produced a stabbing feeling in Cole's ribs. "I thought the same," he muttered, looking to the neatly swept floor.

Taking the pen again, Grimes resumed the scribbling. "I will have to send a detail to this cabin. Where did you say it was?"

"How come?"

Cole's question stopped the pen. Looking up from the paper, Grimes seemed almost startled. "As I said, I am the provost marshal. I can't have people, white or other, being killed in these hills while on my watch. Is there a problem with that? Everything is as you say, isn't it?"

Able only to nod, Cole slowly drew another long breath.

"Well, then. Where is this cabin?"

"Maybe five miles south of here. It's kind of snugged in the trees. It ain't easy to find."

Grimes had another smirk on his face. "Perhaps you could lead the detail there."

"I got business up north."

"This won't take long."

"It's important I go," Cole blurted, instantly realizing that shot would draw more fire.

Grimes put the pen back in the inkwell. "Why is that?"

His heart pounded harder, even more than when he faced a gun pointed at him. The colonel's piercing grin wasn't meant to be friendly. Cole gave a thought to drawing iron, but surrounded by soldiers, he knew his chances of making it out the door alive were as bad as a rooster's in a mountain lion's den.

"There's a matter in Chicago city that I was called to do."

"Chicago? That's quite a distance. Is it a family matter, Mr. Hayes?"

"You could say that. A friend of mine asked me to carry a story to those that needed to hear it."

"What story is that?" Grimes asked, clasping his hands together and leaning back in the chair.

Ideas flew through Cole's mind like a windstorm. Major Miles Perry was never a friend. Had he not been killed by Comanches in Texas, the soldier who had pursued Cole for five years would be the one to parade Cole to Chicago in chains. Before Perry's

death, an alliance was made between the two to tell
the story each claimed was the truth. The mere mention of Perry's name to an army colonel would attach
to Cole the same blame that had followed him around
like a barking dog—about his part the day that Custer
fell at the Little Bighorn. The real purpose for his ride
to Chicago was to be able to give his side before an
honest court in a fair trial. If he told that to Grimes,
he might as well draw iron and point the muzzle at
his own head.

"It's private," said Cole with a stern face. "Not one
I feel the army has a part in."

"I see," Grimes replied with a nod. "I understand
the need for privacy." Cole's relief at the statement
didn't last long. "However, there is still the matter of
the child that you brought here. If the mother is dead,
as you say, then I must find it a new one."

Cole glanced to the shaded window. "Should be
plenty here that would take it in."

"On the contrary. It isn't a habit the Indians share.
To take a lone orphan in isn't the same as most Christian folk would do. No, I think I should ask you to
take us where this woman was killed. Perhaps she
has relatives that would take the baby."

"But I told you. I got business up north."

"And I said this wouldn't take long." Grimes stood,
his tone leaving little doubt that he wasn't asking po-
litely anymore.

"You must have hundreds of Indians on this reservation. You can't find one mother to take it in?"

The suggestion brought a smirk back to Grimes's
face. "Perhaps I should show what I mean." Grimes

picked up his hat and walked around the desk. At the door, he turned to Cole, who remained in the chair. "Come with me, Mr. Hayes." At the command, Cole reluctantly stood, unsure exactly what the officer had in mind. Grimes pointed through the door with open palm. Cole went through the doorway, noticing the squaw at the desk cradling the child, but still without a loving embrace.

As bright sunlight glared in his eyes, Cole put on his hat, as did Grimes. The colonel slipped on his gloves and Cole went to the palomino. The young lieutenant stood just yards away as Cole gripped the reins.

"That's an interesting weapon," Miller said, stopping Cole's boot from entering the stirrup. A glance at the scabbard confirmed the subject of the remark. "May I see it?"

The thought to bark "hell no" came first to mind. However, Cole didn't have any friends on the post. Slowly he drew the rifle. With a polished oak stock, the pump-action gleamed in the sunshine. Cole tossed the rifle to the young officer, who admired it with the eyes of children presented with ribboned boxes. Miller turned the underside up and, once noticing the hole, looked to Cole. "What's this for?"

"Ammunition."

"Single-shot? Why the pump?"

"Takes a magazine that holds nine rounds."

A smile grew on Miller's face. "Very sweet," he said, shouldering the stock. "Unusual design. Where'd you get it?"

The answer wasn't a simple one. Not more than

six weeks had passed since Cole had retrieved the rifle from the shattered rocks of south Texas. The designer was a foreigner named Serge Mouton. A braggart, Mouton was not one to let the opportunity pass to fill all the ears on the grounds with how he had more smarts than any other—had Cole not killed him.

"I got it from a fellow who was from across the seas."

"Oh, yeah," Miller said, lowering the rifle and tossing it back to Cole. "Looks like a fine piece. I would think it would be effective at more than a thousand yards."

"I seen him hit cactus blooms with it at more than two thousand," Cole answered, returning the rifle to the scabbard, then toeing the stirrup.

"Must have been a fine fellow to part with it," Miller said as Cole pulled himself into the saddle. He eyed the young lieutenant and spoke in a firm tone so as to let the younger man know his place.

"He didn't need it anymore."

"Lieutenant Miller." Grimes's call was met with an immediate salute. "We'll be riding to the northern section. We should return for the lowering of the colors." With a nod, Grimes looked to Cole and swung his horse to the north. Cole did the same.

With her hat tilted to the side and wearing the last dress she owned that could be seen in public, Maud lugged her only bag through the Colossus's doors for the final time. As she walked down the boardwalk, what was left of the sparse population had gathered in the street to gossip about what they had seen and what they thought they knew. From the corner of her eye, she noticed Norman Yater cross the street, hands in his black waistcoat.

"What went on in there, Maud?"

"If you're looking for more business, Norman, you're too late. They already took the body for a reward." Although she kept walking past him, he continued after her.

"Who took it? And what body?"

"I don't know, Norman. Find out for yourself."

"Well, how am I going to find out if everyone is dead?"

"Kate ain't dead. Ask her when she comes to."

"Now, Maud, this ain't fair. We've always been able to talk."

His words slowed her pace enough for him to stride alongside. "Okay, you want to know? Some cowhand named Marlowe was the only son of a bitch who had any money in the place in weeks, and come to find out, the reason he did was 'cause he was rustling cattle in Texas. Two bounty hunters caught up with him and shot him dead, slapped Kate near dead, then talked about going after another fellow name of Rainmaker or something like that. They parted like two dogs, one with the rabbit, the other without, and all I got for my trouble was a lousy five dollars. There, you have the story, Norman. Now you can spread it the way you want it. Right now, my feet are as worn out as my butt. I'm hungry, I ain't got nowhere to sleep, and I got to get out of this town, but I ain't got a horse. All you need to know?"

"Rainmaker? As in '*The* Rainmaker'?"

She stopped hoping to end his questions once and for all. "Yes, So what?" Her casual confirmation drew a shroud of fear over his thin blond scalp, through his spectacles, right into his green eyes.

"Did these bounty hunters say he was near here?"

"I don't know. Maybe. The one named Wheeler said he thought he was coming this way. Why would that make a difference to you? Oh, I forgot, your business is plotting what is left after one of these killers come, through town." She turned around. Sun-dried brush, which she had to travel through, lay ahead of her. At once, she came to a solution and twisted about with a friendlier attitude. "Norman, didn't you say you had a horse for sale?"

He nodded and shrugged. "Yeah. The old chestnut gelding can't pull the hearse anymore. I ain't got the heart to kill it."

The admission seemed out of place. "Norman, you bury people, for Pete's sake."

"Yeah, but I don't kill them. That animal served me faithfully for thirteen years. Seemed a sin to just to kill it because I can't use him anymore."

"Why, Norman," she mockingly exclaimed, blinking her eyes and delicately brushing her palm on his lapel. "Since when has sinning ever bothered you?" Her advance instantly reddened his face.

"Oh, Maud," he said, gently pulling her hand from his coat. "People are watching."

"Oh, who cares. It ain't like they don't know what I do. And it ain't as if they can avoid dealing with you sooner or later. I have a proposition for you, Norman Yater." Her left hand edged up his protruding gut, past his chest, then his throat, to tickle his chin. "For that wore-out old nag," she said while her right hand crept below his belt, heading farther south, "I'd be willing to give you a going-away present. Just for old times' sake." A slight squeeze, bringing him to a quiver, sealed the deal.

Chapter Four

From the crest of the hill, Cole saw the lodges below. Grimes rode just ahead, almost triumphant in his approach to the village. As they passed by the first lodge, two Indian men wrapped in blankets stood by with wary eyes. Cole reined in, slowing the palomino to a trot. As he rode past, memories came back of numerous raids he had been a part of, both as a trooper and a scout. However, the first notion to hit his head was the difference between those camps and this one.

Unlike the nomads he had come across before on the plains, this tribe hadn't been here for more than one or two seasons. The high grass was trampled into dust by constant foot traffic in the same place. Once they were in the center of the camp, a pungent odor came from one of the lodges. He knew it as the scent of death. As more of the tribe came out into the light, the filth on their robes made it clear this group wasn't accustomed to living in the spot no matter how long they had been here, and they were not proud about who saw it.

A few times before, he had happened on the camps of the Sioux, the Cheyenne, and even the Comanche. Even on reservations, those tribes had signs of life buzzing around their tepees, although none of them took kindly to soldiers being about. None of that appeared here. These people didn't have contempt for the white man etched on their faces, as did so many he had seen in the past, but rather a look of indifference—a resolve to accept their fate to be penned up in the squalor of a foreign prairie.

Grimes dismounted and tethered the reins of his horse to a dried bush. Seeing the colonel's casual manner, Cole did the same. "Who are they?"

Grimes took a moment to survey what they had ridden by. "A once-proud people." His eyes turned to Cole. "There's someone I want you to meet, Mr. Hayes." Cole followed the officer to the edge of the camp. Three older men with hair in braided strands squatted around a fledgling fire with puny twigs piled by their side. They displayed the same response to the approach of the white men as the others had. When Grimes stood above them, he removed his right glove and extended his hand to the one in the center. "It is good to see you again."

One man watched the hand with the same placid expression Cole had seen on the others. After a moment, he slowly stood and took Grimes's hand. "Clay

Hayes, this is Crooked Stone of the Nez Perce. I have come to know him well." Cole noticed the calm, yet not joyous, clasp of hands. He wiped his palm against the back of his pants to offer it to the older man. Crooked Stone looked at the open hand but didn't accept it. Feeling like a fool, Cole slowly withdrew his hand.

Grimes broke the awkward silence. "Mr. Hayes has brought a child." He waited an instant to look his friend in the eye. "I believe it is Honor Woman's child."

This brought life to the Indian's cheeks and drew the other men's attention away from the dwindling flame. "Where?" asked Crooked Stone.

"The child is at the post." Grimes frowned at what needed to be said next. "Mr. Hayes said he found her in a cabin with a white man"—he paused—"dead. I'm sorry, Crooked Stone."

The men's eyes pointed like arrows at Cole's heart. "It weren't me."

Grimes looked at Cole and nodded. "No, it wasn't this man. But apparently it was a miner in the hills south of here. I will send a detachment to find her for you." The explanation didn't seem to cut much into the older man's angered brow. Cole felt surrounded by enemies just as darkness settled from the northern clouds that had climbed high enough to shade the sun. Only after a few moments did Crooked Stone look to the dirt. "Why do you tell me this?"

"Because you are my friend," Grimes replied.

"A friend would not bring such a story." The older man crouched down again, followed by the other two.

Now Grimes hung his head. About the time Cole figured it was time to ride back to the post, the colonel knelt. Finding himself standing while all the others were seated on the dirt, Cole knew they weren't about to return to the army headquarters, at least by daylight. He sat on the ground next to Grimes.

"I understand what you mean. But part of my purpose of coming to you was to tell the story to Mr. Hayes. For you to tell the story." With Grimes's words, Crooked Stone began eyeing Cole. "When he brought the child to me, I knew he would have to listen to you first."

What was said seemed a blur to Cole. "What are you getting at?"

Grimes turned to him. He took a breath, as if what he had to say was stuck in his throat. "Four years ago, I served under Colonel Nelson Miles. We had been assigned the task of herding the Nez Perce onto a reservation. Although, some of us protested that the action was unnecessary, we knew we were assigned orders and it was our duty to obey those orders." Grimes glanced to Crooked Stone.

From his time wearing the uniform, Cole knew of the tale. But fear of admitting too much kept his mouth closed and ears open as Grimes continued.

"At the time, we knew the Nez Perce as friendly, but as always, as more land was settled near their homeland in the Wallowa Valley of Oregon, skirmishes flared up. Washington grew very nervous about the prospect of lives lost. It had only been a year since the Sioux had—"

"I know," Cole interrupted. He remembered he

should keep his mouth shut, but he had already blurted the words and felt he needed to finish what was in his mind. "I know what happened at the Little Bighorn." Knowledge about the incident was all too common, and Cole's announcement didn't seem to cause any alarm with Grimes.

"Then you can imagine what it was like to be there." Colonel Grimes had no notion of just what impact that statement had.

"Oh, I have a real good idea what it was like."

Grimes nodded. "So, with that heavy in our minds, we pursued our orders. Crooked Stone, Looking Glass, and Thunder Down the Mountain, a man we came to call Joseph, waged a campaign against us better than any opponent we had ever faced. We had read the dispatches that told of the hit-and-run tactics of the Nez Perce, the defeat of Captain David Perry, the failures of General Howard and Colonel Gibbon to capture them. From June to October, they kept moving. Colonel Miles knew they would attempt to escape to Canada, so we marched day and night so as to surprise them. We stopped them less than forty miles from the border and cut off their escape. After two weeks in the cold snow, I was part of the party when Joseph handed over his rifle and proclaimed he would 'fight no more forever.' " Grimes's face was lit from the fire's glow. His eyes glistened. He put his hand on Crooked Stone's shoulder. "When you get to know your enemy well, you often can understand why he fights so hard." He looked back at Cole. "My father was in the army all his life, as I have been. My only son was at The Point. All I know to do when I am issued orders is to follow them. But sometimes more need be done than just to follow them." He looked again to his friend. "Tell him the story," said Grimes.

The old Indian returned the colonel's smile of friendship, then turned his eyes to Cole. "You found my Honor Woman."

Cole nodded, unsure what to say. "That I did. And I'm sorry she was your daughter. I mean, I'm sorry for the fact that your daughter was killed." Still not right with his reply, he decided to hush before he offended anyone any further.

"I am not sorry." Crooked Stone's remark surprised Cole, but a glance to Grimes showed that he wasn't surprised. "She is home, with those we have seen die before us." He looked into the fire. "Since the white man was brought to us by the Bird Woman, we have always been their friend. My father's father told us all the stories of when it was cold in the mountains and the valley of still water kept us warm. Our people fished in the river, the Shoshone brought us their ponies, and at times the traders came. When the whites came to us, we showed all of them we wanted to learn. We helped them fight their wars, for the promise that we would never be at war with them. But when the whites took our valley, they wouldn't listen to the promises made by their fathers."

He turned to the white-haired elder by his side, who slowly raised his head. With a prodding from Crooked Stone in his native tongue, the older man spouted off the words, which Crooked Stone repeated in English.

"I am a white man. I am the promise made by my father. I carry the shame of his nation. When the young chose to fight, Joseph remembered the promise not to sell his father's bones, and we followed him away, so we could return to there someday. But the blue soldiers chased us like prey. We fought only when we had to, but they blamed us for the fight. The women and young walked through the snow, so the fighters could lead the blue soldiers away. The snow was deep, and the game hid from us. Those that did not eat, we left where they died. They would go back home."

The old man picked up a twig and tossed it into the fire. Grimes, too, placed a stick into the flame, as did Crooked Stone. Cole knew the custom. A fire was a shared wealth, and it took all those around to keep it going, much like a peace offering. Without any wood near him, Cole ripped the dead grass sprouts from the ground and flipped them onto the coals.

The white-haired elder continued. "Those of us who had lived in the valley knew that for the young to someday return, we could not," Crooked Stone said in translation. "We went to the land of the great mother. But the blue soldiers blocked our path. They kept us in the cold. My brothers and sisters died with their children. We knew we would die there, too. Joseph said if we surrendered, we would go home and die. But the blue soldiers' father lied to us. He sent us here to die."

Grimes dipped his head when the elder stopped talking. "I told you I was on that hill, Mr. Hayes. Colonel Miles made the promise to return these peo-

57

ple to the Wallowa. But General Sherman overruled the decision, citing the hostilities of the previous years. He knew as long as there were whites settling the land, the fighting would continue. And Washington wanted the land settled. So the Nez Perce were ordered here."

Reminded that just minutes before he had thought he knew the story of Chief Joseph and the Nez Perce, Cole realized how much he didn't know. He leaned closer to the colonel.

"He said he was the shame of his father's nation."

"He is to them," Grimes replied. "His name is Daytime Smoke. He is the son of William Clark. The same man who, with Meriwether Lewis, was the first American to discover the Nez Perce and pledge the eternal friendship of the United States."

The night continued with more remembrances of the misery the tribe endured while evading the cavalry. As the hours passed, Cole looked into the face of Daytime Smoke. He had heard many such stories, witnessing firsthand the many tribes that had been uprooted from the land for the sake of settlement to civilization. The sadness in the elder's eyes told more than the words coming from his mouth.

The pile of twigs dwindled. The small fire battled the brisk wind from the north. Cole didn't feel much of a chill.

Daytime Smoke detailed the retreat. The numbing cold of the falling snow, the broken hearts of their surrender, the burial of the children and parents, the bitter disappointment of the betrayal by the army to return to the Wallowa Valley. He described every step to the trains that would take them to an unknown land.

"When we came here," Crooked Stone said in his own words, "there were no rivers to fish. We must take the grain of the white man as our food. It was not our food. We were still many, but many would not eat." He paused to survey the dawning light over the camp. "Now we are not many." He eyed Cole. "You brought the child of my Honor Woman. I do not want this child."

The words surprised Cole. "She's your kin. Why wouldn't you want her?"

Crooked Stone turned to Grimes, who wore an expression of despondent agreement. "Sometimes, it's better not to know what happens to your loved ones, Mr. Hayes." The soldier looked to Cole. "Rather than know what will happen to them."

"I don't know what you're talking about."

"He wants you to take the child." Grimes's blunt words stunned Cole even more than what Crooked Stone had said.

"There ain't no way that can happen. I ain't no keeper of kids."

"You can travel beyond the territory. They cannot. If you were to find the child a home, one willing to take care of it—preferably not an orphanage, for it would be an orphan all its life—"

"No," Crooked Stone blurted. "You must go back home. That is where the Nez Perce live."

"It's over fifteen hundred miles," Grimes answered his friend. "The journey is too far."

The old Indian looked deeply into Grimes's eyes,

attempting to sink his message into the colonel's soul. "Not too far for us to come here."

"You two ain't listening," Cole said. "I'm on my way to Chicago city. I ain't got the time to be searching for a home for no kid. I'm sorry for all the troubles your people have had to put up with, but it ain't my doing."

"I can supply you with what you'll need, but I can't pay you," Grimes said.

Cole scoffed. "Like I said, you ain't listening."

"Haatya pik'uunpa." The utterance by Daytime Smoke stopped Cole from continuing his protest. He knew the words as the Indian girl's dying breath. "What did he say?"

"Wind in the river," Crooked Stone answered. "It is where my people lived."

The feel of the girl dying in his arms rushed like a wave through his body. Realizing what her message to him meant—a plea from the girl to take her baby back to where she had meant to travel; a trip she would have made had he not shot her—Cole silenced his argument. However, the notion was still foolishness. "I can't do this. Like you said, it's too far. I don't know nothing about taking care of kids."

"Perhaps you can find someone to help you," Grimes said. "There are plenty of people along the way who would show their kindness toward a man with a child." Cole shook his head, knowing that most Christian folk didn't take to those not of their own color. The more he thought of what it would require just to make the trip on his own, the supplies needed, the cold of winter, the terrain that would be crossed, the more he shook his head.

Sunlight breached the sky, still leaving the camp shrouded in shade. The last twig dissolved into ash. The flame shrank into the glowing embers.

Daytime Smoke rose and uttered an order to Cole, who looked to Crooked Stone for the meaning. "He wants to show you Honor Woman's brothers and sisters."

Not one partial to meeting with folks with whom he didn't share likes, much less those whose lingo he couldn't understand, Cole reluctantly stood, as did Crooked Stone and Colonel Grimes in respect for the elder. Daytime Smoke turned and walked slowly away from the encampment. Cole followed, the other Indian and the soldier close behind. They shared the same look of reluctance that Cole felt, but it seemed clear it wasn't for the same reason. The elder led the party over the small hills of dried brush, his braided hair blown by the morning breeze. Once beyond the small leafless trees, the old man came to a quick stop. Cole came to stand at his side.

Daytime Smoke pointed to the prairie, but there were no lodges. With the sunlight edging over the horizon, all that was to be seen were the tops of the grass and plots of cleared ground. As Cole surveyed the plain, the purpose of the elder was evident. The chilled wind whipped into Cole's face as he stared at the resting place of those he was meant to see. Although Daytime Smoke spoke in his native tongue, Cole understood what was said. This is where the girl's family and likely most of those her age who originally had been sent here ended up.

With the sight before him, the message was clear. Had the young girl named Honor Woman not escaped from the reservation, this is where she would have been buried. She and her child. Now she was buried beyond the camp by his own hands. His stomach churned at the view, and his chest burned at what the girl had wanted for her baby. The breeze howled in his ears. The cries of the dead pleaded with his heart.

"I'll do it."

Chapter Five

Cole tightened the saddle cinch. If he was to keep his cargo steady, it would have to have a firm foundation. He flipped the stirrup down just as Rebecca brought out the child. He took it under the arms and placed it, blanket wrap and all, gently into the rope noose loop tethered to the horn. It wasn't the most comfortable way to travel, but it was secure. As he pulled the knot taut, he looked into the young eyes and noticed the courage behind the innocent stare. He wished he were so confident.

"It appears fair weather is ahead," Colonel Grimes said as he stepped off the headquarters step. Cole glanced at the morning sun and the cloudless sky. The north breeze hadn't stopped since the previous day when he had seen the graves of the Nez Perce. The thought spurred him to get started.

"We'll need it to make it far today." He stepped into the stirrup and climbed atop the saddle. With the child at his belly, he lifted the reins over its head.

"I had the quartermaster supply you with flour, cornmeal, some hardtack, coffee . . ." Grimes paused while Cole glanced behind at the pack mule with the bundles strapped to its back and a droopy-uddered goat leashed to the bundles. "And some essentials for the little girl."

"Girl?" Cole peered down at the black bowl-cropped hair of the child. "Are you sure?"

Grimes's smirk could be seen below the brim of the straw hat. "Yes. I didn't tell you? She's about eighteen months old."

Traveling with a baby wasn't a smart idea at the outset. A baby that was a girl seemed a worse one. "I ain't never tended to no females."

"Well," Grimes said as he walked to the side of the palomino. "I assure you they have the same natural functions of any male." He thought for a moment, then whispered, "All but one."

"Yeah, I know about that one. I ain't looking forward to it." Cole took the reins of the mule and turned the palomino toward the gate. He was stopped by the offer of the colonel's hand.

"I want to thank you for this, Hayes. It means a great deal to me." Cole obliged him by taking his hand. "I wish you luck."

Cole nudged the palomino. "I'll need more than that."

* * *

Amid the Abilene townspeople who stopped in their tracks, Choate rode past with the body of Curtis Marlowe strapped across the saddle of the horse tethered behind. He reined to a halt in front of the door with barred windows. Once he was dismounted, he ignored the stares, stepped onto the boardwalk, and opened the door. At a desk was a thin man with a mustache and stringy chin whiskers, wearing a star on his coat. The lawman dropped the pen in his hand in surprise from the intrusion.

"What do you want?" he asked while leaning back in his chair to open a bottom drawer.

"I got Curtis Marlowe outside. I come for the bounty."

The lawman peered at Choate. Then his eyes darted to the window. "You sure that's him?"

Choate nodded.

The lawman rose, eyeing Choate as he went out the doorway. He went to the body and gripped the bloody scalp and yanked the head up to view the face. After a moment, he released it to sag against the animal's girth. He came back to the door, scratching his cheek as if in some disbelief. He eyed Choate again from head to toe and went back inside to sit at his desk. "That is him, all right. Can't pay you the full amount since you shot him in the back, though."

"Papers said nothing about that," Choate said.

"Well, that don't matter. I can't pay no darkie to shoot a white man in the back."

Choate stepped in front of the desk. "Ain't no darkie. Now, you pay me five hundred dollars."

"Don't sass me," the lawman said as he stood. "It's

Frank Beck you're talking to. Sheriff Frank Beck, and I don't take to being sassed by no darkie or anyone looking like one." A moment passed as the two men glared. Slowly, Beck took his seat. "Why did you shoot him?"

"To kill him dead."

"I'm not in a mood for jokes."

"I don't know jokes. Don't want them none."

Beck frowned. "So, what made you shoot him?"

"Had to. Marlowe pointed a gun at a fellow, about to kill him."

"What fellow? Where?"

"Wheeler is his name. They were both in Ellsworth. I came in and fired. Killed him dead."

"Bill Wheeler?" Beck asked.

Choate shrugged his shoulders, and Beck shook his head.

"Wheeler wasn't here more than two hours ago, claiming it was him that shot Marlowe and the body was stole from him while he was pissing in the bushes. Don't ask me why, but I didn't believe him then, and still don't." Beck's grin turned to a wrinkle of remorse. "Look, I don't know what to tell you, but if I pay you five hundred dollars, I'll have every white man in Kansas running in here with a rope for me and you both. It ain't like Marlowe didn't deserve exactly what he got. I have no argument for that. But he was only wanted for thieving cattle. Had he been killing women and children, then you'd be a hero."

It wasn't the first time the threat of white men with ropes had been made to Choate. "I am a Crow, not a black man. I have hunted men for the army and for federal marshals. I have hunted and killed many white men and have been paid the same as all others."

"Federal folks, huh. Well, we don't cotton to them much, either. But I tell you what I'll do. I haven't a penny in this office. I can sign a voucher for half of the amount, which you can take to the bank when they open at nine. I'll talk to the judge, which will take a week, and if he says you're due the whole five hundred, then I'll sign for the rest. It will be his neck then. Sound like a deal?"

Cheated by most of his dealing with the whites, Choate took in a long breath and let it out slowly. Two hundred and fifty dollars was better than arguing for the rest in a week, which he figured was the sheriff's plan all along. More than likely, it was the lawman's scheme to keep the rest. Such was the luck of a redman in black skin. There were other men to be caught, and richer bounties. He nodded once and stood at the front of the desk, while Beck took a slip of paper from the desk and scratched the pen across it. When he was done, he slid the paper to the front.

"Make your mark."

Choate took the pen and wrote his name in English on the drawn line. Beck again looked surprised.

"You can write?"

Choate scowled at the remark.

"Don't take no offense. I just haven't seen many darkies that could, that's all."

About to shout, Choate stopped his tongue. He hadn't the time to educate the sheriff on how the Crow had been schooled in the ways of the whites.

He snatched the paper and turned for the door, but a poster on the wall stopped him. It was the same one Wheeler had shown him. As he read, Beck chuckled behind him.

"I don't think you want any part of that one. The Rainmaker is a deadly shot and don't mind killing people in the back, neither. You'd do best by sticking to the cattle rustlers."

Choate turned about to the sheriff. "Rustlers only pay half."

Beck's chuckle stopped, and Choate left the office.

Maud Price slid off the gelding, her rump feeling swollen. Two days without sleep had left her groggy and mean. Even a gal in her line had to use a bed for what it was intended, but only endless grassy field had been in view since she left Ellsworth. As she tethered the horse, the clomping of boots on the boardwalk drew her attention. It was the large black bounty hunter she had seen in the Colossus. Quickly she faced about, not daring to be seen by the man, unsure what feelings he may still hold toward her. Women in bonnets across the street slowed their step to gaze upon her. Feeling a bit loose from their disdain and not wanting to attract attention, Maud straightened her blouse to a more respectable fit. The clomping passed, and carefully she peeked to see the determined stride of the tall black man as he continued farther down the boardwalk.

Breathing a sigh, she realized how far she had come just to dodge another ill fate, possibly at the hands of the same man. However, the deep breath led to a yawn, and her knees began to buckle. If she didn't get any sleep, she feared she'd slip to the ground and take her snooze on the street. She winced in the morning's glare, then spotted the broad banner sign of the hotel staring her in the face. Her single bag in hand, she stepped up to the boardwalk and proceeded into the lobby.

Smoke filled the room from the seated suit-clad men reading their newspapers while puffing on their cigars. The aroma made her yearn for a drag, but it was too early to solicit any gentlemanly offers. She trudged the short distance to the front desk, where a thin, black-coated clerk shuffled message cards in and out of the pigeonholes. "I need a room."

The clerk peered over his shoulder and a sneer grew on his lip. "We haven't got any."

"You don't got one room?"

The clerk sneered again, resuming his attention to the pigeonholes. "Not for you."

After a peek to her blouse, she was sure all the buttons were fastened. Her reflection in the polished wooden desk revealed smudges in her makeup caused by travel on the trail. She rubbed them with her thumb, only to smear the two-day-old rouge, but there was little she could do about it at the moment. "What does that mean, sweetie?"

The endearment hung in the air like a threat, twisting the clerk to face her. "We don't take your kind in," he answered, his palms flat on the desk in the manner of a preacher at a pulpit.

"What kind is that?"

"You're a prostitute, am I right? A harlot? Tart? Whore?"

With each word, his voice became louder. Maud grew indignant at his high and mighty tone, but she couldn't risk antagonizing him. "Of course not," she replied in mock shame, which did little to change the clerk's demeanor. With more attention of those in the lobby drawn her way, she played the last card in her hand. "I'm here to meet my husband, who's traveling on a different train." She gazed into his eyes the best she could, but the thin man didn't seem to respond to her needs. A better strategy was to respond to his. "You see, my husband has all our money," she continued, slowly edging her palm over the back of his hand. "And I am traveling all alone. It isn't safe for me to wait for him on the streets, for what if he missed the train and didn't arrive for days? Then I would have to depend on the kind company of any strong man that would come along. Do you know what I mean?" She ended with a wink.

The clerk withdrew his hand as if it were in a snake-pit. "You'll have to leave. This is a respectable establishment. We threw all of your type of trash across the tracks ten years ago. Most of them have left westernwards, but I see your 'husband' didn't know that. Get out before I have you thrown out."

With her meager bluff called out in the open, she frowned. The clerk's attention drifted to the Negro maid with a mop and bucket in hand coming down the stairs. "Martha, did you finish in twenty-six?"

The maid nodded with fatigue and indifference, her eyes sagging. Maud knew exactly how she felt.

"Yeah," Martha replied. "Dem walls still have the stink of that drunk dying in dere. I scrubbed dem good clean, but I left the window open 'cause it'll take two days for the smell to leave."

The clerk nodded and turned to the pigeonholes, taking the key from the pigeonhole marked twenty-six and slipping it into his vest pocket. He turned to Maud, who still stood at the desk. He resumed his preacher's stance.

"That's okay, honey," she said, dipping her eyes to his trousers. "I'm too tired to look for it anyway." With a bit of a swagger, she twisted about and walked for the door.

Slowed by the mule and goat, Cole stopped the palomino under the shade of an oak atop a small grassy rise. Once he was dismounted, he carefully pulled the girl from the saddle and sat her on the ground. The day was at least half gone, and only four miles had been covered at best. Little was to be gained by attempting further travel, at least not without feeding the child and stock.

The goat quickly took to the wild growth, still green despite the changing season. The mule showed no interest in eating, another sign of the lack of smarts given to the breed. Despite the bit, the palomino sought the tender blades to nibble. Cole's attention turned to the baby girl, then to the vast terrain before them.

Along the ride from the post, he couldn't clear his mind of the foolishness of this idea. The journey had poor odds of success with him alone. Dragging the pack mule and goat, and with frequent stops to seek suitable shelter for the girl, only fueled his desire to find another caretaker. Colonel Grimes's suggestion to give the child to a Christian family seemed the smartest choice. Still, the Kansas border wouldn't be crossed for another day, and then it would still take some slick talk to get white folks to take in an Indian, no matter how young.

As he was pondering, the thought of feeding the child came to mind. A glance showed her still sitting on the grass with a puzzled face. He drew a tin cup from the pack and proceeded to the goat.

Many years had passed since he'd milked a cow. The goat appeared to have the same parts. Scratching his stubbled chin to consider his approach, he finally took a firm grip. Instantly the goat attempted to flee, but Cole's hand kept the animal still, despite its loud protest. "I ain't enjoying this neither."

With his left hand holding the cup and the goat squirming, he tugged on the teat, but even multiple efforts produced no milk. He placed the cup on the ground and held the goat's hind leg so as to stabilize the animal. Lessons learned long ago told him that the softer the touch, the more likely he was to get the milk out. He pushed back his hat brim so as to put his forehead to the goat's back. He gently tickled the nipple just as he thought a calf's lips would so as to encourage nature to provide.

With one calm stroke after another, he stroked the teat down. However, the goat's pained twitch and baying told him that his grip needed to be more subtle than that applied to a gun butt. Easing his hand a bit stopped the cry. Several more kinder squeezes brought a white drop, which hit the dirt. Fearing he would lose control of the animal if he released the leg, he aimed the teat over the cup. Another drop hit the tin's bottom.

This small success encouraged him to continue. As the drops turned to small streams, the gray bottom of the tin turned white. Memories of his days on the farm, when he was called to the duty of milking cows soon after they calved, came to mind. He sensed the rhythm of hands smooth to the cadence he recalled from those days long ago. The level rose slowly. Each squirt eased his grasp to a circle of his thumb and a single finger.

With the tin nearly half full, Cole stopped milking. Slowly he rose, careful not to tip the tin, preparing for the task of getting the child to slurp it down. A glance in the girl's direction found only grass.

Scanning to the right didn't find her either. His heart beat a little quicker. Thinking she was behind the tree trunk, he put the tin to the ground and scurried around the mule. A peek behind the tree produced the same result.

He took a deep breath in an attempt to compose his mind, and this gave him a moment to think of where she could have wandered. On the slope below was a sea of high grass that could easily hide her small body. If it would have done any good, he'd have shouted her name. However, at such a young age it wasn't likely the girl would respond. Then he was reminded him that she didn't have one to call.

Kicking the grass, he peered through the blades. A

dark object caught his eye. He reached in and yanked the babyless brown blanket. His heart beat a little quicker. Besides the hill, only acres of dormant prairie surrounded him. He charged back up the hill to gain a better vantage point, but no motion in the grass could be seen, and the burden of finding a witless child made his shoulders collapse.

More ground could be covered with the palomino. After mounting the horse, he nudged it into the grass. "Girl!"

With every step of the horse, he felt his heart go from beating to pounding. He recalled the sorrowful faces of Crooked Stone and Daytime Smoke. Colonel Grimes's sly smile at having convinced Cole to take this fool mission only made him mentally kick himself, especially when he realized that the entire plan may have failed only hours after it had begun.

Fear became anger. Why had he been saddled with this hardship? If it hadn't been for one reckless act of his gun, he would likely have been halfway to Chicago city by this time. Why didn't he refuse? The morning's sun dawning on the graves of the young had reminded him why he had changed his mind.

Steering the palomino in a circle back to the tree gave him a glimpse of the sun, now angled to the west. At best there were two hours of daylight left. Besides the lack of light, the bitter north wind would bring the chill of the night.

Maybe it was for the best? If he left the child to fend for itself, might she find a place to sleep? The foolish question was washed from his head. However, if she was hungry or cold, might she cry? Could he find her easily if he left her to cry? The notion of something else finding her first came to mind. Especially in the dark, the small girl would be easy prey for a better night hunter. Coyote?

"Girl! Where are you, damn it!"

The cool air filled his lungs, but he wasn't able to take a deep breath. Each twist of his neck to survey the plain produced no sign. He could feel his blood boil. It would serve the child right if she were left behind. She deserved it. The vengeful thought only recalled the dying breaths of the mother named Honor Woman. Pained by the bullet in her back and knowledge of her own oncoming death, her single concern was for her daughter—the concern only a mother could show under such circumstances, even to the man who had put the bullet in her back. It had been left to him, once an orphan himself, to take care of this one. If he didn't find her, the mother's ghost would haunt him the rest of his life.

The tipping tops of the seedheads revealed a barren spot where only short wild growth had sprung. A black round head of hair popped up between the shifting blades. He kicked the palomino to a trot, then reined in hard at the sight of the little girl sitting among a patch of toadstools. When the little hands pulled one from the marshy soil, Cole swung his leg off the saddle. As the white stem met the girl's lips, he snatched it away. The girl quivered, then her face cringed at Cole's sudden appearance.

He grabbed the small shirt and lifted her to eye level. His fist clenched, he peered into the tiny brown eyes. Grown men who had caused him such anguish often were dealt a punch to the nose. The whip of the breeze reminded him at whom he was staring. He inhaled deeply, and exhaled a warm sigh.

With his left hand he took the reins, and he clutched the girl to his chest with his right. "You are a bear. A little bear, you are," he muttered. As he was about to mount, the words melded in his head: *Little Bear.* He peered at the small child. "That's you from now on."

He stepped into the stirrup and rode to the top of the hill. His mind went back to the task he was planning before he had lost sight of her. As he pulled up and dismounted, he saw small dry twigs protruding from the tree. A fire would have to be started, but first the child needed food—before she stuck something more deadly in her mouth. A glance at the goat and the empty tin tumped to the side slumped his shoulders.

Chapter Six

Two days of seeing to the needs of the baby girl equaled a month on a cow trail. Forcing food down her throat and scrubbing the mess from her drawers drained him of his spirit and his fresh water. Dim street lanterns ahead signaled a small relief. After paying a hefty price to stable the horse, mule, and goat, he walked along the boardwalks of Abilene toward the hotel.

Once he was in the lobby, he headed straight for the desk. A slim clerk wearing a black suit coat scribbled on the book before him. "Need a bed for the night," said Cole.

The clerk first looked up with a polite smile, only to dart his eyes to the small child resting on Cole's shoulder. "I'm sorry. We're full."

"You sure?"

"Positive. We have no vacancies." The clerk's full attention was drawn to the baby.

Cole paused, knowing that he didn't have much chance of getting a bed elsewhere in town, and tired after two restless nights on a bedroll, his eyelids now drooping, he felt more could be done to find him a place to stay. "I just need it for the night."

"I'm sorry, you'll have to go."

Cole felt the young girl reaffirm her hold around his neck. "It wouldn't be because of this young'un, would it?"

The clerk pursed his lips. "It's an Indian. A savage. We don't allow them in the hotel."

"Well, I've got this one under control. So how 'bout a room?"

"I'm sorry. No." The clerk put both hands on the desk, propping his shoulders up just like a hawk.

In no mood to dicker, Cole let out a breath. He drew the Colt pistol and aimed it to the side. A flick of his thumb opened the chamber gate. A nudge spun each cylinder. "How much did you say a room is?" he asked with a peek to the clerk, whose shoulders sagged and whose eyes were wide open.

"But, but, but . . . Ten dollars. That's the price."

After counting a full load of bullets, Cole snapped the chamber gate closed and holstered the pistol. "I got six."

The clerk pushed the register in front of Cole. "That'll do. I think I do have one room. If you'll just sign in."

The book had lines of scribbled names. The clerk prodded Cole with a pen, and it was no time to attempt to scratch words on paper. Writing wasn't something that came natural, even his own name. "Hayes. You can write that down, can't you?"

"Yes, of course," the clerk answered, sliding the book back and scribbling on a blank line. "And how long will you be staying with us? One night, I hope." With the awkward question, the clerk raised his head at Cole. "I didn't mean that the way it sounded." A moment later, the clerk reached into his pocket and drew out a key. "Number twenty-six. Up the stairs at the end of the hall on the right."

With a nod, Cole reached into his pocket and pulled out six silver dollars, then took the key and climbed the stairs, careful not to jostle the girl. He was close to sleep, and if she awoke now, he would spend another four hours trying to get her back to sleep. At the top of the staircase, he crept down the hall, watching the room numbers increase one by one. Finally, his bleary sight focused on a two and a six.

With his right hand, he steadily slipped the key into the lock. A twist of the key freed the latch, and Cole put his toe to the base to nudge the door open. The pitch-black interior of the room made him ease his hand into his coat pocket. His fingers nimbly picked a single match from the box without rustling the rest. Rolling the stick upright in his palm, he stuck his thumbnail into the tip and struck it lit.

The flame flared, then settled peacefully to lick the wooden stick. Cole squinted into the dark to see a stub of candle on the wall. Passing the fire on to the wick illuminated the room. Quick motion drew his attention to the far wall.

A figure stood from the bed. Cole's left hand took the match, and his right dropped to his side. He gripped the Colt but didn't draw, focusing on what moved. The dim light showed the form of a woman. The more the light penetrated the room, the more her eyes widened as her quivering hands clutched the sheet that draped all but her bare shoulders. A tall gal, her hair hung to just past her neck. Intense heat at his finger made him drop the match.

"Please, please—" she begged.

Cole put his aching finger to his lips to hush her, then dabbed it on his tongue to squelch the burn. Once the pain eased, he pointed that finger to the girl on his shoulder and shook his head. The woman seemed to understand and whispered.

"Please, don't hurt me."

Cole gestured with his open palm in a way suggesting that he meant no harm. "My mistake. The fellow downstairs must have given me the wrong key. I'll leave you be," he said, retracing his steps out the door until she stopped him.

"No. Please," she said, her face releasing a nervous grin. "There's no need for you to do that."

Confused by her change of heart, Cole again shook his head. "It wouldn't be proper."

The grin faded, and the open mouth of despair returned to her. "No. It's all right." She let the sheet slip enough to reveal her cleavage. "I don't mind sharing the bed."

He was sure her action was no accident, but he was

unsure of the purpose. "I don't know who you are, ma'am. But what you got in mind, I ain't no taker. Now, I'm going back downstairs to tell that fellow that he give the wrong key. We'll just call me coming in here a mistake and leave it at that." When he turned again, she spoke in more desperate terms.

"Please. Don't."

Cole faced about again, again careful so his motion wouldn't unbalance his sleeping cargo. "Don't what? Leave?"

The woman took a long breath and let it out slowly. "If you tell him I'm here, he'll throw me out in the street. I snuck in here two nights ago and have been sleeping since, but that rat carpetbagger down there wouldn't let me stay. I crawled in the window."

Her story seemed true. A glance told him that she wasn't a woman of quality, and not the sort allowed to stay here. Little Bear snugged Cole's neck, reminding him that he himself likely wouldn't have gotten a key had he not hinted at gunplay. With a cautious step inside, he closed the door behind him. "I'll take the floor."

"No. It's all right. I don't mind you in the bed." Her suggestion stopped him. She noticed his caution. "Or I can sleep on the floor."

He shook his head. "No, I need the bed for this child." The remark made her look fondly at the girl. The distraction relaxed her grip on the sheet, and the flickering light gave Cole a dim view of her white flesh with defined darker spots. Like a soldier, he abruptly about-faced. "Damn, ma'am. Don't you have nothing on?"

81

"Sorry," she whispered. The rustling of cloth didn't last long. "All right. You can turn around now."

As he did, he saw that the sheet was back on the bed, and that the woman stood in her bloomers above her knees with an untucked top strapped over her shoulders—still not the dress of a lady. His sagging energy cut into his sense of decency, and he approached slowly. The woman's arm reached out.

"Let me hold the baby. Is she yours?"

The offer alarmed him, more over the risk of waking the child. He glared at the woman. She retracted her arms. "Get in the bed," he said. Like a frightened coward, the woman retreated back onto the bed. Cole stepped to the side, motioning the woman to scoot to the far side. Gently, he laid Little Bear on the bed and pulled the sheet over her. The woman looked startled that his order was for that reason. Cole leaned over the child to stare the woman in the eye. "If you wake her up, I'll throw you out in the street myself."

Her nod told him that his message was understood. On his toes, he crept back to the door. After a last look at the distance to the bed and a quick survey of the sparse furniture, he cupped his hand around the candle flame and blew it out.

Bill Wheeler pulled on his boots just as the sun peeped above the landscape. He hugged his coat's collar tight around his neck and huddled around the smoldering embers from the previous night's fire. Little heat was gained to thaw his fingers. It would take at least two hours for the sun to warm the air from the night's chill. Without time to build another, he saddled his horse and mounted. Little time could be spared if he was to locate his next reward.

For two days he had ridden south. With the bigger of the two rewards already gone, he hoped he had started on this journey with enough time to get the remaining one, even if the pot was a mite small. As the horse clopped through the grass, his mind settled on his quarry.

George Gross had been a member of the Sam Bass Gang. With terms of employment on both sides of the law, it was the lure of mining that attracted him most, even if he seemed adept at mining on other owners' land. Sam Bass had found money in South Dakota, but when more people started showing up, shoveling ore from the streams, the idea of taking it from them rather than finding his own was too attractive. Gross fell out of favor with Sam when Sam found George's hand in his own pockets, and the two parted company in a hurry. George was too old to drive cattle, even if it was simpler than digging holes in the dirt. When he met Curtis Marlowe, the younger thief talked the older one into stealing steers from the locals outside Fort Worth. The two had made enough of a name for themselves for Texas Rangers to post papers for their capture.

It had been six weeks since word got around of the daring twosome parting over the split of the loot. Marlowe was an easy track, even if it took following him all the way to Kansas. Wherever there were cattle, liquor, and women, with the least law around, you could find Marlowe. George Gross liked the seclusion of mining. The easiest claim could be had from those who didn't live on the land. Government land was used mostly to keep white folks safe from Indians, but most in the trade felt it a waste of a resource. If there was a nugget to be found, George Gross could sniff it out.

When Wheeler crossed the Canadian River, he felt the terrain slowly change from flat prairie to rising and sloping hills. For most of the day, he followed his instincts toward the jagged rocks found in the Arbuckle Mountains. While steering his horse up the rocky inclines, a column of soldiers less than half a mile to the east in a flatland below caught his attention. Normally not one to socialize with Federals, he noticed what appeared to be bodies strapped across saddles. His instincts told him this was in line with his business.

He turned the horse down the rocks and kicked it to a gallop. As he approached, the column halted, some of the soldiers having drawn their pistols. Wheeler raised his empty right hand while holding a stiff grip on the reins with his left. "Hold your fire," he called out. At an amble, he went to the head of the column. The pair of single bars on the officer's uniform seemed new. Wheeler figured the experience of the young man was just as fresh. "Lieutenant, the name's Wheeler." He pointed at the two bodies. "Who you got there?"

"Mr. Wheeler," the officer said with some bewilderment. "I'm not at liberty to say."

"Mind if I have a look?" Again the officer looked to his troopers with some hesitation. It was an opportunity to exploit. "I'm looking for a fellow that's wanted in Texas for rustling cattle. I figured he was in these parts, and well, since I seen you with these bodies, I figured you may have saved me some trouble."

The lieutenant's look of confusion became a scowl. "You're a bounty hunter, Mr. Wheeler?"

"Yessir," Wheeler replied without remorse. Before the officer could make known his opinion of the profession, Wheeler took charge of the conversation. "More than twenty men I've caught. Sixteen have been hung, and the others are waiting for their day to come to meet their maker. That's twenty criminals that ain't going to harm nobody no more, nor steal their stock. All done legal-like." Wheeler paused a moment to eye the rest of the column, then looked again at the lieutenant. "Seems to me we're in the same business: keeping folks safe. So why don't you let me have a peek at them two. Won't be a bother for more than a minute. What'll you say?"

The officer again looked to his men, an action that signaled to Wheeler that he wasn't used to making decisions. Wheeler didn't wait to be told no. He dismounted and went to the first horse. He untied the ropes that secured the slicker cloaking the body to reveal the dirt-smudged face of an Indian girl. With the view came a waft of decay that forced him back a step. This wasn't who he wanted. He went to the following horse, and once the slicker was free, he pulled up the head of George Gross, his gray whiskers full of soil. "That's the man I'm after."

"And who might he be?" asked the lieutenant.

"His name is George Gross. He's wanted in Texas for cattle rustling and a few other places for various crimes. I'll take him back to Texas, though. Ain't worth the trouble to take him any further. Looks like they been buried."

"That's right. They have," the lieutenant said. "And I'm not letting you take him anywhere."

Wheeler stopped rubbing his hands of filth at the reply. "What you mean? This man is wanted. What are you going to do with him?"

"We're taking them back to the post."

"But you can't. I mean, I've got to return him. Texas Rangers are looking for him."

"My orders are specific, Mr. Wheeler. I'm to return these bodies." The officer motioned the corporal behind, and a moment later the enlisted man unsnapped the cover of his side arm. The act alone didn't scare Wheeler, but he knew that trading lead with a squad of cavalry was suicide.

"How 'bout I tag along. Maybe I can have him after you're done with him."

The suggestion seemed to puzzle the officer. "Suit yourself. You can speak to Colonel Grimes about the matter. My job is just to bring these bodies back."

"Much obliged." Wheeler tipped his hat as the lieutenant motioned the column forward.

Chapter Seven

Blinking in the daylight, Maud yawned, then froze still. The threat from the strange man during the night flashed in her mind. Cautious, she peeked to the side to see if she had disturbed the sleeping baby, only to find she was alone in the room. With a sigh of relief, she gulped in panic. Even though she was still alive, the thought hit her that her presence in the room might have been told to the desk clerk.

Throwing the sheet to the side, she sprang from the bed. She took the crumpled skirt from the floor and stepped in, tugging it past her thighs and hips until it hung from her waist. She slipped on her blouse as fast as she ever remembered doing so, nimbly snapping the buttons. Next, she took her stockings, but fearing that time was not on her side, she rolled them in a ball and tucked them into her blouse. She plunged her bare feet into her shoes and tied the laces just enough so as not to trip over them, yet they were anything but tight. She ran to the door, only to stop and retrieve her bag. On her way back to the door, she passed her image in the single portrait mirror.

Her hair was a snarled crow's nest. Her cheeks still wore the smudged rouge. She straightened her blouse, unsnapping the buttons to realign them with the appropriate holes; then she looked again. She appeared to have three breasts. Quickly, she took the rolled stockings from her blouse and threw them into her bag. Finally, she plucked her hat from the bedpost and slammed it on her head. Bag in hand, she opened the door and scurried through the hall to the top of the stairs. Like a sign from above, she had been saved—or condemned. The stranger with the baby in his left arm was at the desk talking to the clerk. There was only one thing to do.

"Honey! I'm ready."

The stranger and the clerk and the rest of those in the lobby all peered up at her. She drew a deep breath, her teeth gritted in a smile. With all other jaws dropped, she delicately took the handrail and pranced down the stairs in her most ladylike fashion. Once she was off the stairs, she approached the stranger with a loving smile, curling her arm inside his. His blank stare didn't deter her from proceeding with her best effort.

"I didn't know you had left the room. Shame on you." The confusion arching his eyebrows began to ebb as they lowered in a crease. She couldn't risk letting him divulge the charade. "No excuses," she said, lurching up to give him a peck on the lips. "Don't worry, I still love you anyway." She turned her attention to the equally stunned clerk. "Are we done here?"

The clerk looked at her, then the stranger, then back at her as if in amazement.

"I told you my husband was coming," she said, taking the key from the stranger's hand and slapping it on the wood top. "You wouldn't believe what he said to me, dear."

The clerk gave the stranger a look as if pleading for forgiveness. "I didn't . . . didn't know. I'm terribly sorry."

"Yes, well, if we had time, we would complain to the manager. But we don't, do we, darling," she said, arching her gaze up to the stranger. "Let's go." She firmly tugged on his arm and led him from the lobby, all eyes watching them parade out the door.

Outside, she continued to pull him from the doorway until she knew the door was firmly shut. It was then that the stranger yanked away from her hold. "What the hell are you doing?"

"You didn't like that? I thought it was pretty good myself."

"That fellow in there thinks you belong to me," he said, pointing at the door.

Maud shrugged. "I had to. I thought maybe you might have told about our little encounter last night, and I didn't want him to get the wrong impression of you."

"Of me?"

It was time for a confession. "All right. I'm sorry."

She paused as she looked into his blue eyes. Apologies weren't her specialty, especially sincere ones. "I thought you might have told him about me. I didn't want to end up in jail. Not in this town, at least not until I got to know the sheriff a little better."

He turned, and the expression on his face seemed a disgusted one. A glance at the townspeople told her they were same the ones she had seen the previous day. The only friend she had was the one who had just turned his back. "I'm sorry. I really am." He didn't stop. She pinched her skirt and ran after him. Once she was at his side, she again pulled at his arm to make him face her. "Hey, I said I'm sorry. Don't hold a grudge."

"I ain't interested."

As he continued walking, she peeked down at her blouse. Unsure if he had the wrong idea, she again scooted quickly to catch him, and again tugged at his elbow. "I ain't selling nothing. I really mean it. You saved my skin back there, and I'm grateful."

The disgust on his face relaxed away to a smirk. "You're welcome."

The moment she needed had come. The gamble had paid off. Feeling that she was on a roll, she pushed out her open palm. "I'm Maud."

He took her hand as if wary of a trap. "Clay."

With a manly snap, she shook his hand. "Nice to meet you, Clay." He nodded in answer to her greeting, then with the same determination he resumed striding down the boardwalk. It was no time to let him go now. "Where you headed?"

"To the livery."

"Mind if I come along?" she asked, trying to keep up with him.

"I'd guess you would if I told you no."

She smiled at his recognition and honesty. "I'd guess you'd be right." He crossed the street, and she followed, dodging the traffic of men on horseback. When she caught sight of him again, he had opened a tall door to the livery. She hiked her skirt so as to run to the door. As it creaked open, she entered the dark stable. The stench of manure made her eyes water. She waved the flies from her nose.

Clay stood talking to the stablemaster, placing coins in the man's palm. Then, taking the reins from the stablemaster, he led out a palomino with a blond mane. A black saddle trimmed in silver was on its back. Clay led it through the tall door, and Maud retreated outside.

"Pretty horse, Clay." Her hope to break into his stiff attitude with compliments produced only rumpled lips on his part.

"Ain't my kind of horse. Little too fancy for my taste. But it was all I could get at the time." The tall door opened again, and the stablemaster led out a gray mule with bundles strapped to its back and a goat not far behind.

"This yours, too?"

He nodded. "Yup. Quite a train, ain't it." Lifting the child onto the saddle, he placed her in a roped loop.

"Oh, so that's how you carry her," said Maud. "Say, where is it you're going?"

"North," he answered, throwing the stirrup into the

91

saddle and tightening the cinch. She would have preferred him to look her in the eye, but she had to try now.

"Yeah? Well, I'm going to Omaha myself," she lied. "What say I ride along with you. Keep you and the little one company. Not in the same way, of course."

He craned his neck at her. "Like how?"

Usually when she offered her company, it was met with a fonder reaction. He appeared to be insulted. "I mean, I mean, like someone to talk to, is all."

He threw the stirrup off the saddle. "I ain't much for talking."

"Oh, come on, Clay. You can't expect a defenseless woman to travel on her own," she said with her hands on her hips.

He glanced at her from head to toe. "Looks like you done pretty good so far," he muttered as he passed by her, taking the reins and walking the horse and mule farther into the street.

"I know you can't mean that, Clay. I see it in you. You and that little girl. A man that would take a baby wouldn't leave a lady by herself."

"Lady?" he blurted. The slight made her dip her eyes to the dirt. It wasn't the first time her status had been questioned. But she knew the little pout had worked when she heard his voice. "I already got one female to fend for. That's my limit. Besides, I ain't headed for Omaha." The more he spoke, the more remorse she heard in his tone. From the corner of her eye she could see his boots. She didn't look at him in an attempt to squeeze his guilt for the answer she wanted. The more silence, the better for her. "Do you even have a horse?"

She twisted about. "I'll get it."

Jeffrey Grimes put down his pen upon hearing a knock at the door. The letter home would have to wait. He glanced to the side to the photograph of his beloved Margaret. His bride had left the post for home in Hartford eighteen months before, unable to deal with the harsh climate of the West. His dedication to duty had always come before his commitment to her, and she had realized that when she took her vows to him twenty years earlier. She departed with disappointment, remorseful at not fulfilling her duties to him as an officer's wife. He never thought of it that way. Now he wrote what he had always meant to tell her, that it was he who had failed her. Another knock interrupted his thoughts. "Come in."

Corporal Stephensen entered. "Lieutenant Miller's detail has returned, sir."

"Very well," Grimes replied. He rose, putting on his straw hat, left his office, and walked outside. The sun shined brightly. He scanned the sky but couldn't find a cloud. He knew the fair weather would be his only pleasant discovery.

The column paraded by the porch. Miller held up his hand to stop and ordered dismount. He snapped a salute to Grimes.

"Sir, the detail found the cabin and have returned with two corpses. I ordered a further search, but we found only these two, sir."

"Thank you, Lieutenant." Grimes took a deep

breath and stepped off the porch. He went to the first body. A peek beneath the slicker confirmed what he had suspected. It was never easy viewing death, even an enemy's. This time it was a loved one of a friend. The thought sunk his heart that he as an officer in the Army of the United States had had a part in it.

He looked to the second horse. "Is that the man that did this, Lieutenant?"

"Yes, sir."

"Any idea who he is?" Grimes said as he went to the horse.

"His name is George Gross."

Grimes didn't recognize the voice. "Who said that?"

"I did." A civilian rider came from the rear of the column.

"Lieutenant Miller, who is this man?"

"My name is Wheeler, sir. Bill Wheeler," the rider answered, sliding off his mount. "This fellow here is wanted in Texas for cattle rustling. I'm here to take him back."

"I don't see a badge, Mr. Wheeler. Are you an officer of the law?"

"No, sir. I am a private businessman."

"A bounty hunter, sir," Lieutenant Miller said with some disdain.

"Yessir. That I am. But I don't see how that makes any difference. Like I was telling the young lieutenant there, Gross here is a wanted man." Wheeler reached inside his vest and drew out folded reward posters. Like a clerk, he licked his thumb to shuffle through each one. "See here," he said, handing a bill to

Grimes. The name was the same, and the description seemed to match.

"You can have him when I'm done with him," Grimes said, handing the poster back to Wheeler, then turned his back on the small man.

"What do you plan on doing with him, if you don't mind me asking?"

The inquiry infuriated the colonel. "At this point I am not sure." He faced Wheeler. With each step he could feel his anger build. "This man Gross killed a friend of mine's daughter, apparently in an attempt to force himself on her. She was only trying to find a better life for herself and her child and happened upon this no-good bastard of a man who ended up shooting her in the back. That is why I'm not eager to allow you to take him away. Now, this is federal land and I am in authority. I will keep him, and if I so choose, I will give him to you when I am ready."

"George Gross was blind in his left eye and near blind in the right. Must have been one-in-a-life shots for him to hit anything."

The casual statement stopped Grimes. At first, he didn't think he had heard correctly. "Say again."

"George Grimes was near fifty-seven. Couldn't see clear more than three feet. Carried a pistol mostly for show."

Recalling the story he'd been told by Hayes, Grimes paused a moment, cleared his throat, and squinted into Wheeler's eyes. "Join me inside." Grimes faced about and walked up the steps to the porch. The clomp of boots on the hollow boards indicated that the bounty hunter was right behind, following him all the way inside. As the colonel entered the office, he turned to see Lieutenant Miller standing in the doorway. "See that we aren't disturbed."

Miller saluted as Grimes closed the door.

Wheeler sat in a chair without invitation. Grimes went around to sit in his chair. Removing his hat, he tossed it onto the desk. "How come you know so much about this man Gross?"

"Everybody knows about George. He's been in the stealing-cattle business for thirty years, then got his taste for mining ore."

Grimes glared at Wheeler. "Yes, but how do you know so much about him? The fact that he was blind?"

A smirk creased Wheeler's face. "That's because I've been in this business for thirty years. I was the sheriff of Johnson County some years ago. You do that long enough, you come to learn a little bit about everyone with papers on them. I heard of George before he joined up with Sam Bass, then kinda kept up with him through meeting other fellows, you know, drinking a shot or two. He partnered up with a young fellow name of Curtis Marlowe. Marlowe wanted to get rich on other people's sweat, and George there knew where there were steers for the taking. So they took them. When the Rangers posted a reward for them both, I decided to go after them."

"How many years have you been hunting men for the price on their head?"

"The last five."

"Why did you turn?"

Wheeler twitched his cheek again. "There were no

turning to it." He removed his hat and rubbed his finely cut hair. "I spent most of my life putting these fellows in jail, risking my life and that of my family, not to mention staying up to all hours of the night for twenty dollars a month. When I seen that them I was putting in jail were eating on a regular basis, had enough money to fetch what they wanted, and wouldn't even be in jail had it not been for one mistake, maybe two, I decided I'd give this a try. After a while, these fellows that turned to banditry rob and steal enough that the law makes it worth a man's while to risk what he has to."

"And what is that?" Grimes's question made Wheeler look to the desk. His hesitation in answering surprised the colonel. Most men in the profession of hunting others weren't much more above the law than those they chased. Wheeler inhaled deeply, then looked Grimes in the eye. "I got a wife and daughter back in Texas, Colonel. I ain't seen them in near two months and don't plan to for at least another two. When a man takes a job, he ain't worth his spit if he don't finish it—that's just the way I was raised. The girl, she ain't seen me much in all these years, and she's getting old enough now to be eyeing young fellows as prospective husbands, as young girls do. I think a father should be around at those times for his family, but he also has to provide for them. When I'm out, away from home, when all I have to keep me warm is a puny fire hardly big enough to melt the snow surrounding it, I try to remember both of them things."

Grimes peeked at his wife's photograph. "I can understand what you mean, Mr. Wheeler." After a moment's thought, Grimes returned his attention to the matter at hand. "You said that this man Gross couldn't have shot the woman."

"I didn't say he couldn't a done it. I just thought it must have been a hell of a shot. George was never known as a crack shooter."

Grimes leaned over the desk. "Have you ever heard of a man named Hayes? Clay Hayes?"

Wheeler shook his head. "Hayes? No, I never heard the name, nor seen it posted. Why you ask?"

Hesitant to share details on the matter with the bounty hunter, Grimes convinced himself the man on the other side of the desk wasn't much different than himself. "Not more than a week ago, a man named Hayes arrived here with a child. He told a story of finding the child after there was a fight between this George Gross and the Nez Perce squaw." Grimes dipped his eyes for a moment. "Her name was Honor Woman. She is the mother of the child and the daughter of a friend of mine." He looked up from the desk. "I would be very interested in what exactly happened in that cabin."

"He told you a story of George shooting the squaw?" Grimes answered Wheeler's question with a nod. "What did he look like?"

Grimes sat back in his chair. "A large man. I'd say perhaps six and a half feet tall. A bit unkept, you know. It appeared he hadn't shaven in some time," he added, then realized how his remark might be understood after taking a better look at Wheeler. "I beg your pardon. I didn't mean to imply—"

"No offense taken, Colonel," Wheeler replied, rubbing his own whiskers. "Don't run into many razors, myself."

The admission relieved Grimes. The more he spoke, the more comfortable he became with this bounty hunter. "As I was saying, Hayes struck me as a man traveling through the territory, as I have seen many times. He carried a side arm on his hip, and also had a unique rifle I had not seen before."

"What kind of pistol he carry?"

"Forty-five Colt. Much like the old issue six or seven years ago. I couldn't be sure—he never removed it from the holster."

"Which side did he carry it on?"

"The right," Grimes answered.

Wheeler's brow lowered, as if he was concentrating on details. His inquiry sounded much like that of a prosecutor.

"What about his face?"

Grimes peered to the ceiling in thought, trying to recall anything remarkable about Hayes. Flashing the image in his mind, the one feature he had noticed came into view. He touched his right eyebrow. "He had a pronounced scar, right about here."

Wheeler's face lit up. The bounty hunter reached into his vest pocket to remove the posters once more. He singled one out and handed it to Grimes. "He look anything like that?"

The description resembled what Grimes recalled. The charges against the wanted man appeared to be the acts of a desperate man. Grimes's heart sank when he thought of giving Honor Woman's daughter to Hayes. "The Rainmaker? Is that who you think this man was?"

"Could be. I've been looking for him ever since that was posted. Heard he passed through Fort Worth maybe thirty days ago. Thought about going after him, but I found out Marlowe and Gross had rustled steers from ranches out of Wise County and were driving them to the railheads in Kansas. But I never lost sight of that poster. With money like that, a man's got to keep his options open."

"Hayes left here the day before yesterday," Grimes said, handing the poster back to Wheeler. "I even requisitioned two weeks' supplies for his travel."

"Why would you do that, Colonel?"

With a sigh, he answered. "The child that I mentioned was the granddaughter of a Nez Perce chief that is in detainment here." The reason wouldn't be easy to convey. "This is neither an easy place to govern nor to be governed. I had heard of Honor Woman's intent to leave this reservation. Normally, it would be my duty to intercede." He paused. "However, after the years I have spent here, witnessing the suffering of these people, I thought it my moral duty to look the other way when her absence was reported to me. Now, in light of what has happened, I wish I'd done something. If I had, she would be alive today."

Wheeler tucked the poster back into his vest. "Colonel, let's you and me have a look at that cabin."

Chapter Eight

"Can't we have a rest?"

The woman's constant nagging gnawed at Cole's concentration. "This ain't no day trip for a Sunday picnic. If you didn't want to ride, you should'na come."

"But I've been on this horse all day. I'm not as young as I used to be. Can't we just stop for a little while?"

Cole kept his eyes to the front. The Indian summer was a fortunate advantage. It would be a waste not to use it as long as possible. Although the grass had turned, red and yellow leaves were still on the trees. The next stiff wind would wipe the branches bare, and the more ground they covered the less likely they were to be caught without shelter in a storm. Yet a peek down showed Little Bear slumped to the side.

He took a deep breath, realizing he had to take into account that he wasn't alone.

After emerging from the trees, he spotted a small pond in the clearing. Water was hard to pass up. Knowing that little more ground could be gained once they stopped, he looked to the sun and figured he had only a couple hours at most before dark. He reined in. "We'll camp here."

"Thank God," she moaned.

Cole dismounted, then gently lifted Little Bear into his arms. "We need a fire," he said while Maud struggled off her horse.

"Where are we?"

"At least a day off the Nebraska line is the way I figure. I'm going to find wood." He handed her the child. "Let her sleep."

Maud stood, confused, and retracted her arms as Cole held out Little Bear. "I ain't a nanny."

"You said that you were going to keep us company. Here, keep her company." He prodded enough, forcing Maud to accept the child despite her cringing glower. "See, you two do make a pair," he said with a grin, then turned to mount the palomino. "Be back soon," he said as he gave the horse a nudge. A peek behind showed Maud holding the little girl at arm's length. He couldn't help but feel a grin cross his face.

A small slope took him down where tall oaks stood, as well as some that nature had laid down. The wood appeared rotted, but still solid. Without an ax, he would have to ride farther for easier pickings at dry branches. Continuing down the grade took him into a small valley. Oaks, cottonwoods, and a few juniper bushes dotted the grass. He pulled up at an oak with a ten-foot-long low-hanging branch without any leaves.

He got off his horse and grabbed the branch, thinking he could easily snap it from the trunk. Yanking down only made the branch sag. Another yank produced the same result even when he lifted his feet and hung from it. The act recalled days when he was a youth on a farm doing the very same to see if he could fling it into the air. After a few moments, he reminded himself he wasn't ten years old. Putting his boots back to the dirt, he released the branch and peeked to be sure that no eyes saw how foolish he must have appeared.

A long glare at the branch convinced him this was the one he had to have. It could be broken into smaller logs, and once the fire was started, the green wood would last the night. He just had to have it. It was a matter of pride.

Spitting in both hands, he took another firm grasp. If he couldn't pull it off, he would push it. He swung the branch back and forth, but couldn't get enough motion at the base of the branch. For greater leverage, he took the end. Shoving the branch to one side produced an aching groan. Encouraged by the sound, he pushed harder, his boots slipping on the grass. To keep his balance, he kept his legs moving. A louder groan came, and he was convinced one final shove would break it. The brittle end cracked, sending him facefirst into the ground.

Disgusted at the two-foot log now in his hand, he heard a whinny and turned to the palomino. When he focused on the lariat strapped to the saddle, he felt like a bigger fool than when he had hung from the branch. "Why didn't you say something before?"

With some pride still intact, he rode the palomino back up the hill with the branch in tow; it was the strength of the horse that had ripped the branch from the trunk. As he crested out of the valley and up the slope, his attention was drawn to gleeful sounds coming from the pond. He reined in.

Only her bare shoulders showing, Maud held the little girl above the water, gently dipping the child into the water. As the two continued the play, Cole nudged the palomino and approached the bank. Maud's turned her attention to him with a smile. "Come on in, Clay. You look like you could use a bath too."

"I like taking mine in private."

"Oh, what fun is that?" she said, bobbing up above the surface enough to show her breasts, then submerging them. Cole dipped his head to view the dust. "You don't have to be shy, Clay. I'm sure a grown man like you has seen a woman without clothes before."

"Usually not in a place like this," he replied, still keeping his eyes to the ground.

"Well, then, if you're not going to join us, I guess we'll have to get out. Would you be a honey and hand me my clothes?" Cole slid from the saddle and retrieved the bloomers and lace top from the small brush near the shore. Still with only her head above the surface, Maud carefully moved toward him, with both hands on the little girl. When she neared, Cole reached out the clothes and Maud casually stood, showing bare flesh without a hint of shame while wading out of the water. "Can you take the baby?"

Trading clothes for the child, it would not be right for him not to look and be sure of a firm grip on the wet child. Maud passed him as she walked up the bank, and Cole kept his eyes out on the pond. A few moments went by, with the sounds of cloth being stretched and pulled, before he heard her voice. "You can turn around now."

When he did, she had on the skirt and blouse.

Bill Wheeler followed the lead of the lieutenant. The tops of the tall oaks sprouted above. As he bobbed his head through the heavy brush of the rocky woods, the surroundings seemed a fit for George Gross. As the incline grew steeper, the deeper into the scattered scrub forest he and the soldier escort rode. As they crested a hill through the thicket, a clearing could be seen below with two open graves.

"That's where we found them, sir," Lieutenant Miller said to Colonel Grimes. "The shack is shortly up this hill."

"Very well, Lieutenant," Grimes answered. "Let's have a look."

Miller nudged his mount up the hill into another batch of trees. Wheeler positioned himself right behind. The grade became a sheer ridge, and Miller ordered a dismount to the troopers behind him. Anxious to have first sight of the house, Wheeler whipped his horse's flanks to charge up the hill. At the top, he saw the small shack hidden in the shadows of the afternoon sun.

Off his horse, Wheeler warily approached the front of the shack with his right hand on the gun butt, unsure if tramps had found a roof for the night. He peeked behind and spotted the troopers leading their mounts over the ridge, then booted the door open. Inside, two dried blood pools were the first things to catch his eye. He knelt next to the one on the right. A wipe of his finger and a sniff told him what had happened.

Grimes strode through the door. "Is this where it happened?"

"Yessir," Wheeler replied as he rose. "That is where the squaw died."

"And how do you know that?"

He faced the officer. "All them years I told you about, you see a lot of blood. You get to know the difference in the smell of it." He pointed to the other pool and walked to it. "And this is where old George bought it." He looked to the three holes in the far wall. Aiming his hand like a pistol, he gauged the angle to them from over the stain. "That appears to be his handiwork."

Grimes's face turned somber. "And that's where he shot her."

"I don't think so. What I saw of her body, the wound didn't show the markings of a close shot. When a bullet is fired at this range, there'd be a powder burn on the clothes. Didn't see none on her. But that ain't what really tells me old George ain't the one that killed her."

Grimes's jaw drooped open, and he appeared surprised at the idea. Wheeler knew how to convince him. He lifted his boot and scuffed at the glass shards on the floor.

"A bullet that comes from the outside spreads glass inside." The colonel's mouth shut and his brow furrowed. "Who did you say this man was, Colonel? The one that you give this squaw's baby to?"

"Hayes. He said his name was Clay Hayes."

Wheeler shook his head. "I can't say I know that name. But I 'spect he is the Rainmaker."

Grimes stared at the bloodstained floor. "Do you think the child is still alive?"

"That's hard to say, sir. Most men on the run can only think of what's best for them. Can't imagine a desperate fellow taking the time to fend for a little one. Not with winter coming on. No, sir, I wouldn't give you a snake's chance in a stampede that the child is alive. But there's always that chance."

The officer let out a long breath. "Mr. Wheeler, it seems I have made a grim mistake. A mistake that is mine alone." He stared Wheeler in the eye. "I'll supply you with whatever you need, including Gross's body, if you go after this man you think is the Rainmaker and bring that little girl back."

"Won't have time to take George back if I'm going to catch up with this fellow. You'll do me a favor by burying the body until I can return for it to take to Texas." Grimes nodded, then removed his glove and offered it to Wheeler.

"Consider it done. I know my conscience won't rest until I know that child is safe."

Tim McGuire

* * *

The night's fire popped and sizzled. He stirred the pot of beans over the flame, then doled out some on Maud's plate and on his own. She picked through them to find any meat, but there was none. She wrinkled her nose between bites.

"Taste bad?" he asked.

"No, but it's only beans."

"I could throw some jerky into it."

The prospect of wadded and cold beef wasn't encouraging. She shook her head. He continued to shovel his spoon into the pile. "You think we'll be in Omaha in two days?"

He shrugged his shoulders between gulps. "If the weather holds." He looked out into the dark. "You never can tell this time of year."

She looked in his face amid the glow of the fire. Blue eyes beamed out from the reddened face. Despite the creases cut into his cheeks, he wasn't a half-bad-looking man. She had spent several nights with some she didn't want to see. As she gazed, the child rustled on its blanket, which lay next to him. "You never did answer me back in Abilene."

"What's that?" he muttered with a mouthful.

"Is that young'un yours?"

He shook his head. "Nope." He shoveled in another mouthful. She wasn't going to let that answer stand.

"Well, then, whose is she?"

Once he swallowed, he grunted his throat clear. "She's an Indian girl's." He took another gulp.

"I figured that," she said, disgusted. "Why do you have her?"

Rubbing his sleeve along his chin, he faced her with a furrowed brow. "Been asking myself that question for the last hundred miles."

Once she was sure his anger wasn't aimed at her, Maud smiled. "Then how come you have her?"

The simple remark seemed to cut into him like a knife. He took another bite, as if to consider his answer. While he did so, she took one of her own. Finally, he swallowed the beans, reaching out to the coffeepot on the spit to pour himself a tin cup full. He raised the tin to his lips, blowing the steaming surface.

"An army colonel asked me take her."

The reply appeared simple enough, not one that would take so long to consider. "Why did he ask you?"

"The mother got shot," he answered quickly, shoveling the final bite into his mouth.

"That's it? She got shot, so he picked you." The explanation made her chuckle. "Would you do it, Clay? Did you shoot her?"

His brow furrowed once more, but no words followed. This time it appeared the glare was meant for her. Before she could say any other words she'd regret, she stuffed a healthy portion into her own mouth. As she swirled the beans in her mouth, a cool gust blew on her back, but it wasn't the only reason she shivered. The subject needed to be changed.

"Where you from, Clay?" she asked, hoping that wouldn't spark further flames from his eyeballs. A peek showed him placing the plate to the dirt and rubbing his hands together as if readying them for another duty. With his hands free, she took a firm grip of the spoon, not sure if she might need it as a weapon. He placed his right hand in his coat pocket. She squeezed the spoon, trying to steady her quivering hand, ready to jab it into his eye if he lunged at her. He pulled a pouch from his pocket, unfurled it, and opened the flap. Drawing a single paper, he sprinkled it with tobacco.

Maud eased her grip on the spoon, then swallowed the beans she forgot were in her mouth so as to inhale a deep breath. Slightly shaking her head, she felt like a fool for her fear. She was becoming as jumpy as a schoolgirl at a barn dance. Relieved that he wasn't about to do what she thought, ashamed at what she did think, and delighted to see him roll the smoke, she put down her plate.

He stuck the roll into his mouth, lapping the end to coat the paper and slow the burn. When he took a twig from the fire to light it, he drew on it. The end glowed red. It was too enticing, so she plucked it from his fingers and took her own deep drag. A tingle replaced the quiver. Exhaling the calming smoke, she gave it back to him. "I asked you where you are from."

First he looked to the side, then up at the stars. "I was born and raised here."

Maud looked about. "Here?"

"Due east, 'bout a hundred miles or so. Outside of Fort Scott." The muscles in his face eased. "Me and my ma lived there on a farm. My pa was a soldier most of the time. Every time there was a fight, he put on a uniform. He was gone most of the time." He paused to take another drag, then handed it to her. She took one of her own. "Just before the war, my ma died. My father was what they called a Jay-hawker, but he never liked the term. I went with him, not knowing much and expecting even less." He shook his head and exhaled a breath. Staring into the fire, he seemed pained at the memory. "He was killed in Texas," he said matter-of-factly, then turned to her. "Then I went off and joined up with the army. I haven't been back here since then." He took the smoke from her. "What about you?"

Memories flooded her mind, most of which she wanted to forget. "I ain't got much of a story."

"Go on, now. I told you."

The encouragement, along with the way she now felt, thanks to the smoke, made her relent. "Well, I'm an eastern gal. I was raised in Erie, Pennsylvania. There weren't much to do there, and I got tired of going to school each day, so I did what most of us in the trade did: I jumped on the first fellow that told me he would take me from there. Gave him my virtue right when he said those words: 'I love you.' I was raised a Quaker and he was a Presbyterian, but that didn't stop me from marrying him at a justice of the peace." She paused to take the cigarette from him for another drag. "The no-good son of a bitch."

"Stay with him long, I guess?"

"Oh yeah," she scoffed. "All the way to seek his fortune in the cattle business. We got as far as St. Louis, when Horace decided he could get a stake to buy cows by playing cards. It didn't take him a single day to lose the two hundred and sixteen dollars that we had. And do you know what he did to me after that?"

Clay shook his head. Maud threw the smoke into the fire.

"He sold me."

"Sold you?" he asked in doubt. It spurred her to convince him it was true.

"I'm here to tell you. A fellow named LeClerc staked Horace twenty dollars on one hand at faro. Faro! Ain't no more crooked a game. And Horace staked me. And do you know my husband didn't have the guts to tell me. When I found out about it, Le-Clerc was knocking at my door from a sound sleep. He had a bottle in one hand and a note from Horace in the other. I never saw Horace again." She paused, thinking about the rest of the story. "Of course, once I got over the indignation, I have to admit, LeClerc at least brought the goods. Best night with a man I've had to date." She looked to Clay, who cackled at her. "That was ten years ago. But I'm still a young woman ready for new experiences."

He stopped his cackle, then tipped his hat back, revealing his whole face from the shadow of the brim. "So that was your start?"

"Oh yeah. I was on my own in St. Louis for two years. I joined Hildegard Prescott's girls. 'Hildy the Till,' we called her. She took seventy cents of every dollar, and I had to pay two dollars for the room. 'Bawdy Maudy,' I was come to be known." She shook her head and looked into the flame. "Boy, thank the Lord my mother died soon after I left. My worst fear was she would have found out. Anyway, I left St. Louis for the cowtowns with cowboys with money spilling out of their pockets. But the local societies kept getting too proud to have us. So I went where they drove the cattle, until I ran out of money and couldn't get there." Inhaling a deep breath, she let out a long sigh. "Can't go nowhere there ain't misery at every door."

"There is one place," he said softly. His face relaxed and he smiled contentedly. It was as if a fond ideal had struck him. "In New Mexico, east of Santa Fe, is a town called Nobility." He looked at her with his smile changing to a sly grin for only a moment. "You'd find a lot of work there. But a little further out from the town is a farm. A widow and her boy and girl live on it. When I first got there, I didn't have a notion to stay. After a while, it was the closest I come to settling put. It took me back to the days when I was a kid, with my ma, living near Fort Scott." He paused looking into the fire, jerking his smile about at her once more. "We built a barn. Wasn't the best one ever built, but it was the best one I had ever. Me and the boy did it." His eyes returned to the fire and his voice softened to a whisper. "Noah was his name. I sure enjoyed it there."

"Why didn't you stay?" asked Maud.

The question made him stare at the fire for a moment. Only after a long exhale did he reply. "A man who has been the places that I have draws a lot of fellas you don't want around those you care for." His jaw clenched. The memory went from fond remembrance to pained recollection. "It was one of the hardest things I ever had to do, but it was the right thing."

Maud stared into the fire as well, not wanting to draw further anguish on him. She sat on the log, trying to imagine what the journey to Omaha would require and what she would do once there. Then there was the idea of just staying warm during the night. The child seemed at peace in her dreams, rolled in her blanket. That was dandy for her, but a woman would require something more than a small cloth to keep warm. Her eyes darted to him. There was nothing to equal a man to keep a gal warm on a cold night. She peeked at him. With his hat pushed back, his reddened face had the features not of a gruff man she had shared a bed with more times than she could count, but rather one who'd known a rugged life. The trick would be to convince him it was best for them both. Yet he hadn't shown much interest in her brash attempt to earn his affection at the pond. A subtle approach was needed, one she hadn't had to practice before.

"Did I tell you he saved my life?"

His announcement jerked her head up at him. "Who?"

"The boy. Noah." He huffed a single chuckle. "That's how I met him. I was in a bad way. I was in the desert. I had to put my horse down, and the heat started to play tricks with my head. An outlaw on the run had caught me unaware. To confuse the posse chasing him, he had me strip my clothes off."

"Oh, really," she said, imagining the sight. "I would have liked to see that." She regretted the saucy reply for only an instant. Subtlety wasn't her best virtue. "I'm sorry. What did he do then?"

"He had me put on his clothes."

"Oh," she moaned in disappointment.

"Then he shot me. With my own gun."

"What!?"

He nodded and pointed to the scar above his right eye. "Right there. An inch over and it would have killed me dead."

Her eyes locked onto the healed gash. At first, she was shocked at his near miss with death. Then she remembered a description she had read. It took only an instant to recall exactly where she had read it. The wanted poster that the bounty hunter Wheeler had shown her and the black man back in the saloon. Suddenly, the fire was no match for the shiver crawling up her back.

"It was the boy Noah that pulled me out of a waterhole that weren't two inches deep," he continued with a spry smile. "I would have drowned or bled to death had he not found me."

All this time she had been traveling with a man-killer. She wrapped her hands around her shoulders, trying not to let him see her shake. She knew of stories of men like this who killed women at the drop of a hat—especially whores, due to the fact they had no menfolk to look out for them. Her quivering chest forced a huffing breath.

"You cold?" he asked in a consoling tone.

She shook her head, then changed it to a nod. "Just a little. I think the wind turned." She meant more than just the breeze.

"I guess it is getting about the time to turn in," he said as he rose. A small shriek of surprise peeped from her.

"You okay? You're awful jumpy in a hurry. You ain't getting sick on me, are you?"

Again, she shook her head.

"Good. I wasn't sure if it was the beans or me." His fingers wrapped around his gunbelt buckle. In doing so, he drew the pistol, and Maud could feel her eyes bulge. A flick of his thumb and the belt fell loose, but the pistol remained in his right hand. He tucked it in his pant waist, then unfurled his bedroll. It was just earlier that she had thought of cuddling close to him, but now all she wanted was a way to the nearest town of any kind.

As he slipped off his boots, she eyed his every move, but nothing in his manner appeared a threat. Finally he lay on the roll next to the child, only feet away from the fire, his right hand firmly on the butt of the gun. He slumped his hat over his brow, only to bend the brim up and peek at her. "You going to sleep?"

"I thought I'd stay up awhile," she nervously answered.

"Suit yourself," he replied, snugging the brim over his eyes.

Like a cat frozen at the sight of a dog, she perched on the log, ready at any instant to run screaming into the dark. Moments passed, and his exhaled breath gave every sign that he actually was beginning to sleep. Perhaps she had made a mistake. She had ridden to this spot with him, and if he had thought about doing her harm, there were several gullies along the way for him to have left her. The more she pondered, the more unsure and guilty she felt. Many men had scars on their faces or chests, and some in places that only a gal in her line or a wife would find. However, before she could feel at ease to close her eyes she had to know more.

"Clay?" His "hmm" told her he hadn't fallen asleep. "This place in New Mexico? Is that the last place you been?"

"No. I spent some time in Texas, too."

She cringed upon hearing the words and recalling the poster. "What did you do down there?"

"I helped some folks."

The statement surprised Maud. "Helped them?"

"Yeah, a woman doctor and some foreigners. They was looking for, well, let's say they were looking for something special to them."

Although normally she would pry more into the purpose of his help, the end result worried her more. "This woman doctor, is she—is she alive?" The nerve of the question shocked even Maud. Slowly he bent the hat brim again.

"She was when I last seen her," he answered with a puzzled face. "Why you ask?"

His curled lips shrank away her curiosity. She relied on feminine excuses that men always accepted. "Oh, don't pay no mind to me. I was just wondering if I was the first woman you ever traveled with. That's all." When his hand let loose of the hat brim, her heart started beating again.

"Nope," he said with some exhaustion. "You ain't the first."

Claire Rhodes again found herself staring out the window at Baltimore Harbor below. The wonder she recalled as a young schoolgirl urging her father for permission to climb the tall masts came to mind. And those days when, as a young spirited adolescent, she resented her father's strict insistence that she adhere to well-laid rules of duty for young ladies weren't to be forgotten. He wanted her to be educated at Smith College, while she yearned to take her lessons from life itself.

Now, after a rebellious marriage to John Rhodes, who chose to seek his own fortune rather than share hers, bearing witness to his murder while avoiding death's claim of her, the role as owner of the family shipbuilding business was a greater test of her abilities than any she imagined. Her father's death only six months before had thrust her forward into the man's world of business, when all she wanted was to be at her husband's side as his private confidante. She had come away from it all with the most precious gift John ever gave her. She felt a small grin crease her face as she recalled her thought that hanging from a cliff in Colorado was no match for the birthing of a child. However, her experience while in the West was the true test of her maturity. It was there she felt like a grown woman all the while she was in the care of a man she hardly knew.

Today, Stuart was more than eighteen months old.

Those days when she was responsible only for herself seemed decades ago.

Her attention drifted back to the desk. There were bank drafts to be signed and contracts to skew in the company's interest. Steamships had replaced the sail. She had to steer the company to the future. Despite her father's disappointment at not having a son, he had taught her the ways of business and she had always been a quick study.

A knock at the door interrupted her concentration. "Yes. Come in, Penny."

The maid of the house entered the study. "Forgive the intrusion, madam. You have a visitor at the door."

Since her reprieve from mourning, many a visitor had come calling, attracted more to her wealth than her charm. However, suitors normally chose the formality of Sunday. Tuesday meant that whoever it was likely was without a job. "A visitor? Who is it?"

"A young woman. She says her name is Jane Reeves. Dr. Jane Reeves."

The title seemed peculiar. "Doctor?" Penny nodded in reply that she was sure. "Well, did she say what she wanted?"

"No, ma'am. Just that she had something to share of a personal note."

Still confused, Claire thought the interruption a welcome break from the dull duties of business. "Well, tell her I will see her. In the south drawing room, if you please, Penny." The maid nodded and left the room.

Claire stood, inspecting her dark blue dress. At times when she wore the dress, she felt adorned in the uniform of a naval captain; however, it made clear her lack of capriciousness and demanded the respect she had to have from her managers—a facade she knew was necessary, yet one she regretted. While heading for the door, she glanced at her image in the mirrored coat tree and saw a woman of age. With her palms she brushed the loose strands back in place. Vanity deserved at least a small consideration. However, the time needed for a proper entrance would take too long. She gave up the charade and decided to receive the woman doctor as is.

Toward the staircase, she allowed herself to peek inside Stuart's nursery. Her son was safe and well into his nap. Certain pleasures had a calming effect, and the sight of her only child fast asleep always did the trick. When she was down the stairs, she walked through the foyer. Quickly at the south end, she made sure all seams and cuffs were straight, pulled aside the drape, and entered.

"Dr. Reeves, is it?"

A woman with red hair and wearing a pastel-brown coat and dress all buttoned in front faced about. "Yes. You're Mrs. Rhodes? How do you do?"

Claire stepped farther inside and offered her hand, which the woman gracefully took. "How nice to make your acquaintance. Please do sit." The women sat on opposite ends of the small love seat. "May I offer you some tea?"

"Yes, that would be nice," the woman replied.

Claire picked up a small bell on the end table and rang. "So, Dr. Reeves. I understand you've come on a personal matter. I admit I was confused when my maid first told me. Is this about my mother? Do you know Dr. Patterson?"

"No. I apologize if I alarmed you. I'm not a medical doctor. My degree is in archaeology. I am attending Professor Hall's seminar on psychology being held at John's Hopkins University."

The connection eluded Claire. Penny came into the room, and that allowed Claire a moment to order her mind and think of an association. None came to mind. "And what does that have to do with me, Dr. Reeves?"

The young woman's polite face changed to one of worry. Although Claire was only slightly taller, the doctor appeared perhaps a year older, two at the most. However, she showed every discomfort of a youth addressing an elder. "I'm not sure exactly how to say this."

"Say what?" The idea that this woman had something to say which strained her frustrated Claire. "Please do tell me whatever it is." The more she stared the woman in the eye, the more the doctor avoided speaking. "Come on, please. You're worrying me."

The woman met Claire's stare. "I read the letter. Your letter."

Jane's words were sounding more like a confession, and Claire was still bewildered. "What letter?"

"Your letter to him. Your letter to Clay Cole."

Claire fell back against the arm of the couch. Like a bolt of lightning, the news from this woman's mouth stole away her breath. "I see."

"Forgive me. I know how private a letter is meant

to be. And I would never intrude. But he did ask me to read it."

Struggling to recall all of what was written, Claire rose from the seat and went to the far side of the small room. The stranger was correct; Claire felt like something private had been intruded upon. "I wrote that letter two years ago. How do you know him?"

"He led an expedition I was part of in southern Texas."

"Expedition?"

"A research expedition of sorts." Claire faced about as Dr. Reeves tried to explain. "I was involved with a Lord Nigel Apperson on his quest to find the lost treasure of the Aztecs. It is known as the gold of Cortés. We came upon a letter written by Cortés himself which led us to believe that it was in Texas."

"I see. So you have a habit of reading other people's mail, Dr. Reeves." Claire's snipe appeared to dispirit the red-haired woman.

"The people involved in that letter have been dead for more than three hundred years. By the way, we did find the treasure."

"Really? I am surprised I haven't learned of such a discovery," Claire said, then took the tray from Penny.

"Well." Dr. Reeves sighed. "It pains me to say that it was all lost in an explosion."

Claire stopped in midpour. "Explosion? It sounds dangerous," she said, resuming her filling of the cup and handing it to her guest.

"It was," the woman said. "He saved my life."

Although Claire knew she shouldn't be surprised at

such an announcement when she first heard Clay Cole's name, the idea that she had shared the same experience didn't comfort her. When she finished pouring her own tea, she couldn't sit next to this strange woman and so resumed her place near the drape. "How did that come about?" she asked, and took a sip.

"I was in a cave that filled with poison natural gas. I became unconscious from the fumes. The next thing I knew, Clay had pulled me from the cave just before it imploded."

"How awful," Claire remarked, recalling her own experience.

"Yes. It was." Dr. Reeves stirred her tea but didn't drink. "I understand from him that you, too, may owe your life to him?"

The question sounded more like a hint. "Did he tell you that?"

"I asked him when I read your letter."

The subject had been broached once too often. "I must say, Dr. Reeves, I don't care to discuss this. Why did you come?"

The doctor put down her teacup. "I'm sorry. It wasn't my intent to offend you. I just thought you would like to know where he was. Please accept my apology." She rose, holding her handbag close to her chest. "I think I should leave."

With her back to her guest, Claire Rhodes felt ashamed of herself. A petty jealousy had made her rudely treat a woman who had come only to share news of a man to whom Claire herself had been so indebted. The maturity she thought to have gained with the recent tragic events in her life appeared to have vanished.

"Is he alive?" asked Claire, facing the drape.

The doctor looked to her. "Yes."

"Please, don't go," she said, stopping Dr. Reeves at the drape. "It is I who should apologize to you . . . Jane, is it?" She held out both her hands as a gesture. It took only a moment for the woman doctor to accept it. Like lost sisters, the two women stood clutching their hands. "So where is he?"

"I'm not sure. I last saw him in Texas. He and an army officer—"

"Major Miles Perry?"

"Yes. You know him, too?"

"Oh, only too well. A thorn in the side when I met him. I imagine he is still?"

Jane's smile faded and her eyes drifted from Claire's. "He didn't survive an Indian attack."

"Oh, poor man. Even if he was a sour person, I regret to hear of his passing."

"Yes, well," Jane said. "He and Clay agreed to settle their dispute. When I last saw Clay, he said he intended to honor their agreement. I think he was going to surrender. To go to trial. To clear his name."

Claire released Jane's hands and stepped back. "You know he is innocent."

"Yes. I believe him."

"Then we should work together to help him. If indeed he has turned himself into the law, I pray he is safe."

"I agree. Anything I can do, I will," Jane said. As the two women joined hands again, Claire felt relief.

In front of her was another believer in the man who had saved her life and made it possible for her to bring her son into the world. Now he inspired the forging of a new friendship bound in the belief of his innocence. She breathed deeply. She felt young again.

Chapter Nine

Though the breeze was gentle, it was the snap of cold that drew Cole from his sleep. He peeked at the morning sunlight. A glance above his head found Little Bear still sound asleep. Craning his neck over his shoulder, he looked for Maud by the log stump. She wasn't there.

At first he thought she had strayed for a warmer place by the fire, but when he sat up, a scan in all directions didn't spot her or her horse. Did she leave or was she taken? He drew the Colt and stood. As he went to the stump, he peeked back at the child to be sure she was still sleeping.

The ground around the log showed no proof of a fight: no torn cloth, loose buttons, or blood. Peering about at the dew-glistened grass and calm pond, he noticed no signs of any movement. "Maud!" Only the echo of the call came back over the plain. With nothing to indicate otherwise, he stood convinced the woman's absence was her choice.

He returned to Little Bear and gently rubbed the girl's back. As the child stirred, he lifted her, careful to keep the blanket wrapped tight to block the cold. "I guess we're back on our own," he muttered. He pulled her close to his chest inside his coat. "Didn't need her anyway." His momentary bliss changed with the wind and a whiff of what the girl had produced during the night.

When he was done rinsing the soiled flesh and clothes, he built a small fire to dry them. The flame quickly took to the remainder of the previous firewood. His skill milking the goat had improved, and a little more than a half hour's work had produced a tin full for the girl's breakfast. The fatty liquid didn't have the cream he remembered raw cow's milk having, yet it washed the scratch from his throat when he tasted it. Not knowing how long the weather would hold, he forewent morning coffee and quickly tethered the bedroll to the back of the saddle. After cinching the saddle to the palomino, he filled the two canteens and loaded the bundles and child on the beasts.

As the sun rose, his stomach began to rumble—he had eaten only a meager bean dinner the night before. His hand went into his coat pocket, and he drew out a pouch of jerky. With clenched teeth, he bit into one end while ripping the other free. He swirled the piece with his tongue from side to side to soften the hard beef. His eyes on the sloping terrain in front, he felt a subtle tug at his hand. True to her name,

Little Bear reached out her tiny paws at the hand that had dangled the meat close to her nose.

"Not for you. Got to have teeth with roots to handle this." Despite his own words, the girl's persistence yanked at his heart. Slowly his hand crept closer to her reach. Once she had it in her clutches, she quickly put her lips on the jerky strip. With a firm pinch, he held it steady so she couldn't swallow it but she could suckle the salt and beef taste. "Probably spoiling you. It wouldn't be something I would have got when I was your age." The girl's attention was locked onto the jerky, but talking helped pass the time.

"When I was a young'un, my ma wouldn't give me the taste of something she knew I couldn't have. She'd rap my knuckles with a spoon. But that was after I took what it was I wasn't supposed to have." He saw the image of his mother's mischievous smile. Despite her strict nature, there were times when a slice of pie would be left alone on the table as a test of his obedience. More than once, he held his appetite back, knowing she would miss the single piece on the plate. After she returned to the house she would delight in seeing the piece still intact so she could say she had left it just for him.

During his thought, Little Bear stopped her suckling of the jerky long enough to gaze up at him. "But she would have a hard time not giving in to those brown eyes. If she had to deal with those, likely she would have give in to let you have the whole pie."

He pulled the coat snug around his shoulders. Although the sun climbed across the sky, the air grew colder. The clouds seemed to stay in place, as if smeared against the blue with a butter knife. The view made for a wary anticipation that later came true. The lack of clouds brought colder nights. Each time, it became a trick how close to settle next to the fire. Fearing that the child might creep closer to the flame and an errant spark might jump into the dry cloth, Cole had to sleep light. The catnaps took their toll during the next day's ride.

Waterholes became harder to find, particularly when his eyes grew heavy. An occasional jolt when the palomino missed a step was all that kept Cole from falling asleep and off the horse. Rolling hills flattened out. The terrain made clear that the days spent in the saddle had led into the Nebraska prairie.

Cole allowed the stock a chance to graze on the dormant grass, and a glint caught his eye. He knelt next to it and found a shard of broken glass. A brush of dirt revealed the face of a clock. The wood surrounding the face had withered from years of water and wind. The more he dug his fingers into the dirt, the more he noticed of the frame. Finally he recognized what was there. A grandfather clock lay buried in the ground. There was little doubt how it got there.

He'd heard the stories. Easterners moving west along the trail to settle the valleys of Oregon had shed their belongings for the sake of having less weight to carry. Heavy snows met those wagon trains that left Missouri in late summer. The oxen could hardly pull the prairie schooners, so sacrifices had to be made. This must have been one of them, abandoned nearly forty years before.

Scanning the flat plain, he figured he may have

traveled farther than he first thought. If he followed the same path, he might be able to fulfill the promise he had made to Colonel Grimes. What was at the start a fool's notion now had a little more hope. While he was pondering, another glint sparkled close to the clock. Scraping away more grass and dust, he unearthed a small box of brass with four small legs. A wad of spittle and a rub of his coat sleeve polished the engraved detail.

The faces and wings of two cherubs emerged from the caked dirt. As more tiny clods crumbled, a lever crank protruded from the side. He blew away the loose specks. This was a music box. He spun the handle three times, but there was no sound. Its long term in the ground, barraged by rain and baked by the sun, likely had warped the springs and wheels inside.

He stood, intent on cleaning the dust from the box enough to see the seams of the lid, but the hardened dirt wouldn't allow the lid to open. He sunk his nails into the slot, but still it wouldn't budge. With his frustration building, he wandered closer to the palomino. Finally, without any success, he slammed the heel of his hand against the lid, hoping it would pop free.

Three chimed notes broke the silence, slowly followed by four more. Surprised by the sound, Cole saw it had also caught Little Bear's attention. With the spring laboring, five final notes came from the box to a haunting inconclusion. Cole shook it and again pounded his hand against the brass, but no music sounded. Still, the melody interested the child, and she reached for the box. It was the first time he had seen her show any affection for something she couldn't eat.

"You like that, huh? I guess that's all you get for now." As she continued to reach, he noticed the sun above. It was past midday, and the need to find better shelter for the night forced him to resume the ride.

He climbed into the saddle, the young girl's eyes locked on the music box all the while. With only enough hands for the two sets of reins, he relinquished the box to her. She clutched it in her fingers like claws around prey. Then she tried to put it in her mouth. The grainy taste of dirt wrinkled her face. Cole chuckled as he nudged the palomino's flanks. "That ought to break you."

The sun was directly overhead when Bill Wheeler rode into Abilene. The first place he steered for was the sheriff's office. Once he found it, he slid off his horse and strode into the doorway. "Howdy, Frank."

Sheriff Frank Beck rose out of his chair and welcomed his old friend. "Bill Wheeler, you old dog. What's brought you back?"

Wheeler took Beck's hand, then tugged at Beck's stringy chin whiskers. "I come to chop off this silly thing. It haunts me in my sleep." The joke didn't amuse the sheriff, who placed his palm over the whiskers. "Oh, don't fret. I didn't really come here for that. I got business to tend to and thought I'd stop by and see if you can help me."

"Somebody in town I don't know about?" asked Beck as he returned to his chair.

"For who I'm looking for, that'd be too much to

ask. But he may have passed by here." Beck reached into his vest pocket and drew the Wanted poster. "This fellow."

"The Rainmaker?" Beck said with some surprise. "You after him, too?"

"What you mean, 'too'? Who else is after him?"

Beck huffed a chuckle. "Besides every other man-hunter this side of the Mississippi, there was a darkie in here not more than a week ago eyeing that poster on the wall." He pointed to it, and Wheeler glanced over his shoulder.

"Big fellow? Look a little like an Indian?"

"That's him. Brought in Curtis Marlowe across the saddle. Had to pay him half the reward and likely the rest once the judge comes back. Remember? The one you claim to have shot and got stole from you."

"Yeah, I remember."

Beck laughed and clapped his hands. "You said you were—"

"Yeah, I know what I said. That reward was right-fully mine. I captured Marlowe in that saloon. He was rightfully mine."

"Oh, yeah? He said he saved your life by shooting Marlowe."

"He did no such thing. I had everything in hand. I got no time to talk about him. I'm here to learn if you know anything about the Rainmaker."

Beck leaned back in the chair, scratching his chin, eyes blinking while he gazed at the ceiling. "The only thing is . . ." The pause drove Wheeler to tap his foot on the wooden floor. Once he counted ten, the break became intolerable.

"Spit it out, Frank."

"Hold your water," Beck replied. "It's on the tip of my tongue and you done scared it off." The sheriff resumed his pose in deep thought, until his face lit up and he shook his finger in the air like a schoolmaster. "I know it. There was a gal came in here yesterday, babbling about some man she met had a scar like that described in the poster."

"Where is she?" Wheeler asked, anxious to pursue the clue.

With a shrug, Beck replied, "Got no idea."

"What!? Someone tells you a wanted man is in your jurisdiction, and you don't go after him?"

"Hellfire, Wheeler. I can't go chasing every fool story of a badman that left a shadow around this town. They don't pay me to leave these folks here alone just to gallop off to smell where some coyotes marked some bushes."

Wheeler realized little was going to be gained with the old sheriff. "Did you at least see which way she headed?"

"No," Beck answered, snatching the pen from the inkwell. "I don't make a habit of watching women's behinds. Especially those which have as many hands on them as hers must have had."

"What are you getting at?"

"She was a floozy. Probably still hung over from business in the alley. You know we don't allow that sort of thing in this town anymore. Upset too many of the womenfolk. Couldn't keep their husbands at home."

"A whore? She was one of them?" Wheeler asked.

"I don't say them words. But yes. She was if I ever saw one."

One face came to Wheeler's mind—that of the only woman he knew who had seen the poster and who fit the occupation Beck had mentioned. "I got to find her. I'll see you, Frank." Wheeler marched through the doorway. Faint words from behind came from the old sheriff, but Wheeler didn't care to stop his mind from wondering where to find the woman. The problem with Abilene, it was in the middle of nothing with a lot of nowhere to go. A deep breath followed by an inner sigh gave him time to consider just where to go next. While he weighed all the options, his eyes fixed on the answer.

The old Cattlemen's Saloon drew his conscious attention from the parade of men in through the doors. Whoring and drinking might have been outlawed, but faro was still a staple of the town. Where men drank and wagered their wages, the need for a woman's attention was always in demand to celebrate a windfall or console the downfall.

Into the street he stepped, dodging the wagon traffic to cross the main thoroughfare onto the opposite boardwalk and through the batwing doors. Despite the smoke drifting above the tables and the hollering over near wins, Wheeler surveyed the room like an engineer. The only two women in the place were wearing aprons rather than feathers or thin undergarments. They weren't on the laps of the patrons, but instead doled out liquor from a jug. Convinced he had chased a bad hunch, he turned for the door— until a familiar cackle silenced all the clamor.

He faced about and strolled cautiously into the room. Most of the faces weren't familiar, and although he kept his right hand near the butt of his revolver, he didn't notice any hoglegs strapped to any hips. Still, an old acquaintance could emerge from the smoke at any moment, and he wanted to be ready in case it turned out to be one holding a grudge for being put behind bars.

From side to side, he sighted everyone in the place as he got to the last table. Four men and a very remarkable woman dressed in a soiled brown dress buttoned only to the bust and without any lace to cover her divide sat at the single table at the rear. She dealt cards to each of the players, careful not to tump the three balanced stacks of coins in front of her. "What do you say, boys? One more hand."

"Sorry, gents," Wheeler announced, turning all eyes his way, including those of the woman, whose smile soured. "I'm afraid I've got to call a halt to this game. This woman is in violation of the local ordinance banning female solicitation."

"I ain't soliciting nothing. Don't listen to him, fellows."

"I'm a federal marshal sent here to arrest her."

"He is not. Don't let him fool you. He's a low-down bounty hunter."

"Bounty hunter?" one of the players questioned. "Who you after?"

Wheeler fought back a grin at the opportunistic inquiry. "Her."

"What!? He's lying, boys."

"Who is she?" asked all the players.

"Belle Starr," Wheeler answered to their amazement, as they all looked at her. It was time to get on with the business, but the players seemed enamored to be in the presence of a legend. "She killed a man in Missouri. Teased him with promises of fornication. Waited until his britches were around his ankles, then produced a pistol from under her skirt. Took aim at the biggest part of him."

Awe and disgust at the fabled act were etched on the players' faces, and chairs scooted across the wooden floor in retreat while the rest of the room continued in their play. Wheeler turned one of the empty chairs backward so as to sit while resting his arms across its back. "Howdy, Maud."

"You no-good bastard. What did you run them for?" she asked, flipping the deck to the table.

"I needed to talk to you in private."

"The price for that is customarily ten dollars." She glared at him. "But I've already told you that. I forgot. You're a five-dollar man."

"I told you before, I ain't a buyer for that. I come for word you were spreading about meeting a man with a scar." Wheeler noticed that his question shrank the disdain from her cheeks.

"I already told the law about him. Didn't seem to care, so I left it be." She moved her attention to the stacks of coins.

"Yeah," Wheeler said, taking a firm grip of her hand. "But I'm willing to listen." He tightened his grip, forcing her eyes to meet his. "Where is he, Maud? You know who I'm talking about."

She yanked her hand to escape, but he maintained his grasp. "Let go of me. I'll yell."

"In here? Who'd care? Now. There's a share in it for you if you tell me where I can find him." As he watched her consider the offer, a shadow came over her face. Her eyes fixed on an object over his shoulder. He peered behind him.

A tall, burly figure with a straight-haired beard glowered above him. Instantly noticing the man's broad shoulders supporting thick arms the size of small logs, Wheeler realized he had miscalculated the gallantry of the locals. "Back away, friend. This is a private conversation."

"I heard the lady complaining," the burly man said. "I think she don't like talking to you." He looked to Maud. "You want to leave, ma'am?"

Maud nodded. "I'm grateful for your assistance," she said in a sweet voice as she rose from her chair.

"Sit down," barked Wheeler. When she looked to him with a indignant scoff, he drew his pistol and tucked the muzzle under the chin of the burly man. Maud froze stiff. "I am a lawful agent of the federal government in pursuit of a criminal who has crossed state boundaries. This woman is a witness as to the criminal's whereabouts. I'm authorized to seize property and to arrest anyone who can aid in the capture of a fugitive in unlawful flight from justice." Noticing that all eyes in the saloon were on him, he thought it time to make his resolve known and clear the room. He pulled back the hammer. "Go home to your wives, all of you."

The burly man was first to ease backward. Wheeler

didn't move the pistol, which allowed the man to step away in peace. The other patrons folded their greenbacks and swigged the rest of their drinks. Even the barkeep didn't mount much of a protest as long as Wheeler had the pistol drawn. Once they all had filed through the batwings, Wheeler placed the Colt on the table, then turned his attention back to Maud.

"Like I was saying, where is he?"

"I don't know. He could be anywhere by now," she answered, fingering five coins and tucking them inside her bust.

"Then why did you tell Frank Beck that you seen him?"

"I was scared. That's all." She slipped other coins into her shoes. "I thought he might have followed me back here, and I didn't want to be killed. If that's a crime, then drag me off to jail. Otherwise, leave me be." She finished with the ruffling of her skirt as if it were being hiked above her stockings. Wheeler didn't figure she had a gun, so he didn't peek below the table, and when she snatched the last four coins and her hand sank out of view, he didn't bother to see where they ended up.

"Now you listen. I'm offering you a share in the reward."

"Ha. Like you did Choate? I ain't working for no fifty percent."

"Damn you, woman. If you'd just shut up, I'll tell you." His growl silenced her. "This is what I need. You tell me where he is and I'll pay you a thousand dollars. That's all you got to do."

She snarled her lips. "That ain't even thirty percent."

"But all you're doing is telling me where he is."

"And when do I get paid?"

"When I have the Rainmaker in chains and collect the reward."

"So I'm just supposed to wait here while you go off. What if you forget about me?"

"So you're saying you want to come along? Fine by me." His dare put the play back in her hand. Her eyes darted back and forth from his eyes to the table. The indecision made him confident.

"I'm not sure exactly where he is. I left in the middle of the night. He said he was heading north, so I told him I was going to Omaha. But he made it sound like he wasn't heading in that direction."

"He ain't. Did he have a baby with him?"

Maud nodded. "How'd you know?"

"I met up with an army colonel said he give the baby to him so as to bring it back to its native land. I didn't figure he'd still have it with him, though. Can't think he will keep it much longer."

"I think he will," she replied quickly. He sat confused at the conviction of her tone. "Don't ask me why. He is a scary sight, but there is something about him. About how he talks about living a simpler life. I think he is a different fellow than you might think."

"Well, don't you be fooled. I've seen many a man show a peaceful side, only to draw a gun and put a bullet in a man's back. Hell, it's said Jesse James is a Bible-toting deacon."

She dipped her eyes to the table. "Maybe you're

right. He sure looked mean. Didn't care for me none, I'll tell you. And I showed him every part of me I have and he didn't try nothing. That ain't normal."

After a moment, Wheeler thought it best to avoid her example. "Here now. You listen to me. You're the only one that's seen him. You and me will track him down. You point him out to me, and I'll take care of the rest. You'll be a thousand dollars richer."

"You're going to shoot him?"

"Only if I have to. But it's best to keep wanted men under control. If that means killing them, then so be it." His statement made her take a long breath and finally nod.

He clutched her hand with a softer touch. "Let's ride."

Chapter Ten

The aroma of burning wood guided Cole for most of the morning. Atop a large plateau, he sighted a burgeoning settlement below. Thick plumes of smoke and steam climbed into the sky from stacks well above the rooftops. This was no boomtown.

For the last two days he had passed farms and fields full of cattle and corn. He wasn't far from white folks. He breathed a heavy sigh of relief at the view. Food and rest were less than an hour away.

While leading the mule and goat down the slope, he had time to consider what he was to do while in this town. The provisions he'd been supplied by Colonel Grimes had all but disappeared in the three-week journey. Money, what little of it he had at the start, seemed to slowly drip from his pockets with the purchases of additional blankets and clothes for Little

Bear. As he neared the edge of the town, the more he saw, the less relief he believed he'd found.

He first took notice that this place was different from ones he had known when the palomino's hoof met the hard brick street. The coaches and wagons appeared to be in greater numbers than El Paso had on its busiest day. Only other riders on horseback did not clog the streets.

As he ambled the horse and jerked the reins of the reluctant mule, people slowed, as if he were on parade. It was unwelcome attention. The unease made him search for a livery so as to secure the stock, then find a place to stay the night. All the pens he came to were full of the stink of short-horned cattle, so he continued farther into the town.

Every house he came by had at least two floors, some three, all adorned with fresh paint. Every roof had a bricked chimney. He saw not a single black metal pipe of a potbellied stove. Mules or draft horses pulled the hefty wagons down the streets from one building to another. More than one church steeple pointed to the sky. He didn't recognize the type of settlement he was familiar with.

At the merge of two streets, he steered left and headed down what appeared to be a less hectic part of the town. He halted the palomino at the first spot he thought was safe to tether the reins. When he had dismounted, he took Little Bear from the saddle and walked on the boardwalk. It wasn't the wide landing found in most places. His curiosity getting the best of him, he garnered the courage to seek information from a bonneted young woman with her daughter's hand firmly in hers.

"Beg pardon, ma'am," he asked, tipping his hat. She stopped, although her face showed discomfort at his interruption. "Mind telling me where this is? The town, I mean." Mumbling the question in such polite terms only confused her. It was best to spit out what he needed to know. "What is this town?"

"Why, this is Lincoln. Lincoln, Nebraska."

Not having spent much time in the territory, he stood bewildered at first, trying to imagine the location on a map in his mind. "So this ain't Omaha?"

"Of course not," she said, eyeing him as if he were as dumb as his reply. "Omaha is fifty miles to the east. This is Lincoln. The state capital."

Realizing his mistake, he nodded and tipped his hat again. "I see. Appreciate the help, ma'am." Her eyes darted to Little Bear.

"Have you brought that for the orphanage?"

"That?" He followed her eyes, which were fixed on the Nez Perce girl. "Oh, you mean her."

His correction didn't seem to change her tone. "If you call that a girl. I mean, it isn't yours, is it?"

The remark made Cole peek at the woman's daughter, who was barely as high as her mother's waist. Despite the color of their hair and skin, the two young girls both were females to him. However, the woman made it clear she didn't hold the same attitude.

"No, ma'am. She's not."

She continued while he stared at the daughter.

"The reason I asked is I thought you might be bringing it to the Indian orphanage. The Institute for Abandoned Indian Children."

His eyes jerked to the woman. "What might that be?"

"It is the orphanage, as I said. They take in Indian orphans and raise them to be respectable. You understand, they educate them, teach them the customs of their betters. It's the only decent thing to do with them."

Taking mild offense at the remark, he bit his tongue. It wasn't long ago he thought the same. "Where might I find it? That is, if I was looking?"

"It is on the far end of town. On the other side of the tracks." She pointed to the west, then pinched her skirt to continue her walk. Cole tipped his hat for the last time as she passed him.

Although he didn't care for the way she had said them, her words held truth. A place that taught Indian kids might not be so bad. With all that was ahead of them, it may be the best not only for Little Bear, but for him as well.

"Get out of the way, black boy!"

At the yell, Cole twisted about. A draft wagon was stopped in the street, and a craggy mulewhacker stood in the box. The target of his tirade was a colored man in a white man's waistcoat. He held the reins to an empty single horse buggy that was angled in front of the team of the draft wagon.

"You ignorant nigger, get them out of the street. You shouldn't be in that seat if you can't steer."

The colored driver avoided looking the teamster in

the eye. Never one comfortable with a bully's rant, Cole first thought to stay out of the incident, but seeing the simple solution, he secured his grip on Little Bear and stepped into the street.

"If you'll hold your horses, he'll have a chance to turn his."

The mulewhacker turned his stringy-haired head at Cole. "Mind your business, stranger," he said tersely.

"If you took better care of yours," Cole replied, gripping the harness of the single horse, "then none of this would be needed."

"Don't sass me," the mulewhacker said, raising the whip in his right hand. "I'll lash this across your back just the same as I would his. I wouldn't mind it none, seeing you deserve it for stepping into affairs not of your concern. You can't hide behind that baby."

Cole released his grip of the harness and switched Little Bear to his left arm. "You wind that whip at me and you'll be eating that leather." Cole moved his coat from his right hip, all the while keeping his eyes on the old man. Showing his side arm made the man lower the whip and eventually drop it. "That's the first sensible thing you done." Cole again took the harness and led the horse around to the side of the teamster's draft wagon. As the old man shook his reins, he spat at Cole, but the spittle hit the street and Cole ignored it.

Cole looked to the colored driver, who knew better than to show appreciation in front of the townsfolk. Cole stepped back onto the boardwalk, wondering what price he would pay for his defense of the black man.

"Allow me to shake your hand."

The offer twisted him about again. A man with a thick but trimmed mustache, wearing a dark suit coat and pants, eagerly extended his open hand. His broad smile showed nearly all his teeth. "That was very brave. I admire men unafraid to take up for the innocent," the gentleman said.

His skin was pale to the point of looking sickly, and his voice had the blare of a bugle. Cole shook the man's hand, noticing that more people had collected around them, most with smiles. The gentleman continued.

"Let me introduce myself. My name is Roosevelt. And you are, sir?"

"Clay Hayes," Cole answered, becoming more comfortable with the name.

"So good to make your acquaintance, Mr. Hayes. I'm afraid the incident was of my doing. I asked Hector here to stop to allow me to dash into this shop. I saw the buckskin clothes in the window and couldn't wait for him to pull the carriage out of that terrible man's way. Once I came from the store, I delighted in witnessing your dealing with the matter. I am in your debt."

"Weren't nothing."

"Oh, I disagree. You put yourself in harm's way for a complete stranger." He leaned closer to Cole to whisper. "And an inferior, if you know what I mean." He straightened, and put his eyes on Little Bear for the first time. His smile grew even bigger. "What a beautiful child. Is she yours?" he asked. He knew the truth would lead to longer explanations, which Cole

didn't feel comfortable giving while surrounded by
white folk.

"Yup."

"I've heard about men such as yourself, the taking
of Indian brides, the joining of their customs and the
sort." The more Roosevelt spoke, the more edgy Cole
sensed the crowd became. It wasn't that many years
before when hostiles were taking scalps off some of
these folk's kin.

"I need be going."

"Oh, please allow me to invite you for dinner. I'm
staying with a good friend, Senator John Buttram. I'm
a guest in his home and I'm confident he would enjoy
your company, as would I. Would your wife be coming?"

"Don't have one." The answer appeared to give all
in attendance a poor impression of his morals. "The
child's mother was killed not long ago."

"Oh, how awful. Please accept my condolence for
her loss. I couldn't imagine how I would respond to
such a terrible event." It took Roosevelt only an instant to regain his smile. "So can we count on you? I
would enjoy it so. Where are you staying? I'll have
Hector take you to your hotel." His questions came
at Cole faster than a rattler can wiggle its tail.

"I don't have a place—"

"Even better. Why, Senator Buttram's home is
more than adequate to house you and your daughter.
So, have you transport, or should we take you there?"

Cole nodded and arched his thumb behind him. "I
got a horse."

"Fine, then. Follow the carriage. It's just at the end of town."

As if slapped, Cole stood stunned as the gentleman climbed into the buggy. The broad smile never slackened as the colored driver turned the horse in the opposite direction. His first thought was to mount the palomino and escape this town. Little out of the ordinary had occurred while he was here. However, the offer of food, and free at that, was too great an opportunity to leave behind.

He was soon on the horse, keeping the buggy in sight despite the people and wagons crossing his path. The tall buildings grew less numerous with each street, and he came upon a yellow house shaded by at least a dozen oaks. He slid off his saddle at the fence, unsure if he was to follow the small road that led to the front of the house. With a wave of Roosevelt's hand, Cole took Little Bear from the loop, tugged on both sets of reins, and walked up the gravel road until he reached the porch. Two staircases flanked each end of the porch. Both led to an upper balcony that stretched the entire width of the house.

The owner came from the front door. Roosevelt proudly introduced Cole, recalling the events in the street and adding details that Cole didn't remember happening. Cole shook John Buttram's hand and was invited inside. When he told them he needed to tend to his horse and mule, Buttram assured him his stablemaster would see to the animals' needs.

The first thing he noticed of the house's interior was all the shiny wooden furnishings. The stair rail with a middle landing that curled to the upstairs was made of the same grain as the legs and arms of the chairs and couches. The foyer led into a main hall, where there was a red rug with black and yellow swirls resembling broad leaves every two feet for the complete length.

When it was suggested he rest before the evening meal, Cole appreciatively agreed. He was guided up the stairs. A maid asked to take the sleeping Little Bear. When Cole told her of the child's needs, the woman smiled and assured him she had raised four boys and a two girls. A servant brought him to a narrow door. He opened it, and inside was just as narrow a bed. However, when Cole sat on the edge, his back began to hurt him more. He unbuckled the gunbelt and let it drop to the floor, tossed his hat onto the solitary chair, and put his head on the pillow.

A knock at the door woke him. Told two hours had passed, he knew it was time to prepare for supper. Although the meal was still cooking, a tub was provided for him to scrub the grit of the trail from his flesh. His scruffy beard met the first razor it had encountered in two months. The first set of clothes brought to his room were made for a smaller man. He knew "proper attire" was a must at the dinner table, so he finally found a coat with a white shirt to fit his brawny frame. The servant helped him knot the tie.

Still not as comfortable as he would have been in his own duds, he walked down the stairs with care, fearing the tight pants would shorten his step and send him tumbling to the ground floor. Off the last step, Cole turned about and headed to the main room.

First to greet him was Roosevelt. The first order of

business was to accept his hearty handshake. "A fine grip. A sign of a robust man," said Roosevelt, beaming as usual.

Not sure how to answer, Cole just nodded and shook Buttram's hand. A long table with a white linen draped across it stood under a hanging lamp with more than two dozen branches, all with lit candles. The servant pulled a chair from the table and opened his palm as a signal for Cole to sit. He obliged.

"Mr. Hayes," Buttram said as he took the folded white cloth napkin off his plate and put it in his lap. He had a finely trimmed mustache and chin whiskers. "My guest tells me you are what he calls a 'frontiersman.'"

"I ain't sure exactly what that means," Cole answered. "If it's what I think, about living all my life in the West, then I guess the name would fit."

"Precisely what it means, Hayes. Precisely," Roosevelt said with the vigor of one who has just shown a winning hand of cards. "I've been telling John about what I've observed while on my trip. I've been quite taken with the type of men that it takes to live in such a sparse existence as the area provides."

The words didn't have any meaning for Cole. "What'd you say?"

"The survival nature of the people. It's not like this in the East. There are mills and factories. Where I'm from in New York, there are ample food and shelter. If one needs a meal, they simply go to a market and purchase it. But not here. I've seen men such as yourself that hunt for their food. I say, I admire that."

"We aren't just the primitives that you think,

T. R.," Buttram said. "We have our own industry in this part of the nation. Look no further than behind you." Both Cole and Roosevelt arched around to see a cart with a silver dome being pushed by a colored fellow with a white coat buttoned firm to the collar. When the dome was pulled off, a side of beef steamed on the large plate. "I trust you like prime rib, Mr. Hayes?"

"I ain't sure exactly if I ever had it cooked like that, but it sure smells just as good."

Roosevelt and Buttram laughed at the remark.

"You see what I mean about our industry here, T. R.? Without the cattle industry of the West, you easterners would still be gnawing on pigs." They huffed a chuckle as their plates were filled with sizable portions of the beef. Cole watched the colored servant slap a slab on his, then place a smaller plate with three green stalks and ladle a sauce with the smell of lemon over them.

Although not schooled in manners, Cole knew enough to wait for the host before he dug into the grub. Buttram lifted his knife and met Cole's eye, motioning for all to start. It was all that was needed. Plunging his fork deep into the red meat, Cole sliced through it with surprising ease. The prongs of the fork were covered with beef, and Cole quickly stuck it in his mouth. The savory taste was like that of fresh churned butter.

"Don't misunderstand, John. I didn't mean to imply that there isn't an economy here," said Roosevelt as he cut and diced up a tiny piece. "However, there is a different spirit among the people here, men and women equally, that seem to define the adventure of what it is to live on the prairie." He delicately placed a morsel on his tongue, then closed his mouth. It was hard for Cole to believe that a man with the belly of Roosevelt ate with such small bites. "Would you agree, Hayes?"

The piece of beef still stuck in his throat, Cole choked out, "I ain't sure what you're getting at." Finally, with his throat clear, he thought to explain. "Most all the folks I know only do what they have to. Eat. Stay dry and warm. Have water around regular. I don't mean to take a difference with what you're trying to say. But I'd have to say that most folks don't know to do any different than what they're doing."

Roosevelt put down his fork. Unsure whether he had offended the easterner, Cole stopped cutting another bite. It was only after a small grin creased Roosevelt's lips that Cole breathed a little sigh of relief.

"Spoken like a scholar," he said, clapping his hands. "Simple. To the point. Bully for you."

The word didn't seem to fit the smile. "Bully?"

"Yes, of course." Roosevelt seemed to strain for an explanation. "I trumpet your achievement in putting words so simply to such a complex issue."

"Trumpet?"

"What he is trying to say, Mr. Hayes," Buttram said with a smirk, "is that he agrees with what you said. My friend T. R. here hasn't mastered the idea that not all of us graduated from Harvard."

"Harvard?" After his blurt of ignorance, Cole put another bite into his mouth to stop another.

"The most prestigious school in the country," Roosevelt said with some pride.

After a nod, Cole tried to think of a way to squelch the subject. Finally swallowing, he thought a smile might do the trick. "Sounds plenty important."

"Of course it is," Roosevelt replied quickly, but a grunt from the host turned the easterner's mind. The big smile returned. "Well, no matter. I didn't invite you here to talk about myself. What about you, Mr. Hayes? Where do you hail from?" Although he knew the question wasn't about a storm, Cole wasn't sure how to answer until Roosevelt made it plain. "Where are you from?"

Relieved, Cole sliced into the beef. "I was raised in Kansas."

"Oh, are you a farmer?" Roosevelt's question was met with a disapproving eye from Buttram.

"T. R., not all westerners are farmers. Just look at the man's dress when he arrived."

"No," Cole said, holding a forkful of beef. "I was raised on a farm. A small one." The recollection made him pause. The simple days of youth came to mind, but further memories of the loss of those days pained him. "Became a trooper soon after that," he said to change the subject.

"Aiding in the noble effort to settle the country. I commend you, sir." Roosevelt's remark ended with a salute of his knife. However, Cole didn't accept it as due gratitude.

"Just doing what I was paid to do," he answered. Then he put his attention to the green stalks.

"Do try the asparagus," Buttram said. "They're

fresh. I had them brought from a grocer in Iowa." His encouragement held the same pride Roosevelt had for Harvard. Cole nibbled at the end of a stalk, but the tart sauce sent a distasteful wave through his tongue. "A different taste, Mr. Hayes?"

Still with his mouth full, Cole only nodded at the truth of the senator's words. He swallowed, and took a gulp a water from the glass to wash down the sauce. With the taste still lingering in his mouth, the thought of talking—to work his tongue free of the taste—occurred to him. "The duty of the army when I was a trooper was to keep folks safe. It wasn't up to me to see where they settled."

"Yes," Roosevelt said, before taking the final bite of his fork. "But it was men like you that allowed for such settlement to become possible. Where did you serve?"

"Fort Laramie. It was my only post. I served my hitch there, then lighted out on my own."

"I've heard of that fort. A remote area, I understand. A lot of engagements with savage Indians, I've come to learn." Roosevelt put down his fork and knife.

"One thing I've come to know," Cole said as he finished the last of the beef, chewing with his mouth half open. "When it comes to fighting for your life, it ain't nothing but savage on both parts."

"Really," said Roosevelt, tossing his napkin on the table. "I am surprised to hear you say that, Hayes. Of course, I agree that when one is faced with danger, one reacts accordingly. But to describe soldiers and savages as alike shocks me."

"I meant no offense," said Cole, finally swallowing the beef. "Only meant that there were some things I saw that didn't make me proud to wear no uniform."

"Such as?"

Roosevelt's dare made Cole lean back in his chair. There was only one event that came into his head. "In seventy-three, we was ordered to round up a band of Cheyenne that had been blamed for the loss of twenty head of cattle and killed a rancher's wife and son. When we was told how bad these folks were hurt, ears and fingers lopped off, there weren't a man not foaming at the mouth to take after those that did it. It took us three days to catch up to them. It was dawn, and we charged into the camp. Our orders were to shoot, not take captives. When you're ordered to shoot, you ain't looking to wing anybody, you shooting to kill them, for fear that if you just wing them, you're likely to get shot back at."

He paused, and saw both men's eyes focused firmly on him. "Now, I was a young fellow then, and learned the one thing you're drilled, and that is to follow orders. I shot every buck who stood with a bow or gun, either one. Long about the third one I put to the dirt, I noticed that these weren't Cheyenne. I saw them as Shoshone. Their color ain't the same, and the way they mark their horses. These didn't have no white man's cattle, not an easy thing to hide. Besides the fact that many of the tribe had been known to scout for the cavalry. I knew it wasn't the band we were after. So I rode to the commander, Colonel Everett Jamison. I told him what I just told you, and he looked at me as if I just pointed a gun his way. His words were 'lice had no color.' His orders were to wipe out any band he came upon. It didn't take but ten minutes. When the firing stopped, I noticed all the bodies. Most were women with their young, their blood pouring so much, the dirt couldn't soak it up fast enough." He took a long breath. "Our orders were to dig a hole big enough to bury them, and that's what we did. It weren't hard to figure that the longer I stayed in the army, the more I would see of that, so I left when my time was up."

Cole calmly wiped his mouth, trying to clear his mind. He glanced at the two men, their faces equally solemn.

"A tragic event, indeed," Roosevelt said, unsmiling. "I am sure the sight must have been quite disturbing." He grunted his throat clear. "Nonetheless, the result was necessary despite the brutal means."

"How you mean that?" asked Cole, unsure if he understood what the portly easterner had in mind.

"Come now, Hayes. Surely you understand the need to civilize the country. These natives, besides their peaceful behavior at times, must adhere to the rightful ownership of the lands they occupy, and those rights were bought and paid for by the citizens of the United States."

"I must agree, Mr. Hayes," said Buttram. "Your tale is an awful occurrence. But the Indian nations have no place in our society," he continued while the colored servant took away his plate. "After all, they aren't 'people.' "

With deep breaths, Cole tried to calm himself. He watched the servant take his plate. "I've heard that before." His eyes then turned to the two men. "Custer said the same sort of thing."

"You knew the General?" asked Roosevelt, his puffy cheeks again drawn back.

"Oh, yeah. And he was a colonel last I saw him," Cole answered, quickly realizing that further confessions would lead him to another pained remembrance.

"How so?"

"Oh," Cole mumbled. "Me and J. B. Hickok rode together for a while. He was once a scout for him and would tell me about him."

"Wild Bill Hickok?" Senator Buttram's curiosity lit up not only his own face, but Roosevelt's as well. The more Cole said, the deeper into a mudhole he felt he was sliding.

"The same. I never knew him to call himself that, but he did answer to it."

"Fascinating character," said Roosevelt, facing the senator. "I once had the good luck to meet him at a performance in New York—a Wild West show, they called it. One of Buffalo Bill Cody's shows. He, too, is a captivating fellow."

Mention of Cody's name made Cole recall what Hickok thought of the man who claimed to have fought so many Indians. *If the Indians had paid better, Cody would have fought for the other side. No greater lover of money had yet been born.* "Don't believe everything you hear."

Both gentlemen turned to him. He had failed to heed his own warning, and now he felt near knee-deep in that mudhole.

"I heard them shows weren't exactly how it really is, is all."

"Of course not," Roosevelt agreed, grinning. "I realize it was all for show. After all, they were on a stage. However, I did find them fascinating in the yarns they told. Especially one fellow—whose name escapes me, though. Hickok reveled in his exploits with this other man. Said he, no other pistolier had the calm of nerve to point a pistol at another that rivaled himself except this one man." Roosevelt tapped his head as if to nudge his memory. "I'm sure it will come to me."

"Well, while you're trying to remember, we should retire to the front room," Buttram said as he rose. Cole scooted his chair away from the table. When he stood, Roosevelt's blaring voice almost buckled his knees.

"The Rainmaker!"

Cole twisted about, expecting lawmen to crash through the windows. Standing like a crouched statue, he eyed Roosevelt, whose big smile had returned.

"Have you heard of such a man, Hayes? You said you knew Hickok."

His heart went from stopped to pounding. "I, uh . . . I only heard the name."

Roosevelt's disappointment at Cole's response curled his brow. "Pity. I would have enjoyed to know more about him. I understand he is still alive."

"I think you're right. So far, he is."

The three men left the table. Cole tried to take in deep breaths to settle his nerves. While in a lawmaker's home, any more slips of the tongue might cause him to spend the rest of the night—and his life—behind bars. The senator led the way to the front room while Roosevelt came alongside Cole.

"Quite a dangerous fellow, I understand. It's legend that he's killed as many as thirty men."

Never one to count how many men he sent to the grave, Cole thought that number was double the truth, but disputing it would require proof. This time, he remembered better. "Like I said, Mr. Roosevelt. Don't believe everything you hear."

Chapter Eleven

Maud kicked her horse to come alongside Wheeler. "Can we stop for a little while?"

He looked at her with unconcerned eyes. "Did you whine like this when you were with him?"

She faced away from him. "No." A strong thought made her look at him once more. "I'm having you try to see how the horses need rest."

A smirk broke his face, but he kept his eyes forward. "Horses? Why, I would have thought you were worried about something else's backside."

Maud felt her lip curl. "Ain't going to do no good if we catch him and you're dead tired."

"Don't you worry about that. You just point him out. I'll be plenty ready when the time comes."

There was no reasoning with him. Every idea she had to bring him to her way of thinking didn't budge him from his. "Why is he so important?"

Wheeler slowed his horse and glared at her. "That's my business."

His stern answer only fueled her own anger. "Well, according to you, it seems like it's my business, too." Turning his face back to the front, he nudged his horse. Not to be ignored, she did the same. "So, what is it?"

"I just told you, woman."

"Told me what?"

Again, he faced her. "That's the business I'm in. It's my trade."

She wasn't surprised by the words, but she was by the answer. "Is that all?"

"That's it," he replied. Then a more solemn reflection came over him. "It's how I put food on the table. For near thirty years I came home every night, but I didn't bring much with me then. Every day I'm out here, I try to remember those days."

"But why him? Why the Rainmaker?"

"Five thousand dollars is a lot of money," he answered matter-of-factly. "I don't know him. Don't want to know him. He's only a name on a poster to me. Ain't even a name, at that. But if bringing him in gets me the money I need to be home with my family, then that's my business."

Maud thought of the face of the man they pursued. Clay had much the same look. Much the same determination. Much the same reason to continue. The factors leading to her being on a horse covering the same Kansas dirt in twice a week weren't of her doing. Fate had put her between two men who didn't know each other, but a piece of paper put one as prey and the other as hunter. She tried to have a mind like Wheeler. It was business. The right and wrong wasn't left to her to decide.

The morning brought a clear sky. Due to the stiff wind, Cole covered Little Bear's head with his coat. A breakfast of eggs, ham, and biscuits had settled his stomach, but not his mind. The three days of rest at Senator Buttram's hospitality had given his aches time to heal. During that time, another annoyance had pained him more than all of those in his joints combined. Today, he had come to the decision to rid himself of the burden he had carried for five hundred miles.

He stepped off the porch and headed for the barn. The stablemaster already had saddled the palomino. He put the young girl into the loop like he had done it all his life. With thanks given to the stablemaster, he mounted and steered the horse to the gravel road and off the property.

Unsure of which day it was, he knew by the traffic filling the streets that it wasn't Sunday. The stares of the passersby reminded him of when he had first come into the town. He hoped it was due to being a lone horseback rider and not because of the little girl roped to the front of the saddle.

Heeding the directions given by Buttram, he followed the street through the center of town. Carpenters busily hammered fresh lumber into new structures. Brick and mortar were slapped and stacked around sturdy frames as tall as four stories.

Merchants displayed their goods on the boardwalk, attracting buyers by forcing them either to sidestep the baskets and racks to walk in the street or to buy items just to clear the way.

A scan in front and behind told him he was surrounded by the emergence of civilization. He took no comfort from the observation. The gawking citizens made him feel unwelcome—their ways and habits along with their new ordinances meant to squeeze out undesirables. He couldn't help but consider himself part of that group.

The palomino stepped over the train tracks, and Cole glanced over his shoulder. Somehow, he felt more at ease knowing eyes wouldn't follow him this far. Looking again to the road, he couldn't help but notice another scene. To the right, the station bustled with travelers on the platform. Their formal dress left little doubt as to their purpose: either to seek a fortune in the West, or to return east having witnessed disappointment firsthand.

As the horse continued on the road, a large lone structure came into view. At its center stood a dominant building rising what appeared to be four floors high. Single floor wings sprawled to each side. The brick wasn't a jubilant red or green, but rather a windblown dusty brown. As he approached, he noticed tall iron fences surrounding the property. The grounds were void of trees, and the sparse grass was a short-cropped yellow. At first, he thought he had taken a wrong turn and found a prison. Nearing the fence, he spotted the youthful faces he expected— dressed not in their customary fare, but rather in white stiff collars and long hemmed skirts of plaid.

He reined the palomino to a stop and stared. The children showed no signs of their tribe. No braids, no beads or feathers. Their black hair was cut in respectable fashion to support the teachings of their white lessons. None showed any spirit or a desire to engage in delightful play. Only drawn faces peeked his way.

Squinting to focus on those nearer the house, he found young boys laboring to clear the dirt with a rake as a farmer would plow the field for early-spring sowing, but with the winds and snow not long away, it seemed of little purpose. The exertions appeared to serve more as discipline than useful work.

He peeked down. Little Bear also watched. Although there was no telling what was truly going on in that tiny head, he'd never seen her so attentive to something she couldn't hold or eat. Almost as if she knew what he was thinking, she peered up. Those squinting brown eyes dug into his soul. Without the courage to continue the stare, he glanced to the side. He sat on the saddle as if nailed to it.

The idea had seemed a sound one at first. The intent was to find a home for this little one, give her a sturdy roof over her head and regular meals. The face of the mother came to mind. Her dying plea was to return the girl to the land where her people had lived for centuries.

The woman he had met on the boardwalk had spoken of the benefit of being raised in white ways. However, this place with the iron gate was another pen the whites had found to hold those they didn't want roaming. Although the orphanage could care for her better, a gnawing in his gut told him to turn the horse. The final straw came when Little Bear returned her attention to the children on the grounds. Cole couldn't help looking too. They were without words, but their stares shouted at him to leave. He gripped the reins and steered the palomino's head about, and a kick to the flanks had him fleeing without a glance behind.

All during the return trip through town, he chided himself for making another fool decision. Just when he was convinced the worst choice he could make was to keep the little girl, now his conscience bound him as tight as if he were hog-tied to a tree. Concerns of food and shelter for them both preyed on his mind. Still, when he gave thought to turning the horse yet again, one glance to the little Nez Perce child paralyzed his arms and kept him on a course straight to Buttram's home.

Upon arriving at the fence, he made the turn up the gravel road and tried to think of an excuse for his absence. As he approached the porch, Roosevelt came from the front door.

"Hayes. We were just looking for you. We'd thought you'd left us."

Cole shook his head and dismounted. "The girl was restless. Thought I'd ride her around. Settles her down. Keeps her mind moving."

"Oh," Roosevelt said with some surprise. "Well, we're glad to have you return. I myself am departing back for home. Must return for the nation's Thanksgiving next week. But, before I left, I was hoping to have a photograph of myself with Senator Buttram. It would be a delight to include you in it."

Unsure of what was expected of him, Cole didn't see any harm in honoring the request. He shrugged. "Guess I got time for that."

"Splendid," Roosevelt said, clapping his hands. He invited Cole in, and Cole, after securing Little Bear, climbed the steps up the porch and went inside. In the main room were Buttram and a man with an oblong box atop a tripod. Roosevelt charged into the room as if he owned it. "John, look who I found wandering in front of the house."

The senator acknowledged Cole's arrival in the house, but not with the same cheer his guest had.

"I thought I would include Hayes here in the photograph. You don't mind, do you, John?"

Buttram at first hesitated, the suggestion appearing to sour his mood, then shook his head as if caught in a stupor. "Of course not," he replied.

Cole felt as welcome as a skunk at a wedding. The maid came to his side, reaching out to take Little Bear from him. With some reservation, he relinquished the child to her.

"Right, then," Roosevelt answered. "Might as well get on with it." He held out his arm and motioned for Cole to join him and the senator in front of the box.

The man behind it busily prepared a small prod with a metal trough on top. With care, he took a can from a table and shook out a white powder from it into the trough. Lifting a black drape at the back of the box, he ducked his head under it. Emerging from the drape, he waved both hands. "Closer together, if you will, gentlemen."

Cole stepped nearer to Roosevelt, but the man kept

waving. Finally, Cole was butted shoulder to shoulder with the shorter man, taking no comfort at meshing with another man. Buttram did the same on the opposite side.

"Would you remove your hat?" the man asked Cole. It took a moment before Cole gripped the brim, pried it from his head, and held it at his side, sorry for not doing so before he came into the house.

"That should be a fine portrait," the man said as he ducked under the drape once more. "Hold that pose, gentlemen."

From the corner of his eye, Cole saw Roosevelt grip his coat's lapel while Buttram took his free hand and tucked it inside his jacket. Feeling more common than the other two men, Cole sought a place to put his free hand, and the first natural act that came to him was to grip the butt of his pistol. With that, he settled into position to stare at the box.

As the man came from under the drape, he lifted a black cap, exposing a glass lens curved like spectacles. "Stand still for a moment, please."

Obeying the order, Cole strained not to move. As he wondered how still he would have kept had the man said nothing, the next five seconds seemed like an hour. A peep from Little Bear drew his focus to her. She gurgled more noise as the maid held her. Cole couldn't help grin. A white brilliance lit the room, then quickly faded.

"That should do it," the man said as he placed the cap over the lens.

With instant regret for moving, Cole peeked at the man. Without a hint of having noticed Cole's motion, he placed the prod back on the table. Cole didn't have the courage to confess.

"I thank you, sir," Roosevelt bellowed. He turned to the senator and shook his hand. "John, I shall always remember this trip. I can't thank you enough for inviting me. Someday, I hope to return with my wife and family to this part of our country." With the same sincerity, Buttram expressed his enjoyment over his guest's stay. Feeling obliged, Cole shook Buttram's hand and thanked him for the room and board. A slap on the back came from Roosevelt.

"So, Hayes. What are your plans?"

Caught unaware, Cole relied on an old dodge. "Ain't sure right now." With a moment's thought about the morning's ride, he reconsidered. "I promised a woman I would head west," he said with a peek at Little Bear.

"A woman? Well, you know what they say, a wink from the right one is worth a pound of gold," Roosevelt said with a wink of his own. Realizing he'd given the wrong idea, Cole was quick to set his meaning straight.

"It ain't like that. I made a promise to get a job done, and I didn't think I would for a time, but now I've to see to it." He reached for Little Bear, who lunged into his arms.

"A good father," Roosevelt said with his familiar gleam. "I think I know just what you have in mind."

The easterner's meaning didn't seem clear, but before Cole could ask, he was out the front door. The colored driver had pulled the carriage to the front of the house with the bags loaded onto the back. "Why don't you see me to the train?"

At first, Cole didn't think the idea practical, considering the time still needed to pack his own belongings. However, when he stepped onto the porch, he saw the mule and goat next to the palomino, all held steady by the stablemaster. He looked to Roosevelt, who again winked. The offer appeared not to have been by accident.

With a nod, Cole stepped from the porch, turning once more to wave his appreciation to Buttram and tip his hat to the maid. He climbed onto the palomino and followed the carriage off the property.

Retracing the journey of the morning, Cole didn't know exactly what to make of this little man from the East, or what the need was to meet him at the train station. Still, Roosevelt had been more than kind, and being ungrateful wasn't a habit Cole liked to find himself practicing. The sluggish mule slowed Cole and he lost sight of the carriage. When the horse stepped over the tracks, the locomotive was already at the depot, billowing its black soot high into the air. Roosevelt had already arrived and was waiting on the landing.

Quickly tethering both sets of reins to an awning pillar, Cole took the child and hurried to the landing. Through the mix of people he recognized the beaming smile.

"Glad you could make it," said Roosevelt, offering his hand as he had with every greeting.

"I'd felt poorly if I hadn't," replied Cole, accepting the hand. "With all you've done for me, I can't thank you enough." The conductor's call to board took away the smile.

"Yes, well, it doesn't seem I'll have time to banter as I had hoped." He reached into his pocket and drew an envelope. "You've appeared to me something of a fraud, Mr. Hayes."

The accusation stunned Cole. "How you mean that?"

"Let's just say, judging from our conversation the other night, my guess is you aren't who you say you are."

"I still don't know what you're getting at," said Cole, shaking his head.

"Take this," Roosevelt ordered as he shoved the envelope into Cole's hand. "It won't change your case greatly, but I think it could ease some matters." He raised an eyebrow at the child. "I know there will be needs where this will be handy."

The feel the envelope suggested something softer then stiff paper was inside. "What are you giving me?"

Before Roosevelt could answer, the conductor issued a final warning.

"I know I appear as a 'tinhorn,' I've heard it called, but I'm quite astute at sizing up men. You don't appear to be this child's father—not to me, at least. What you're doing with her, I haven't the time to discover, nor the ambition," said Roosevelt, in retreat toward the train. "I do, however, know that I recognize in you a trait of goodness, almost a modest chivalry." He took his steps as the iron wheels spun on the track. "Use it well," he said, pointing to the envelope while the train car jolted from the yank of the engine. Its huffs of exhaust boomed over Roosevelt's own awkward voice. With a wave, he peered down at Cole as the car left the station. "I trust we'll meet again."

When the caboose had passed by the landing, curiosity made Cole peel back the envelope's fresh seal. He thumbed through five greenback gold certificates worth twenty dollars apiece. He didn't know which surprised him more, the strange easterner's generosity or the idea that the truth had been so easily discovered. He folded the money into his coat pocket.

With a new spirit, he fondly looked at Little Bear. Her attention became focused on all the different folks milling on the platform. Not discouraged by her lack of interest, he turned for the ramp to get back to the horse and mule. The crowd that had departed the train continued to retrieve their baggage, blocking the path, forcing him nearer the depot building. Battling shoulders, hats, and heads, he twisted through the mob, but his legs stiffened when he recognized letters on a poster he knew all too well. He couldn't move his arms or eyes, able only to stare at the big black letters. Above the letters were a five and three zeroes. Below was finer print; although he couldn't understand the meaning, he was confident there was a description and a story of the past.

He squinted at the type, but he didn't recognize any words that he knew. He stood as helpless as the child he cradled, yet another instance where a long-ago decision not to take up schooling after the war had put him at the mercy of anyone who could read.

If his guess was right, the name at the bottom was offering five thousand dollars for him and it stood good whether he was brought in atop a horse or across the saddle. Despite the many people, he felt alone.

His first idea, of asking someone to tell him what the poster said, quickly left his mind. Just saying the words aloud might strike a match to a fuse in any fellow's head. Then, if that fellow didn't speak the words, it would leave Cole even more in doubt as to whether he stood in danger. He looked to both sides, fearful that someone might take interest in why he himself stared at the poster so long. He slowly walked from it, careful to notice if more attention came his way. If the poster was at a train station, it could be in any sheriff's office.

The reputation that had dogged him for the last five years chased him from the platform. What had started as a day on which he decided to head in a new direction, only to cower at that hard decision when a better prospect dangled itself at the point of his nose, now was ending with him confused as to where to hide.

Instinct turned him to the vast plain. He drew the envelope from his pocket and marched back up the ramp. A woman soon left the ticket window. He drew out the greenbacks and leaned closer to the bars to see the cashier.

"When does the next train west get here?"

Chapter Twelve

While watching the prairie pass by, Cole sat huddled on the bench alone. The girl fell asleep with the continual toss of the car. He'd just as soon she stayed that way. It had taken a solid day sitting in the station waiting on the train bound for Cheyenne. Although she slept when she wanted, he had grabbed only an hour of shut-eye at best. Leaving Nebraska would take the rest of the day, and he hoped to get more.

He was angled toward the window, and that posture allowed him to shield the child with his coat from others who might not be fond of an Indian, no matter the age, traveling with them. It wouldn't be long until she woke. If his luck held, she'd stir early enough to wake him and allow a quick retreat to the livestock car to tend to her needs.

His mind wandered as his eyes grew heavy. Only the third time he had ridden a train, it was a first for him to sit among the passengers. The last instance, more than ten years ago, he had bunked with the cattle on their way to Kansas City. It was not a trip to recall with fondness; the smell of the filthy beasts still filled his nose, and their bawling echoed in his ears. Small naps were all he managed for the entire ride then, too. That and the small earnings to wrangle beeves broke him of his desire to continue that line.

However, the first train ride had been with similar beasts, while learning his first trade—that of soldier. His experience crowded in a single car with a bevy of troopers, recalling their moaning in every white language, little of it English, rivaled that of the steers when he thought about it now.

The long years since didn't bring any sweeter memories. Sweltering days and frigid nights, bouncing from one town to the next, wasn't a prospect he had imagined when he set out on his own.

The remembrance popped from his mind when he noticed that the view outside slowed. An instant later, the squeal of iron pierced the car. A jolt threw all in it forward with the force of a mule kick. He clutched the cold metal rod of the seat in front of him to keep from slamming into it. Once the car came to a stop, he glanced at Little Bear. Still asleep. She'd get her regular nap no matter.

Just as his eyes fixed on her, the rear door burst open. Two men with dusty bandannas over their noses charged down the aisle, their pistols drawn at all the passengers. "This is a robbery."

Cole huffed a sigh at his bad luck. Reflex made him grip the butt of the Colt under his coat, but the men had already marched to a spot in the center of the car. Spraying lead might make return fire come his way. He couldn't afford a stray bullet finding Little Bear, buried under his coat. Besides, it was unlikely these two were the only ones to stop the train.

They ordered all to surrender valuables, and the waistcoated men and bonneted women nervously complied with the thieves' demands. Watches and billfolds were collected in a canvas bag. One of the robbers admired an older gentleman's boots. The pair didn't appear ever to have met mud, so they were quickly extracted from the gentleman's feet.

The one item not to be thrown into the bag was a gun.

A shriek from the side brought all attention to a lone young woman. Her black hair reminded Cole of another beauty he'd met in Colorado. The black-shirted bandit yanked at her hand. "Give us the ring."

"Oh, please, no," the woman pleaded. "It's my wedding band."

"Give it to me," said the robber, reaching into his pocket and drawing a knife. "Or I'll cut it off."

She yanked but couldn't free her hand from his firm grip. Cole sat and watched, as if he had escaped the robbers' attention. The more the tugging went on, the bigger the fire inside him rose. He was not one to volunteer to get in others' squabbles, but he couldn't help getting riled over the robber's manhandling of the young lady. With the robber's back to him while the other paraded in the front of the car wagging his pistol, Cole saw his chance. He took a quick breath. The move would have to be swift and without hesitation.

He stood and took one step. Swiping his coat to the side, he drew the Colt and poked the muzzle on the robber's head. The robber froze still at the ratchet of the hammer.

"Did you hear that?" asked Cole. The robber nodded meekly. "Then I'm sure you heard her say no. Drop the pistol." The robber let it fall to the wood floor.

The other pointed his pistol at Cole in panic. "Put your piece down, friend, or I'll shoot you dead."

Cradling Little Bear, Cole had only one play. "If that's your plan, say good-bye to your partner."

"Will, don't listen to him. Kill him now," the captive robber shouted.

"I'd just as soon not spill your brains all over the pretty lady's dress," Cole said, eyeing the young woman, who finally pulled her quivering hand from the robber's grip. "It'd be a shame to stain it."

"I'm telling you for the last time, mister," yelled the other in front. "I'll count to three and then you're a dead man. One."

Now Little Bear started to stir. If she fought his hold, his balance would be thrown. Pulling the trigger wasn't a fear, but after that shot he would need another instant to cock the pistol and he wouldn't beat the bullet coming his way. With a deep sense of hatred at being pushed without being allowed to think a matter through, he knew the only act was to stop the pusher.

"Two."

Cole swung the muzzle to aim down the aisle and fired. Before the smoke clouded his view, he saw the red spot on the other's chest. The thud vibrating the floor confirmed that his shot found the mark. Sweeping the muzzle back, he cocked the hammer and stuck it in the robber's ear. "We're going to find the rest of your friends." Despite the screams, he knew he'd been heard. The boom rustled Little Bear. She clawed at his shirt to edge out from under the cover of his coat. He poked his head around the robber's shoulder and met the young woman's flinching eyes. "Ma'am, I need you to take this child."

Slowly at first, she rose with the twitch of a stumbling drunk. Cole kept his eyes on the robber while the woman carefully stepped out into the aisle and took the child. With Little Bear secure, the matter at hand was to find the group that had stopped the train. "How many are out there?"

"Twenty men" was the answer.

Cole shoved the muzzle harder into the scalp. "Lie to me again and there'll be one less to count."

"There's six of us. Five if you don't count Will down there."

"No need to count him anymore." Cole snatched the robber's collar and yanked him to the rear door. "I know they heard the shot. Since they ain't calling, seems they're waiting on you to do the talking." He grabbed the latch and kicked the door open. "Call out to them. Have them show themselves."

He pushed the robber into the sunlight. The brisk wind watered Cole's eyes, but he knew if he wiped them, lead could come from any angle. The single

177

sound was the huff of the distant engine. The only sight was the tall grass bending in the wind. To get a better view, Cole nudged his captive down the iron landing steps and onto the ground. A moment's hope that the others has fled was answered with a loud call.

"Let him go or I'll drop you to the dirt."

Cole couldn't determine the direction of the phantom voice. "You already lost one man. Your take has one less share. Leaving this one behind will double that. Be happy with what you got and ride out." He stepped out farther from the train, but the wider angle produced only the sight of the two other passenger cars, the coal wagon, and the engine. With a glance behind, he made out the two livestock cars. Still with a firm grip on the collar, he bent slightly to peek under the cars, but he didn't spot any legs.

The quiet made him edgy. Keeping the muzzle pressed against his captive's head, he walked toward the front, careful not to stray too far out.

"Just who the hell are you, mister?" the robber muttered.

"I'm the fellow that's going to put a slug in your ear if you don't keep your mouth shut." Several cautious strides put him at the middle of one of the cars.

"You a lawman?"

"Nope. Just someone don't take to ladies being wrestled with."

"How 'bout we give you Will's cut?"

"Ain't interested in any blood money." He scanned behind, but there was still no sign of movement.

"You're the one that spilled blood by shooting Will."

"Better his than mine. You point a gun at somebody, it's as good as firing it. Besides, you fellows don't look like no churchgoers. Ain't got a doubt this isn't you all's first time."

"Mister," the robber said with a nervous quiver. "They're going to kill you. If you don't give up and surrender, they're going to start shooting, and I don't mind telling you I don't care to be near what they're shooting at. Some of them fellows ain't crack shots. Why don't you do both of us a favor and let me loose. I'll tell them to leave you alone, and we'll ride off."

"Didn't I tell you to shut your mouth?" Cole said, edging closer to the front of the passenger car. The breeze drifted the engine smoke over the grass. Darting his eyes to the front, then the rear, and under the train, he kept the pistol steady at the robber's head.

The groan of a window sliding jerked his head from behind. The black-haired beauty popped her head out. "We hear them on the roof!"

Cole peered up. A rifle barrel gleamed in the sunshine above him. Slipping the Colt's barrel off the robber's head, Cole matched its aim to his view and fired. The rifleman took the slug in the gut and doubled over during the drop to the ground. A figure from between the front cars caught Cole's eye. The figure fired. The captive robber cried in pain, the bullet popping his chest open. As the robber slumped, Cole pulled back the hammer and returned fire. The shot hit the figure in the leg, sending him to the dirt. Not dead, the figure fired wildly, one shot spraying dirt, another splintering wood on the car. Cole cocked the hammer and aimed at arm's length, sighting the barrel at the biggest part of the other shooter. He squeezed the trigger. The bullet ripped open the victim's shirt. Blood spurted like a fountain.

Again pulling the hammer back, he waited for the next attack. In the distance, a single rider jumped over the tracks and rode in the opposite direction. At first relieved, Cole thought to trust what the robber had told him.

He crept slowly toward the engine. Revolver poised in front of him, he peeked behind, then moved his eyes in front. He saw a shadow under the car, cast from the other side. Cole knelt. A pair of boots headed toward the rear of the car. Rather than wait at the end of the car, he decided on attack as a better strategy. He took aim and fired. The bullet exploded through one boot, folding his ankle like a hinge. The wounded shooter screamed in pain, reaching for his bloody boot. With the fallen revolver inches away, he hesitated, then scrambled for the weapon. Cole cocked the Colt, which froze his opponent. The men looked into each other's eyes.

"Don't," said Cole. The offer was heeded. Bending under the car, Cole went to other side and retrieved the fallen gun just as the passengers exited the cars.

"Mister, I wish to know your name," said an elderly man with a gray waistcoat and a black bowler. He gratefully extended his hand.

Cole holstered the Colt as he stood over the wounded man. "I ain't no one," he said, not accepting the handshake.

"No one? I daresay you are, man. You're a damn hero. Why, if you hadn't have acted, these men likely would have killed us, or left us for dead out here."

"How you mean, left us for dead? The train ain't dead."

"Just as well be. Ask him," the elderly man said, pointing at the engineer, who nursed the welt on his brow.

"That's right," the engineer agreed. "That bunch tore the rail out. That's why I had to stop, or we would have derailed. That's when they jumped me. I guess they didn't want us reporting this at the next stop. Don't worry, though. When we're overdue, they'll send a party out here to find us."

"Party?" Cole inquired.

"Yes," answered the engineer. "Pinkerton men, most likely."

The news made Cole more nervous than he had been when facing the train robbers. If he didn't make tracks of his own, the hard fight he just won would be for naught. As more passengers approached with appreciation, he silently marched directly to the passenger car. At the landing, the black-haired beauty stood on the steps with Little Bear.

"You mind following me?" he asked her. She gratefully nodded. He continued to the livestock car and threw the latch free. Climbing in, he untethered the palomino and saddled it.

"Who are you?" she asked.

He looked into her eyes. He hated lying to women. They always seemed to know. He focused attention to the cinch. "Clay."

"You're a brave man, Clay. Are you this child's father?"

"You might say that."

"Well, I know she must love you very much. She screamed when you were outside."

Cole turned to her in surprise. "*She* did?"

The woman nodded. "Yes, she did. You must be very proud of her."

The chatter was nice to hear, but the gnawing at his gut that told him to escape made him hurry to finish. Once done, he grabbed the reins to the mule and goat. Determined not to be slowed by stubborn animals, he jumped from the car and tugged the reins until the three overcame their fear of the height and leapt to the ground. Quickly, he mounted, then stared at the black-haired beauty. "I don't mean to be disrespectful, ma'am. But I got to ride." He glanced at the rest of the passengers, who stood in a group and pointed in confusion over his actions.

He leaned and reached down for Little Bear. The beauty gave him the child, then clutched his neck for only an instant and gave him a kiss on the cheek.

"Thank you for my life," she said. Although it was not the first time he had heard such gratitude, he tipped his hat, unsure how to respond. He swung the palomino around and spurred the flanks.

Maud lifted her head from the table to eye the toothless drunk staring at her. His gaping mouth appeared as a dark cave. Long grizzled whiskers grew wildly over his face like sage scrub. His wide eyes showed his eagerness for her company. She hadn't slept in a bed for six days, but she still couldn't convince herself to stoop so low.

"Get up, woman. We're riding."

The order didn't come from the drunk, whose pose continued in frozen anticipation. She tilted her head and saw Bill Wheeler walk to the table. She slumped her head back to the wood top. "I just want to sleep."

"No time for that." His voice held no pity for her. "I just heard that the Rainmaker ain't but fifty miles from here."

She jerked her head up at the news. Managing to get only one eye open, she focused on the stubbled cheeks. "How do you know that?"

"Talk from some fellows down the street. They're buzzing like bees about a single man that killed four men trying to rob the train to Cheyenne. The county sheriff has the last one locked up. That one is still wetting his pants," Wheeler said with a laugh.

"How do you know it's him? The Rainmaker?"

"According to the talk, the one in jail, he confessed to the sheriff that he and two of his brothers and two cousins stopped the train, but the man that put up a fight was a tall man wearing a winter coat and a black hat. The sheriff got word from Cheyenne that the story was true. The man with the black hat rode off, tugging a mule and goat, and," Wheeler paused until Maud opened her other eye, "he had a baby with him."

She leaned back in the chair, unable to believe that her long travel that had seemed so foolish actually had hope. "Where did he go?"

"He took off for the Tetons. Come on. We've got

to get after him before he gets up in them mountains, or we'll never find him."

The rumbling in her stomach reminded her why they had stopped. "You said we were going to eat. I haven't had anything for two days except those hard-tack biscuits. They were hard as rocks when they were baked. I need to eat something."

"Can't afford the time. He gets beyond those hills and he'll be gone for good." He gripped her arm, but she tore away.

"I can't. I won't go until I have something to eat."

"There's nothing in here," he answered as a plea for her to agree.

"Then find something."

Again he took her arm, and again she shrugged his hand free. Knowing he wouldn't and couldn't pick her up from the chair, she felt confident he would relent and fetch some food. However, the strategy appeared to fail when Wheeler booted the drunk's chair, tumping the old man to the floor. Wheeler righted the chair less the drunk and sat, leaving just the two at the table.

"We've come a long way. I ain't seen my family for near five months now, and I kind of like to get this all behind me so I can be with them. I need you to help me. I already said I'd split the reward."

"You said a thousand—" He cupped his palm over her mouth, then peeked behind him, no doubt worried someone in the small room might have heard her blurt. Understanding his concern, she nodded, then spoke in a softer voice. "You said a thousand dollars, Bill Wheeler. It's hardly a split."

"Yeah, but a thousand buys a lot of food." He cocked his eye to her waist. "If you ask me, I think this trip has done you some good."

"Well, I didn't ask you." The comment made her inspect just what he was seeing. "This dress is about to fall off of me."

"It still has a ways to go before that happens."

"Quiet, you." She regained her train of thought. "It's getting cold, too. If I keep following you I'll likely freeze." She darted her eyes at him for some reaction, but he kept the same dead stare without a word. "Well?"

"You told me to hush up."

"Ain't you seeing what I'm telling you?"

"I was just waiting for you to finish so we could get moving."

The lack of his concern tired her even more. She dipped her head back to the wood tabletop. "If I can't eat, then I'm going to sleep. At least I can do that without food."

Through squinted eyes, she saw his grimace, but she couldn't care. She was too sleepy. After several moments sitting in front of her, he wiped his lips, then stood. He buttoned his coat and pulled his hat down. Not sure of his next act, she kept her head still. He stepped from her view. Her first thought was that she had won. Surely, he must have seen her point and gone to fetch her something to eat. The door squeaked open behind her and closed with a thud.

Her confidence waned after first ten, then twenty minutes passed. Slowly, she lifted her head and looked to the door. When she found herself staring at it for more than five minutes, she rose to go to it. With the same squeak it opened, and she peeked outside. Despite the darkness, she saw that the gelding was still tethered to the post—and that Wheeler's horse was gone.

Her stomach ached more, and it wasn't due to lack of food. She closed the door. Facing about, she eyed her prospects. Two men spoke to each other while casting an occasional glance at her from the tattered bar. The only other breathing soul was the drunk passed out on the floor, and she wasn't sure he was even breathing.

She didn't even know where this place was, or its name. Her heart raced. She went to the table and wrapped the shawl around her shoulders. Whatever her chances of finding Wheeler in the dark, they had to be better than staying here.

Chapter Thirteen

The sky was covered by clouds and the wind was at peace with the land. Snow began to drift in his face. His breath came out as steam. Before him lay flat prairie dotted with the winter's first warning not to tread farther. No one was in sight, and a peek behind showed the same, only beyond it trouble waited for him should he return. Soon he'd have to cross the Great Divide. He was aware of the size of the task— and just how foolish—but fate had left him no choice. Bringing his eyes forward, he took a glimpse of the small girl below him, then nudged the palomino.

Despite the stubborn mule, he kept a steady pace. He ducked his head to combat the chill, focusing on the ground in front without allowing his eyes to stray to the view ahead. The coat was wrapped tightly around his shoulders, the slack taken up by the encompassment of Little Bear.

The still silence kept his mind wandering.

The cold wasn't the worst he'd been through. Bivouacked on the Montana plain more than ten years before, during a patrol for the cavalry, took that prize. For six days he had endured the meanest weather the territory threw at him. The flimsy canvas tent was no match for the steady northern gale that kept the colors as straight as a plank. Woolen capes did little to retain warmth. Coffee was drunk straight from the fire; if left off the boil, it became solid in minutes. Two soldiers froze in their sleep. Five others in the troop lingered with a heavy cough, only to return to the post before succumbing to death. Even those renegades they were patrolling for were smart enough to leave the place for better shelter. If he survived that, he would live through this.

The flakes became bigger, usually a sign of a storm, but as long as the wind stayed calm he could keep moving. As the incline grew, so did the depth of the snow. The palomino's hooves sank beneath the white blanket. The mule, without the high step of the horse, trudged through it, leaving enough of a wake for the goat to proceed with ease.

Little Bear caught up on most of her lost naps. Even during the night she didn't stir, allowing Cole needed rest after digging for the warm ground for more than an hour. The mornings only showed evidence of another heavy snowfall.

Despite his hopeful wishes, the menace he'd expected for half a week finally came into view upon cresting a rise at midmorning. Stretched across his path, a white wall of rock rose from the plain, its top hidden in the clouds. No reprieve was in sight for as far as he could see to the left or right. The wind stiffened. He closed his eyes to escape its bitter lash as well as to reconsider.

All the reasons he had used to convince himself that this journey was folly now took shape in those mountains still more than a day away. He opened his eyes and let out a long breath. Never one to back down from a dare, he stared at the challenge, not wanting to admit he'd been bested before he even began. There was still enough food, and from what he could make out from the distance, there was more than enough timber for fire. Little would be proven if he turned tail. Perhaps when he got to the foothills a modest path could be found. If nothing else, the rocks would provide a better break from the wind. The prospect made him kick the palomino to go on.

The valley had to be negotiated with caution. Although the layer of snow appeared uniform, windswept drifts hid gullies that dropped the horse to a neck-high depth, causing equal if not more strain on the mule. More than once he thought he'd lost the goat. The dried scrub made good kindling, but few bigger sticks could be found. He let the fire burn its way to the bottom of the snow, but only when the wind would allow the flame enough relief to catch on what little grass was available above the snow. Small junipers and young firs burned quickly despite their green wood. Digging them out of the snow to hatchet the trunks was a chore.

Each time he camped, the burden of carrying the child slowed him from his work. While sitting around the last fire before the next day's assault up the valley, he finished the first sack of coffee given to him by Colonel Grimes. At first he thought to add the sack to the fire, but when holding both ends of it in front of him, he noticed that it went from his chest to his waist. The vision of Lakota mothers with cradleboards strapped to their backs came to mind. He knew that if he carried the girl on his back he would smother her under his coat, so he cut loops in the canvas to serve as straps, then two holes in the bottom to provide for her legs.

The first attempt to get her to sit in the sack met with resistance. When he slipped the straps over his shoulders, the restriction on his reach made it hard to capture the girl. When he finally had a firm grip of her arms, she defiantly kicked away the opening. With a chilled breeze watering his eyes, he couldn't keep the slit from collapsing against his chest.

A bigger fire raged inside him from the frustration, until he grabbed the girl's leg, forcing it into the sack like a shovel. Soon the other leg followed and she slumped inside the sack. It was then he realized that the holes he had cut were too far apart, leaving the girl bunched like a snake. Carefully, he made the alteration while she was still in the sack, knowing she wouldn't allow him a second chance. The Bowie knife's sharp edge sliced the canvas easily. When the girl's legs dropped through the enlarged holes, her bottom landed with a thud but the remaining stitches held.

The sack was worth the effort to make it. The girl fought to escape it, but when she peeked from the top, the bitter wind quickly forced her to retreat into its warmer confinement. The best purpose it served was for him. When he was lying on his back, the girl now slept on his chest, easing his nighttime worries. The first night with this new arrangement was peaceful.

The early dawn flurry turned into a gust-driven white torrent. The palomino's unsteady steps compelled him to lead the horse and mule on foot. The depth of each stride brought the chilling snow to his thigh. With Little Bear in the sack, he wrapped each arm around the opposing shoulder to seal his body's warmth, all the while maintaining a frozen grip on the reins. The hat's broad brim shielded his eyes from the wind. He slipped the red bandana over his nose. He couldn't afford a glance back to check on the animals for fear the wind would freeze his face.

He peeked beneath the hat brim and saw only a white blur. There was no sky, no mountain, no trees. The incline inched the snow level higher. Once it was at his waist, he trudged through the virgin blanket, lunging to keep from falling backward. He had to be cautious, for if he leaned too far, he would collapse facefirst and quickly be buried.

With his mind focused solely on the next stride, he pressed his blistered lips together, frequently spitting away the flakes that would seal his mouth closed. Even a momentary pause for the strength to continue could prove deadly. If he didn't go on, the cold would numb his mind, convincing him to stop while his body's senses faded. He blew what warm breath he could muster on his brittle fingers.

Again he recalled those days on the Montana plain. There was a time when he thought he wouldn't survive and would be carted back to the post with the rest of the casualties. What saved him then was concentration on the next minute, the next step, the next breath. If only he could manage those now, he would have bested the cold.

The increasing grade, although requiring twice the effort for each motion, was a sign of fortune. Even if he couldn't see it, he was ascending closer to the rocks.

Sunlight leaked past the long cloth rag. It woke Maud. She blinked it in, squinting to focus on her surroundings. Curled like a newborn, she was in a dirt hole. Carefully, she pulled back the rag that draped the hole from the outside. The illumination was blinding. The view gleamed with white.

When her eyes adjusted, she determined that she had found someone's former home or a miner's failed attempt at striking riches. Nearest she could remember, she had ridden into the dark, calling out Bill Wheeler's name in hopes he hadn't gotten too far ahead. She was wrong. When the wind blew harder, she knew she had to find a better place than atop a horse. This red rag, either a fat fellow's drawers or a discarded tablecloth, was the only thing to catch her eye. When she found it, it was all she could do to climb the wall of the gully and pull herself in. Now that she gave thought to it, she hoped her horse survived the night's storm.

Below the edge of the opening was one constant plain of snow. The breaking clouds allowed the sun to emerge. As long as it shone, the reflection of light was painful to see. She wrapped the shawl over her shoulders and crawled out of the hole.

If she jumped from the edge she would sink like an anchor into the sea of white. Her only escape was to climb up to the top. The rag drape was pinned at both ends by large stakes pounded into each side of the opening. She tugged at them, but they wouldn't budge. Her yanking convinced her they weren't coming out, but if they were sturdy enough, she might use them as steps of a ladder. The mild breeze chilling her flesh made up her mind.

She pulled the drape inside, then squatted beneath it and turned her back to the opening. With tiny scoots of her heels, she inched closer to the opening, gripping the drape for balance. When she was at the edge, she slowly stood. Her face scraped the dirt, but her head passed by the top of the opening. When she reached for the cliff above, snow spilled into her face. She shook her head to clear her view. Once her fingers had a firm grip, she pulled herself up, feet scrambling for those stakes. Finally, when she kicked one, she planted her shoe on top of it and balanced her weight. Quickly, her other foot found the remaining stake. She now stood on them both, hands as high as she could extend them.

She inhaled the cold air, knowing she had one chance. When she pushed against the stakes and if they broke, she would tumble down the side of the gully and into the snow below. The last she recalled, the depth of the gully was more than ten feet and now filled with snow, she would either freeze to death or suffocate. If it melted enough, she could even drown.

The consequence scared her. Her chest tightened and her chin began to quiver, but not from the cold. She never admired those women who cried easily, but she felt entitled. As the warm tears streamed down her cheeks, a loud neigh bellowed above. She peeked up and the reins of her horse dangled above, its large head protruding over the edge.

She closed her eyes and gave thanks to her maker. When she reopened them, the reins were still there. She took another breath to consider her plan. When she took her hand from the edge, her balance would be lost and she could fall into the gully. Yet, if she thought about it too much, she'd likely talk herself out of trying. Like a bothersome fly, she reached out to the reins and snatched them. Tugging on them only brought the gelding closer to the edge and kicking more snow into her face.

"Hey yah," she screamed. "Back up, you stupid excuse for a man." The horse stood firm. "If you don't back up your rear end, I'm going to find a way to get up there and cut off what they left you with."

Whether it was the high tone of her voice or the threat, she didn't care once the horse skittishly retreated, dragging her up the side of the gully wall and to the top. Once she was there, the horse continued retreating, plowing Maud through the snow until she let loose of the reins.

Chilled to the bone, she first knelt, then stood.

Even though there wasn't much of a breeze, her wet clothes made it feel like she stood in a blizzard. Taking long quick breaths, she finally exhaled enough to expand her chest and regained a normal pant. The gelding turned about and walked to her.

When it nuzzled at her chin, she didn't have the heart to follow through with what she had planned only moments before. She remembered when she was stuck out on those stakes, and the deliverance brought by the animal. Finally, she relented and patted its neck. "I'm sorry. You know I just said them things because I had to. Weren't nothing personal."

As she prepared to climb into the saddle, towering mountains over her shoulder stopped her in her tracks. She was awed by the sight; the snowcapped hills stood before her as if they were giants close enough to touch. Upon making the discovery, she remembered what Wheeler had said about catching the Rainmaker at some mountains, and surely these must be those. With renewed hope, she stepped into the stirrups and turned the gelding toward them.

The loping gait of the horse tossed her side to side, putting her in a daze. She hated riding. She was raised where respectable ladies traveled by coach or buggy, not by horseback. The thought brought other memories of when she was a feisty sixteen, yearning to find out what lay beyond the green hills of Pennsylvania. When the recollection brought about the many failures of that dream, she blinked her eyes to wash them from her mind. The view ahead was one she never planned to see, and although its beauty was one of those she hoped to find when she set off on her own, there wasn't a faithful husband to share it with, only a former client's gelding.

The more she thought about her hardships, the more depressed she became. She didn't want to think about the past. Every turn of her life had brought new problems to conquer. It was time to set things right. When she peered before her, the mountains came a little nearer. She wasn't sure exactly what was beyond them, but she'd always been told California was a land where fortunes were made. She heard all the stories of how men became rich overnight. It was natural that men and money were made for only one purpose: to serve women. After all, a life spent in saloons with husbands of other wives proved they couldn't live with only bread on their table. She'd been trading herself for only a few dollars a night, and now it was time one of them lonesome fellows spent his riches on her for life. Perhaps, if she continued and somehow got past these hills, California would be waiting for her on the other side.

Although she had kept a steady pace, the sun maintained a faster one. As it edged over the tops of the mountains, the shroud of their shadow crept down the side. The warm rays had dried her clothes, but her undergarments were still damp. She would need to find a place to spend the cold night.

Once the sun left her view, the snow behind her still in the light turned to a red hue, and that in the dark in front of her became more of an icy blue. The hill steepened. The gelding slogged through the heavy snow, but as she passed some rocks, the drifts seemed more shallow. With her backside aching from the long day's ride, she decided to dismount and walk. The lack of sunlight never was more missed. She shivered as she lurched for each step, reminding herself of the new resolve she'd promised herself in the daylight. It was now a test of her will. She never had much of one.

She crouched behind a rock, holding the reins in her shivering hand. Every minute seemed colder and darker. The pain in her legs cried for rest, and her back screamed for a bed, alone.

She couldn't go on. Every breath became shorter. Her arms went from shivering to shaking, but she couldn't move them on her own. Her legs curled to her chest for warmth. If she just got a little sleep and waited for the sun, the next morning she'd warm up again and be fine. Her eyes grew heavier. The smell of wood burning and food wafted over her nose. She could eat while she dreamt. It smelled like soup. Her mother must be cooking at the stove. All she needed was a little sleep, and then she'd wake up dead.

She shook her head to clear her mind of the cold's mean tricks. However, even though she was sure she was still alive and awake, the aroma of food didn't vanish. Sniffing the air brought a stronger sense. It was real.

With renewed strength, she rolled to her belly and peered up. A dim light pulsed above. Slowly she crept on her hands and knees, inching up the rocks. Whoever was cooking likely wasn't expecting company. As she crawled, the essence filled her nose. She inhaled deeply. The warmth was like a wave, filling her body, chasing the chill from her bones. Caution waned with every whiff. Her knees crunched the snow. If she moved faster, she could bathe in it. Once she was past two large boulders, she could see the light of the fire. As she poked her head up, she saw a small cave with a campfire. A kettle sat mounted on a tripod above it. No one tended to the fire. It must have been another divine deliverance. Whatever she did to deserve it she couldn't recall, but it was time to give thanks to above. She closed her eyes and recalled the prayers her mother forced her to remember. A few verses forgotten, she concluded with "Amen" just as gunmetal clicked behind her head.

"Don't move."

She didn't need the cold to be still.

"Who are you?"

The voice sounded familiar—one that was heard not long ago. "Clay?" The momentary silence either sparked a nerve or she was still dreaming. "Clay? Is that you?" While she was still staring at the fire, her heart beat through her chest.

"Maud?"

She exhaled so long, her breath blew the flames to one side. Before she answered, she quickly recalled those forgotten verses. Slowly she faced about with the gun's muzzle now at her nose. "Glad to see me?"

"What in hell are you doing out here?" he asked while easing the hammer to rest.

The first answer in her head was the truth. "I came to find you."

"Out here?"

"Well, that's where you be. That's where I had to go."

He shook his head in disgust. "Get up to the fire, or we'll both freeze." He motioned toward the flames, and she quickly scampered to her feet and near the beloved heat.

Holding her fingers so close she could feel the flame lick at her skin, she backed them away only long enough for the pain to quickly pass, then repeated the same act. He took several moments before he joined her.

"Looks like you got the same horse."

She nodded. "The dumb animal saved my life this morning. But I don't care to go into that." She gazed upon his face as her fingers thawed. The flickering light danced across his face. All the time, his expression was the same one of disbelief.

"Why would you travel all the way from Kansas just to find me? That's got to be near a thousand miles."

The truth could be stretched only so far. "Because I missed you, Clay."

"Then why did you leave?"

His questions not only were hard to answer, but they were coming too fast. The only tactic she knew to avoid them was womanly diversion, but she'd have to start slow. "I'm cold, Clay. I can't think straight. You got any of them victuals left?"

When he reached behind him for another plate, she sat relieved at the break. Her eyes wandered and found the sleepy little girl with her blanket tightly tucked around all but her head.

"She's grown," Maud remarked as he ladled a plate full of beans. His eyes darted to the girl for only a moment, then he looked at her with a puzzled face.

"You see that?"

"Of course. Anyone can," she answered, taking the plate. The steam filled her nose. It was the same smell as before, only now it was much more heavenly. The first bite was quickly followed by the second and then the third before she even swallowed. The food melted the frost from her insides. Even though it was just beans, she relished the taste. It was food.

"I guess you can't see something getting bigger the closer you are to it," he said, his eyes still fixed on the girl.

"Of course not," she slurred while gulping. "My mother would always say how big us kids would get. She would joke about putting a rock on our heads to stop us from growing." The memory made her giggle, but it didn't slow her from finishing the plate. She handed it back to him. "How about seconds?"

The request seemed to shock him, although he ladled out another scoop.

"Just one?"

He dipped the spoon again and dumped the contents onto the pile on her plate. She wasted no time scarfing them down.

"And I guess the further away you get from something, the more it changes."

His comment stopped her mad shoveling. When she peeked at him, his eyes were aimed at her waist. "A girl's got to eat."

"I didn't mean it that way. It's just . . ." He paused, wagging his fingers in her direction. "You seem to have missed a few meals since last I saw you. Not that you look bad or nothing."

Since his tone sounded apologetic, she dipped her eyes to her hips, then her thighs, then her bosom. All during her life she had been bigger than most women. Strangely, it appeared this disaster of near-death escapes and starvation might have done her figure some good. "What are you saying? That I'm skinny?"

"I wouldn't say that." He paused. "But it does appear there's a little less of you. You know what I mean?"

"And you're saying that as a good thing?" she hinted.

It took a moment before he finally nodded. "Yeah. I'll vouch for that."

Suddenly, the beans had lost their taste. There was no need to eat more. She handed him the plate. "I'm full. But those were mighty tasty." Even though she could eat more, another urge struck her. "You got a smoke?"

"Yeah," he said, reaching into his coat pocket. He drew the pouch. "I never had a woman ask me that," he said, as he unfurled the paper and dribbled the tobacco. He licked the paper's edge and rolled the smoke. He took a stick from the fire; the coal end soon set the paper aglow. He took a drag, then handed it to her. A thought came to mind. It may have been time to advance her womanly diversion to a subject that would keep his interest.

"What else haven't you heard a woman ask you?"

The question raised his brow. He rubbed his stubbled chin as she had seen most men do when stumped. When she inhaled the smoke, all her joints tingled, then her head. Her eyes lost focus for an instant. The last smoke she had had was the one she had shared with him more than a month before.

Still waiting for his reply, she took another drag while he drew a small metal box from the coat. "I have to guess I wouldn't know that until they ask it." He drew the knife and poked the point into the box with a slight twist. Her interest in pursuing her delicate questions faded with his action. "What are you up to?"

"Oh," he said with his eyes fixed on the box. "I found this a while back. It only plays a little before it stops. I reckon dirt has got in it and sludged up the wheels inside. I've been tinkering with it. I think I can open it up and clean it out."

"I never thought you much of a music lover." The remark brought that grin that always surprised her.

"Oh, I'm not." He nodded to the sleeping child. "But it keeps her quiet. Keeps her busy trying to figure out why it makes noise. By the time she plays with it enough, she gets sleepy," he said, looking up at Maud. "Then I get some rest."

They both giggled at the idea. As her mouth opened, Maud couldn't help but yawn. The smoke had made her as tipsy as any shot of liquor. The suggestion of rest became more appealing with every breath. Finally, she offered the smoke back to him. He gently slipped it from her fingers.

Her eyes grew even heavier, and she knew the notion of sharing the same ground with him would have to wait. She lay next to the fire. All she needed was a little sleep.

Chapter Fourteen

Despite the stubborn mule, Cole kicked the palomino up the hill. He knew the animals hadn't had much chance to graze and the firs likely appeared appetizing. The supply of oats exhausted, he couldn't allow the time to stop. The blue sky and calm wind wasn't an advantage to be wasted.

A glance behind showed Maud, now wearing his bedroll blanket, struggling to keep her mount moving. It didn't seem to take offense to her insults to its male pride. Some of them were even funny. While he was amused by her berating, he slowed the palomino and glanced at the valley below. He caught sight of a solitary figure.

Cole scanned the valley but didn't spot other riders. Whoever it was, this rider appeared to be following the tracks they had just left, although at least an hour behind. Maud kicked her gelding enough to force the animal to come alongside. Cole didn't see any reason to worry her.

"What are you looking at?" she asked.

"Just checking to see how far we come." He looked at her before she faced behind. "You got control of that horse?"

Her eyes dipped to the gelding. "Him and me, we kind of have a love affair like married folks. I guess I'm the wife and he's the man. I do the screaming, and he does the ignoring until I kick him enough to do what I tell him."

Cole laughed. "I see it still takes him a while to get the notion."

"Yeah. He's like any man. That's why I love him. That and the fact that he's had his manhood taken, so he won't go off and leave me with the smell of the first filly in season. I think maybe some wives ought to have that done to their husbands."

It took him a moment and a hard swallow before he replied. "Wouldn't do much for someone in your business."

"Got a point there," she answered with a grin. "Should keep my mouth shut."

Cole's attention drifted back to the rider in the valley. Only the snow could be seen. "Come on. We need to make some time." He steered the palomino up the hill. As he rode, the mule's ornery behavior irritated him more than usual. Now someone was tracking him.

Frequently, he bobbed his head over each shoulder, looking for any motions or shadows. There were none. He kept the palomino more to the open in an attempt to keep his view clear, but he knew the tactic made him an easier target. His hand on the butt of the Colt, his eyes darted to each tree, then he saw Maud's attention on him. His hand eased off the Colt; he did not want to alarm the woman, causing questions to be asked and answered.

The slope gradually leveled, obscuring the lower valley. Cole felt even more vulnerable. He saw that a dense thicket of fir and pine extended down the far side of the oncoming slope, and he got an idea. He kicked the palomino to stride through the thick powder.

"Here," he said, holding out the reins to the mule. "Take hold of these." Passing the reins to her, and noticing her bewildered expression, he pointed down the hill. "Keep heading this way. I need to get to higher ground to see where we might camp." As he glanced to Little Bear, another problem occurred to him and the solution quickly came to him. "Wait." He slid off the palomino and loosened the loop to take the girl off the saddle. He eased the child over to Maud. The chilled breeze still was mild, and he rapidly untied the knot from the horn and strung the same loop to the gelding's saddle.

"I can't keep this nag moving—now you want me to pull a mule and nursemaid this baby to boot?"

"Just keep a strong hold on her. Give them reins a mean yank. Talk to the mule like he was your own. That ought to get his attention." He wrapped the blanket tight around Little Bear. It wouldn't keep her as warm as when she was in the sack under his coat, but that couldn't be helped. He had work to do. "I won't be long behind. Catch you at the bottom."

Even though she gawked at his order, he waved her on and she complied, only shaking her head and taking out her frustration on the poor gelding's flanks. He watched the procession. A finer match couldn't have been sported better between Maud and the mule. He was sure that should he let her take command of the animal for the rest of the trip, only one of them would survive the contest for most headstrong. Although the mule would be the smart bet, his money would be on Maud.

When her rants began to fade, he swung the palomino about. He spurred the horse to charge up the grade, plowing the snow to the sides. Within a few strides he rode into the cover of the trees. Ducking his head under the limbs, he sought a place where he could survey with clear sight for anyone following up the valley they had just left. The wide-boughed firs were easy to hide behind but difficult to see around. The treetops left long shadows on the white snow. His would blend in should it be cast farther than expected. Finally, he spotted a bare cottonwood that stood tucked in front of three thick green firs. It gave a good view to the front and provided cover to his back.

He dismounted the palomino, tethered the reins to a branch, and drew the rifle from the scabbard. The unique weapon gleamed in the sunlight. The darkwood stock and the blue-finish lock and barrel looked as if they were freshly polished. He retrieved the pouch from his saddlebags, slung its strap over his

shoulder, and took out one of the nine-bullet maga-
zines. Nine months had passed since he had last fired
the rifle, so a moment was needed to recall how to
load it. At once, he remembered the Belgian Serge
Mouton proudly displaying his family's designed combat weapon. During a search for lost gold in Texas,
the foreigner wagged the rifle in Cole's nose, dem-
onstrating its deadly accuracy from more than a thousand yards. Had it not been for the betrayal of
Mouton's thieving ally, Francisco Gura, and a fortunate slip of a knife, Cole wouldn't have this rifle—or
his life.

The hole in the bottom of the lock provided a space
for the magazine to be inserted. Once done with that,
he pulled the side lever, which with a click confirmed
that the first shell had popped into the chamber. He
shouldered the weapon and sighted the barrel on a
distant tree. The delicate crunch of snow crept into
his ear.

He crouched behind the fir to the right, listening
for the steps. He was unsure who would be after him
or their skill with a gun, or even how many there
were. His right finger curled around the trigger and
his left hand gripped the pump handle, ready to blast
the intruder with as many shots as he could fire. The
erratic pattern of steps seemed ones taken with caution, not those of a heavy horse. If the rider was now
on foot, it wouldn't be to rest the mount. The steps
grew louder and came from the left.

Cole steadied his breath. The slightest noise could
send lead his way. He glanced at the sun, its light
shaded by the heavy cluster of limbs above. Shadows

were cast toward the noise. There was no advantage of seeing the stranger's first.

Another slow depression in the snow like that of an aching squeak came directly over his left shoulder. He prepared for battle. Whoever it was would likely have guns drawn, ready to shoot at him. He rose, swinging the rifle to the left, snapping limbs off the cottonwood, taking a dead aim at the target. His finger held still.

The doe stared at him as if confused as to why he stood. Its black eyes locked on his, expressing offense at being disturbed from its search for food. Cole let a long breath. His heart pounded in relief. He lowered the Mouton rifle, letting it sag by his side. The deer sprung away in the opposite direction at his motion. As he watched its flight, he shook his head and chided himself.

He hadn't seen anyone or anything that was a real threat. Likely that was no rider he saw. The poster he saw in Nebraska might not have said what he thought. He turned to the palomino, removed the magazine from the rifle, and shoved it back into the scabbard with self-disgust for fretting himself over seeing shadows. Once he was on the horse, he steered it for the tracks left by the gelding and the mule.

It took Cole more than an hour to make up the time. As he rode up to Maud in a wide clearing, he saw that the mule had mired itself in a deep drift, rearing its head at her determined yank.

"Hold up," he said as he reined in. "I'll push from behind." He slid off the palomino, strode through the heavy snow to the mule's rear, and signaled Maud to pull. Cole shoved, but the animal's legs appeared to have taken root.

"What took you so long?" asked Maud, as she kicked the gelding.

"I got . . ." Cole grunted. "I got hung up in some deep snow." More determined shoves only made the mule rock forward and back, sinking it deeper like a wagon in a rut.

"Well, did you find a place?"

"What?" Cole replied, throwing his back against the mule's rump.

"Did you find a place to camp? That's what you said you were doing."

"Oh. Yeah," he said, finally relenting in the struggle. "I did." He glimpsed the sun. High, thin clouds shrouded its light. "I thought here would be a fine place. Appears a storm could be brewing, and we don't want to be any higher up than this."

"Well, why didn't you say so," she angrily said. She slid off the gelding to land in knee-deep snow. "I nearly pulled my own arm off trying to move this mangy bastard." Her voice matched the harshness of her words. She arched her back, wincing during the slow, anguished motion.

"I didn't know for sure that this was the place I was looking at until I got here." Even though he didn't believe it, he hoped she would. When more than two seconds passed, he was sure either she did or she didn't care.

Another peek above showed the round white ball in the sky. When he had first suggested a storm it was more to convince her of the lie, but now it appeared certain. "Better get a fire going," he said as he mounted the palomino and headed for a bank of trees only a few yards away. After loading his arms full of dried seedheads, limbs, and rotted bark, he returned to see Maud holding Little Bear. He kicked away enough snow to create a pit for the wood, then thumbnailed a match and set the tinder afire. Nursing the flames to lick at the thicker bark, he soon had enough heat to melt the snow beneath. He unloaded the bedrolls, setting them near the fire. The kettle and tripod assembled easily over the flames. He poured in the beans with handfuls of snow to thin out the heavy clumps.

"How much further do you think we have to go?" asked Maud as she sat near the fire, one arm around the child and the other stretched out over the hissing fire.

The question startled him. "Go where?"

"To wherever it is you're going."

"Well," he started, uncertain of her interest. "I figure there's still a long way between me and it. Why you ask?"

"Just wondering."

Her meek reply was one he had heard from women before. A childish answer often hid adult intentions. It sparked his own curiosity. "You never said why you left me back there in Kansas."

"Oh." She hesitated. "I got lonesome for my old roots. Wasn't easy getting used to being away from them. A girl needs her security."

"Ain't the way I recall you talking about them roots." He stirred the beans, then peered into her eyes. "There was nothing waiting on you in Omaha, was there?"

Her eyes darted away from his stare to view the fire, then blinked back his way. "No. I guess I can't lie about it. You had me scared, Clay."

"Scared? At what?"

"The way you look at me sometimes."

Her answer stole his breath for a moment. All at once his wind returned. "The way you were parading about without your clothes, I did everything I knew to keep from looking at you."

"I ain't talking about then." She paused to jostle Little Bear, who seemed enamored of the fire. The ploy was intended to show motherly instincts, but the longer she dodged the question, the more quickly she shook the child.

"You keep that up and she'll toss all over your dress," he said, then held out his arms. "Give her to me."

Maud pulled the child away from his reach. "No. I kind of like this," she said, softening her motion.

Cole abandoned the effort to get Little Bear, but he wasn't going to let his point fade. "Getting back to the matter, why did you truly leave?"

Again, she paused. Finally she blurted her answer. "I didn't know what kind of man you were."

Confused by the accusation, he rubbed his whiskered chin. "Like how you mean?"

"You can be an awful scary sight to a woman on her own, Clay," she said, leaning his way. "That's why I had my clothes off. I thought it might bring out a different side of you. But when you talked about other women you'd been with, and didn't say what happened to them, I got plumb scared. There, I said it."

"Like who?"

"Like when you said I wasn't the first woman you traveled with. You made it sound like you done something with her."

A moment was needed to recollect what was said back in Kansas. "You mean that eastern woman? Claire Rhodes?"

"You never said her name."

He huffed a laugh. "She's back east. Once she had enough of Colorado and the West, she left on a train. I got a letter from her not long ago." He paused during his defense when he thought of the intent of Claire's letter to help clear his name. It was more than he cared to confess. "Anyway, she's safe."

"She's the only one?" asked Maud with a meek voice.

The inquiry made his mind wonder. At first, he didn't care to volunteer the truth, but he thought more than a single example may soothe her mind. "There was another. Another woman from back east. And despite being a woman, she was a doctor. Doctor Jane Reeves. I was leading her and an English fellow. They were after some loot left by Indians years back in Texas. I was the one warning them not to go there due to raiding Comanches. Didn't faze her none, even after I told her about that tribe's habit of taking white women. Told her if she went on, odds were likely she'd have some Comanche pups of her own."

"And what happened to her?"

"She didn't listen," he replied, whipping the beans like a batter. "She was headstrong." He raised an eyebrow. "Not unlike what I seen recently. She and her English dandy boss didn't listen to me, and all I could do was follow. We all near lost our scalps. But somehow we didn't. Last I saw of her, she was still in Texas. Does that convince you?"

"So I'm supposed to believe that. Sure sounds like a bunch of stories to me."

He scooped up beans and slurped from the ladle. "Well, if you don't believe it, you're welcome to leave."

She peered about at the towering mountains on all sides. "Well, I just might do that, Clay. But I prefer to eat first." A wry smile crept across her face. "I never cared much for beans, but I'll swear nothing never smelled better." He dipped the ladle full of beans, then dumped them onto a plate and held it for her to take. With Little Bear still cradled in one arm, she fumbled with the child so as to accept the plate.

"Put her down," he said. Maud looked confused at the suggestion. He nodded and repeated the order. "She'll surprise you." Maud slowly complied, putting the young girl to the ground away from the fire. Once Little Bear's feet touched the dirt, her legs dangling, Maud let loose of her arms, and the child stood. Cole peeked at Maud's amazed face. "We've been working on this."

He handed the plate to Maud and held out his palms, the signal for the girl to take stomping steps to him. Even though she needed only three, Little Bear made the trip and fell into Cole's hands. "That's my girl," he said with a proud wink toward Maud. Once in his arms, Little Bear cringed and began to whine while struggling from his grasp. "It's that time again."

"What time?"

"That time," he said as he rose and went to the palomino. He dug out a flask and returned to the fire. He clenched his teeth on the cork and pulled it free. Spitting the cork to the snow, he dabbed his finger with the liquor. "She has her back teeth coming in," he said, rubbing his finger on her gums despite the girl's struggle. "Here now. It's only going to rid you of the pain."

"I know how she feels. I've had things prodded in my mouth I didn't care for." He peered up at her at the comment. "Well, I have. My mother would force liver oil down my throat. Made me choke, too."

"I ain't prodding. She'll stop once the throbbing stops."

"I don't think it's right," she said between gulps. "You giving that child whiskey. What if she grows up to be a drunk?"

"It's only a touch."

"Don't matter. Some people can't handle a drink."

Cole hesitated at her words. He had gotten the liquor for the girl, and so far had used it only for her. But the smell of the whiskey brought back painful memories he hadn't thought about until she reminded him. The remark was true. There were folks who couldn't keep the taste of liquor out of their mouths. It took him a long time to break himself of it, and he got it when he was young. He withdrew his finger.

"That should do it." He squeezed the cork into the flask neck and tucked it into his coat pocket. He released the child, and she quickly got to her feet to show off her newfound talent of walking. While he watched, Cole felt the urges of nature build. "You keep an eye on her," he said, arching his thumb to a row of evergreens. "I got to . . . got . . . to."

"You gotta pee," Maud blurted. Cole nodded and pointed at her with a wink. "Ain't like it's your first time, I'm sure."

"Yeah," he said as he stood. "But you're normally asleep when I'm handling that business. It ain't something I think a woman cares to think about."

"Don't bother me none," she said, turning her attention to the girl.

Cole trudged through the snow, each step a bit faster than the one before it. With a hop, he nestled behind a tall spruce, loosened the buckle of his gunbelt, and unbuttoned the front of his pants. When the chilled air met his flesh, nature took its course. The relief allowed him to exhale deeply. He did so again, standing as if in a trance.

"CLAY!"

Maud's shrilled call brought him out of his daze.

"CLAY! Come quick!"

When he took a step, his pants sagged around his hips. Another step dropped the gunbelt into the snow. Maud's frantic shout confused him as to what to do first. Further steps would trip him, so he buttoned the single top hole and dug the pistol from the snow. Around the spruce, he charged through the thick powder, retracing his own steps. However, when his legs moved faster than the snow would budge, he collapsed to his knees. He rose, and leapt to the first cavity in the snow, continuing with hurdling strides to the next and the next. In his jarred view he saw Maud still sitting by the fire, huddling Little Bear to her chest. The palomino and the gelding reared against their reins, which were tied to a heavy log. Growls and snarls echoed in the air until finally he arrived close enough to hear Maud.

"They just came from nowhere," she shrieked, and pointed to the wider white plain.

Cole twisted about. Gray and black figures darted in and out of sight from the explosions of snow. At last, he focused on a black wolf, then instantly he sighted gray one, then another and another. They circled each other as if downing prey. The mule's throaty hee-haw turned his head. With bundles still attached, it galloped toward the hill from where they rode, the leash dangling behind.

Cole cocked the hammer and fired, but the swirl of snow in the air from the moving animals confused his aim and sent his shot too high. Again he pulled back the hammer, but the crackle of the loosening log from the palomino's pull drew his attention. He, Maud, and the child wouldn't last the day afoot. He lurched at the reins, snatching both sets with one hand, but both strong mounts yanked him like a puppet.

He tossed the pistol at Maud. "Use it if they rush you," he yelled, seizing the reins with both hands and crouching to bring the frenzied horses down. Once he had them on all fours, he saw the Mouton rifle stock protruding from the scabbard. With his left hand firmly on the reins, he drew the rifle with his right. The magazine absent, he recalled loading the single cartridge into the chamber. Twisting about, he swung the barrel at the white flurry. "Stay down," he yelled while shouldering the stock. As the snow settled, clearing his view, he aimed at the black wolf. Its snout dripping with blood, it stared at him with growling teeth. Cole closed his left eye and sighted the barrel at those teeth and squeezed the trigger.

The blast sent a stream of flame from the muzzle. Red splattered into the air. Upon opening his left eye, Cole saw that the black wolf had disappeared from view. The rest of the pack had scampered with the boom, one of them with a bloody appendage still clamped in its mouth. Reflex made him pump the action, ejecting the smoking shell, but as he aimed and pulled the trigger, the single click reminded him that he had only the one shot.

He faced Maud. "You all right?" Her mouth was still in awed panic, but she nodded. Sure that she and the child were safe, he slogged through the snow. As he neared the spot where the snow had been trampled, red streaks led him first to the decapitated wolf. Only a few yards away lay the carcass of the mangled goat. The throat was mauled open and the belly ripped apart, exposing strands of the insides.

Footsteps in the snow made him turn. Maud approached with Little Bear still cradled in her arms. "Don't come any closer. Ain't something you ought to see." True to her nature, she ignored his warning and came to stand next to him.

"Sweet Jesus," she said, slapping her palm over her mouth, then facing away.

"I told you so," he said.

After a moment she looked at him, her uncovered shoulders quivering in the sunlight. "I didn't even see them. All of a sudden, they were running after the mule," she said, able only to nod the goat's way. "Then they all . . ." She paused. "It was a hell of a thing. At first, I didn't have the breath to call you."

Cole nodded. "I'm sure you didn't. You have no blame in this. They were probably tracking us for some time." He blinked up at the sun, which appeared to have a halo. At first he had used the excuse of an approaching storm to stop for rest, but fate had now called his bluff. "We'll need to get to better cover."

"Ain't we going to finish eating? Might be the last time we get to."

He peered at the goat, then back at her. "Every varmint for ten miles will be here after that. It's best if we leave now. Besides, looks like she's going to go hungry," he said, his eyes dipping to Maud's bosom. "Unless . . ."

She followed his eyes, peeking at herself. "Don't look at these. They've never been suckled by no kids."

Cole shook his head, then headed back to the fire.

Chapter Fifteen

Echoes bounced all around him. Bill Wheeler stared at the mountain range, trying to determine the direction the gunshots had come from. He had heard only two, and he knew the latter must have come from a rifle. He drew his Springfield.

He kicked his horse and resumed the slow trek up the grade. He steered clear of the tracks in the snow. It was a trick he had used as well to attract whoever was behind while he waited farther up a trail in ambush. Still, these shots sounded as if they had come from over the hill.

Wind gusted into his face. He peeked at the sun. Clouds as dark as a bruise crawled across the sky. What had been a bright morning now appeared more like dusk. He scanned about for a suitable windbreak. He wanted to stay close to the tracks before they were covered by the swirling snow, but he knew that exposure in the open could have him riding in circles, slowly losing his wits, leading him off a bluff, if not freezing in the saddle.

As he huddled his coat around his collar, a distant bray pierced the wind's howl. His head jerked up and he squinted through the blowing snow to see the source. A pack mule strapped with bundles stood in snow up to its flanks.

With Maud's hands clutching his hips from behind, Cole strode against the blistering gale through the high drifts that made the grade even steeper. Little Bear sat in the sack against his chest. He gripped both ends of his coat to keep her warm.

"I can't go on," Maud said.

"Just a little further," Cole answered, trying not only to trick her mind but his own as well. "We'll find cover soon." Despite his words, he sensed her grip slacken around his waist. Another lunging step tore her hands from his coat. He twisted about and saw her kneeling in the snow. Her gaunt face stared straight ahead, just as a blind man would. Cole grabbed her arm. "You got to get up."

"Just let me sleep. I'll be better if I sleep."

He ignored her delirium, but looking ahead, he saw only a single white blur. There may be miles ahead before trees, rocks, or any man-made structure could be found. His head dipped, and the blowing snow quickly climbed to his knees. He squinted against the whipping wind, his mind considering Maud's idea, until his better sense flushed the notion from his head.

He focused on the snowbank in front of him, which appeared as high as his chest. His arms already ached from the cold, and he couldn't garner the ambition to carry the woman over it. The more he stared at it, the more convinced he was that he couldn't continue.

He sagged to his knees, and the height of the bank slightly shielded him from the wind. The lower he sank his head, the less he felt its lash. He jabbed his fist through the frosted powder and swiped out an armful. This fueled another punch and another swipe. Three more, and a small gouge appeared.

Frenzied by the prospect of relief, he burrowed deeper. The snow had hardened and did not collapse. Crawling into the hole, he scraped more room for the woman. His hands felt like claws, but after a few more minutes he'd have time to warm them. When he had dug far enough to bring his feet under the shelf of the bank, he retreated back for the woman.

When he wrapped his arms under her shoulders, she moaned. "No. Let me sleep. I'm too cold to walk. Just let me stay here."

"You'll die," he answered, tugging her into the den. On his side, he slid, then drug her into the frigid hole. There was only enough space for the two of them snugged shoulder to shoulder. Once both their feet were out of the wind, he let out a long breath. No matter how hard he tried, he couldn't keep his eyes open.

Little Bear's scratching while changing position awoke Cole. Since he now knew the child had survived, he looked to Maud. She still lay motionless, so he nudged her shoulder. No response. He nudged again. Still no response. Careful not to put weight on the child, he reached around to feel for Maud's breath. His hands numb, he decided to put his nose to hers. Without sensing any warmth and his lips inches from hers, he kissed her. At first the act produced nothing, but as he matched lips with her longer, he detected inner warmth. Finally, her nose crinkled and she retracted, blinking her eyes, her breath steaming from her mouth.

"What are you doing?" she groggily protested.

He slumped back, relieved at her motion. "You're alive."

"Of course I'm alive. You think you were going to get something for yourself if I was dead?"

"I was trying to see if you were alive. If you weren't, there was no sense in dragging you from this hole."

"What hole? Where are we?"

"Under the snow." He peeked between his boots. He saw in the dim light that the wind had calmed, but it had piled drifts beyond the height of the opening. If it stormed during the night, they would be entombed. "We need to go soon."

"The hell you say." She craned her neck to look at him. "I can't feel anything below my chest. I can't move, much less walk. You go if you want. I'm staying here till spring."

Her defiant temper amused him. "Have it your way. Maybe we can stay a mite longer, but if the wind commences to blowing, then this will be your grave." He closed his eyes, waiting for her reply. It took a few moments longer than he expected.

"What are you saying? That you'd leave me?"

"I ain't going to have it be my grave and the girl's."
Her reply didn't take as long as before.

"Well, how long do I have to rest?"

"See no reason to move while the wind's calm. We
can wait till morning. The sun may break out."

"Thank the Lord." She paused, then her voice softened. "Clay?"

"What."

"How did we get in here?"

"I dug it out." He heard the rustle of the snow and
figured she had faced him.

"You pulled me in here?"

"Yup." Then came the longest of her pauses.

"Well, I guess I owe you my life."

"Don't worry about it. Couldn't leave you out
there."

She giggled, but her tone of voice turned less giddy.
"I guess I owe you one. You could have another
smack if you want."

"I may take you up on that someday." He closed
his eyes, centering the slumbering child on his chest.
"But for right now, I think we should keep our
strength for the walk. I still have to find the horses—if
they made it."

With nature's call bringing him out of his latest short
nap, Cole once again peeked beyond his boots to spot
a brilliant light reflecting off the snow. Scooting out of
the hole, he nudged the sleeping Maud. She didn't
respond. Not wanting to test if she was alive in the

same way he had before, he pinched her hip. Like a wildcat, she sprang from her sleep, bumping her head against the snow den ceiling. "Time to go."

"You bastard," she snarled. "What the blazes you do that for?"

"To get your blood moving. You said you couldn't feel nothing below your chest. Now I know you can." Cole kicked the high drift to allow him space to emerge. The sunlight forced him to squint. Although the wind was calm, the bitter-cold air dug into his cheeks like cactus needles. He rose and trudged through the bank, which had risen to nearly waist height. First he had to take care of his own business, no matter how indiscreetly. When he was done, he buttoned up, then unwrapped Little Bear from under his coat. When the cold air met her bare flesh, nature did the rest, despite her anguished cries.

He buttoned, sacked, and wrapped her. His stomach growled, and he knew the child's hunger had to be worse. The cold's only benefit was its more urgent discomfort, but he knew they had to find something to eat.

Maud's complaints grew louder as she wrestled with the snow. Her clumsy exit had her wearing a good part of it. When the air hit her, she shivered, and Cole knew what would come next. "I'm going to turn my back. Hurry up."

"Out here?"

"Figure you can hold it that long, we'll get to some trees," he said, feeling a smirk cross his face. He faced about. More nasty words filled the air. The rustle of clothes concluded the protest. "You can turn around now."

Cole kept his eyes to the front. The tree line stood less than a thousand yards away. He shook his head. If he had only known they were that close, he would have gone on. A distant whinny broke the still air. He looked at Maud. "Come on."

Both of them broke as if being chased by the devil. Each step was a struggle, but with his stride plowing the way, Maud kept up with the pace. Upon reaching the trees, Cole grabbed the limbs to pull himself up the incline. At the crest, he viewed both horses nestled under the shelter of the tall thick pines. Under the canopy the snow had accumulated only up to their forelegs. It appeared there was more to animal sense than he had thought. He approached with ease, not wanting to spook them, unsure of their temperament, but the palomino surprised him. Never having been particularly fond of the horse since he took it in trade for a man's life in New Mexico, he stood with better respect for it when it came to him. He rubbed its nose and patted its flanks while inspecting the saddle. Maud came down the hill like a bull, which made the gelding shy away deeper into the small forest.

"You can't charge at him like that," Cole chided through his gritted teeth. "You want to chase him to Idaho?"

"After what I've been through, I couldn't care a damn how scared he is."

Despite her words, the horse's true nature prevailed, and it returned to the comforting presence of the palomino. "Be easy with him," Cole told her. She

225

slowly crept to the gelding, finally snatching the reins, releasing a sigh of relief. Cole looked at her and winked. "See what a little kindness can do?"

Maud grinned. "I know all about kindness to men, but I'll be damned if I'm going to show all I know to this one."

Cole inspected both of the animals and found they had survived the storm in better health. He put Maud on the gelding, then mounted the palomino, steering it down the slope.

When the sun shone directly overhead, Cole sensed the warmth and unbuttoned the top of his coat to allow the child to take in the brisk air. As they traversed a valley, the loss of the supplies on the mule began to gnaw at his gut and his head. The child wouldn't be able to go three solid days without food.

The question hounded him as the sun came across the sky. The slow pace of the horse provided him time to consider what options he had. Every time he glanced back at Maud slouched in the saddle, he reminded himself that time wasn't on his side.

They crested a small rise, and the answer to the problem made him slow the palomino. When Maud came to his side, she squinted against the glare and gazed at the sight in the far valley.

"What is that?" she asked.

"Elk." He turned to her. "Food."

A smile quickly creased her face. "How you going to get one?"

He glanced down at the Mouton rifle. There was still nearly a mile's distance between him and the large herd. Days of flanking buffalo came to mind, but these animals weren't likely to stand in huddles like those massive beasts. These had more predators to fear. A missed shot would send the herd stampeding for miles. He didn't have the energy for the chase, and he doubted the palomino had much more.

He dismounted and removed his coat. Pulling Little Bear from the sack exposed the child to the chill, so he wrapped her in the coat and handed her to Maud.

"What are you doing? You'll catch your death."

"Just keep her warm and stay here," he said as he remounted. "I won't be gone long." A nudge to the horse's flanks sent it ambling down the slope. As he rode, he drew the rifle and slung the ammunition pouch over his shoulder. Drawing a magazine, he inserted it into the gun and pulled the lever to load the chamber. Careful not to make sudden moves, he circled around the herd, which still concerned itself with pawing the snow for the dormant grass.

Within two hundred yards, he steered the palomino to the rear of the herd, then released the reins. The well-trained mount continued the course. Cole blew what warm breath he had on his right fingers, raising the rifle to his shoulder. Among the thirty animals within easy range, he sighted on a bull elk. As long as he kept an ample distance, the herd wouldn't fear the threat. He pulled the reins back and halted the horse.

With some of the smaller females in the harem scampering toward the center, he sensed that the minor reaction could turn into panic. As more of them picked up their heads, the bulk of them moved like a swarm, one scurrying after another. When the sighted bull rose his head, Cole closed his left eye. If the bull bolted, the shot would be lost. Despite his shiver, he steadied his aim and squeezed the trigger.

The blast boomed through the valley. The herd fled in one fluid charge to escape. He kicked the palomino and galloped after them, but when he found his target lying in the bloodied snow, he reined in.

He waved at Maud, then dismounted. The shot had found its intended mark just above the shoulder and through the heart. He scanned about and saw a grove of firs that appeared to be a suitable shelter. Tying rope around the antlers, then securing it to the saddle horn, he towed the elk up the small hill and into the trees. Retrieving dried branches, he dug a small pit and lit a match to the withered wood and needles. With his Bowie knife, he skinned the hide back and cut strips of meat. Just when he had the fire ablaze, Maud arrived, gleeful. She slid from the saddle and charged at the fire. She handed him Little Bear while her attention focused on the raw meat. She picked it off the spit and bit into a piece, ripping at it with the fervor of a mountain lion.

"You might wait until it's cooked awhile. Be easier to chew," he said.

She shook her head. "I can't wait. It's the first meat I've had in twenty days." She turned to him with blood-smeared cheeks. "One thing a girl has to have."

The rest of the day was spent butchering the carcass and roasting the strips. Maud persisted in taking the strips from the spit no matter how long they'd hung. Once the meat was properly cooked, Cole cut small chunks and gave Little Bear her first taste of solid food that he'd been able to provide; then he ate his fill of the venison, storing the remainder in the form of pemmican cakes in what sparse cloth could be managed. What couldn't be eaten was used to fuel the fire.

"When are we going to get to wherever the hell it is we're going?" Maud asked, wrapped in her blanket.

"If I figured right, I make that we're near the Yellowstone Valley."

"Is that near anything warm?"

Cole grinned. "Well, there is the damnedest thing you ever saw there. Water shooting up from the ground a hundred feet, hotter than any boiled in pot. Must be more than a thousand of them, and they do it no matter how cold it is." The story made Maud raise an eyebrow. "I'm telling the truth. I been there. You can't drink it, though. The taste is salty. Makes you gag. And the stink is worse than sitting in any outhouse in the middle of summer. But it is a sight to behold."

"Well, what say we go there? It'd be better than freezing our tails here. I could use a hot bath."

He shook his head. "Melt the skin right off of you. Besides, we ain't heading there."

"So where are we heading?"

The question didn't have an easy answer. "I'm going to a place I ain't sure exactly where."

"Sounds pretty damn stupid. You mean we're wandering around and we don't know where we're going? I knew I should have stayed in Kansas."

Cole drew the music box from his coat. "It ain't that bad." He pried the lid off the box and resumed the task of removing the dirt from the wheels and springs. "I've been following the range to a place called 'Wind in the River' by the Nez Perce. I was told by an elder in that tribe it could be found beyond the valley the white man calls Twin Falls. Once past that, it's over the last of the Rocky Mountains and up the Snake River until it brings you to a place the locals now call Hell's Canyon. I'm supposed to cross it and continue west until I come to the top of a mountain where the wind comes off the hills down into the Columbia. He told me it's so pretty there, you can't take your eyes off it for at least an hour. Below, there's a valley where the water is still. That's where he tells me to find the home of his people. That's where he come from." His eyes darted to the sleeping Little Bear. "That's where I'm going."

He continued to scrape out the dust from the box, only occasionally peeking at Maud, whose complaints had been squelched by the speech. With their bellies full and darkness falling, Cole's eyes once again felt heavy. He pulled his bedroll on the ground near the crackling fire. As was her habit, Maud was still awake, no doubt used to a life where sundown was the beginning of her day. As he snugged the child close to him, Cole kept an eye on the woman. She appeared as if in a trance. Unsure if his commitment to return the child to a native land was the cause, he rested his eyes, confident the surrounding terrain wouldn't give her thoughts of stealing the food or horses.

*　　*　　*

When he awoke, another bright morning waited on
Cole. Once he was out of the bedroll and had taken
care of his and the child's business, he struck the
camp down and packed the meat in the saddlebags.
Maud snored in the day. When all that could be done
was finished, he jostled her with his boot.

She wiped sleep from her eyes. "What's the matter?"

"Nothing. We're waiting on you."

"Let me sleep until after breakfast."

"No breakfast today. We'll eat while we ride. Can't
waste the weather we got to get past them rocks."

"Damn you, Clay," she said as she slumped her
head to the dirt. "Can't we just rest one day?"

"No," he replied, snatching her blanket. As he
folded the cloth, Maud again cursed the air blue. He
only grinned, knowing the cold would set her body to
do what was natural and get about the process of traveling.

When they were mounted, they headed through
the small forest of trees and set on a course for the
next range. During the ride, he pulled the pouch from
his saddlebag and tore off pieces of the venison for
her and Little Bear. While crossing the open country,
he was nagged by the sense of a presence from behind. Though he cast numerous glances that way,
nothing appeared unusual.

By the middle of afternoon, they had reached the
base of the far range. When the grade steepened, he
glanced at the rocky apex. Following the view to the
bottom, all he saw were boulders lined in his way.

The trip wouldn't be like the others. There didn't appear to be a suitable pass that could be traveled on horseback. "We'll have to walk," he said, sliding off the palomino. Sure he would have to lead the horse up most of the incline, he knew he couldn't climb and tug with the child still on his chest. Removing the coat, he pulled the child from the sack. Little Bear took a shaky stance in the snow. He hurried to pull the sack from her shoulders, then picked up the child.

"What are you doing now?"

"I can't have her strapped to me," he said as he came to the gelding. He tied the loop to the horn, then secured the girl with the blanket and tightened the knot. "You keep an eye on her while I lead us up the hill."

"Didn't think I'd be some nanny to an Indian brat."

"I'm sure if you ask her, she'd make a different choice, too," he said, and slipped his coat. "Try to keep up. If we're lucky, we can be on the other side before nightfall and make a camp."

The reins of the gelding stretched far enough to tether to the horn of the palomino, but the little slack didn't provide for a secure knot. Still, it would have to do. With the reins firm in his hand, he led the palomino, glancing to see that Maud had control of the gelding. Sure of his step on the jagged rocks, he pulled the reluctant animal up the snowy grade. Each step had to be placed with care due to the narrow ledges that wound left and right. A slip of a boot or hoof would put them both over the side.

With every tug, he sensed the weight of the horse

drag him backward. The incline increased with each lurched step. The sun came across his face. Not much time remained in the day and there still was sizable ground to cover before they came to the crest.

When he had to lean forward to drag the palomino farther up the hill, the rigors of the journey had taken a toll. He stopped long enough to view the sunlit snowcaps lined in a row to the south. Below, the green trees dotted through the snow blanket all the way to the valley. Distant smoke rose from the base. No doubt a homesteader had etched a piece of land to farm. Surrounded by the hills, it would be a peaceful place to live.

What he was after must be a sight like this. However, there was no river, and a moment later he realized they were far from their destination. Yet the scene was like a shot of rye to a drunk, making him scan all that was about. But still he did not see it all. He inhaled deeply, but in the thin air there wasn't much of what his body needed. Soon he chided himself for staring so long. Although it seemed only a few minutes had passed, the sun wasn't waiting for him to finish gazing. He had to get off this mountain before the night winds blew him off it.

Maud trudged up to where he stood. "Are we going to rest?"

He shook his head. "Can't waste the time. I don't think we lack but a few miles, then we start down."

"A *few* miles? Hell, Clay, my feet are aching when they're not froze stiff. I got to rest." She sat on a boulder, perched one leg atop the other, and rubbed life back into her toes. Cole glimpsed Little Bear, who sat wrapped warm on the saddle.

Snow rustled its way from the slope above. Only something moving could create such a wake. Cole gripped the Colt.

"Now what?" Maud asked, only to see Cole point a finger at her to hush. Instantly, she understood and silenced her complaints. Cole edged around the palomino's flanks, peeking up the slope for further signs of the slide's cause.

While he crept, he drew the firearm and focused between the trees for any movement. Only shadows with angled beams of light could be seen. From right to left he scanned, knowing whatever was up there had the drop on him with the high ground. As time passed, visions of another deer or other wild animal strolling through the woods entered his mind. The day was being lost to caution. With the sun leaving for the day, cold would soon seize the mountain. The more attention he spent fretting at ghosts, the worse their chances of getting to shelter. About to holster the pistol, he saw the glint of gunmetal between the trees.

A whir passed his ear. The shot boomed through the forest. Smoke puffed into the sunlight. Cole cocked the hammer and fired in reflex. The sting of the recoil felt as if it shattered every bone in his right hand. The percussion so near the horses, they both reared.

He grabbed their reins, attempting to steady them. Little Bear's eyes widened, her cheeks crinkling from the surprise. There wouldn't be time to calm her.

"What in hell—?" Maud screamed. Cole couldn't

turn his head. He cocked and fired again. Another shot from above spattered the snow in his face. He returned fire, cocking the hammer and squeezing off three rounds just to allow him time to draw the Mouton rifle. As soon as he took a step, a squeal from behind jerked his head about.

"CLAY! Help me!"

Maud was gone from the boulder. The horse's skittish jolts loosened his grip. If he let them loose, he'd be an easy target.

"*Please*. Lord A'mighty. I can't hold on."

With only a glance up at the trees, he rose and fired, then dove for the boulder. Both horses bolted away. Cole swung his head up to the trees, then back at the boulder. With a lurch, he peeked down the side. Maud clung to a small fir. The wet boughs slowly slipped from between her fingers. Another glimpse above showed no one.

He took the pistol with his left hand and reached down with his right. He clutched her right arm, but the woman's weight nearly pulled him off the boulder. Planting his boot firmly for balance, he arched his back and pulled. Maud scrambled for a foothold. With each yank he strained to lift her. As she kicked the rocks, her shoe finally stuck in a crevice. She pulled on him for leverage and clawed a grip atop the boulder.

Her panicked face creased for a moment in a smile, thankful for a second chance at life. When she edged secure atop the rock, Cole thought to glance again at the attacker in the trees.

His right arm fell limp. Pain filled his body. Blood

spewed from the hole in his coat. His knees hit the ground. Despite his will to stand, he slumped facefirst into the snow.

"You bastards," yelled Maud.

Aware he'd been hit, he instinctually took a breath, but his chest didn't expand and he coughed, each convulsion ripping apart his insides. Reflex made him struggle to stand, but the tingle in his legs soon faded. Every effort to move met only with numbness. He pulled his left hand from under his body and peeked at his reddened fingers. Maud's hand came into view, taking the pistol. The ripple of a shot blasted into his ears. When his head dipped into the white powder, a final gunshot was the last he heard.

Chapter Sixteen

The scent of food brought him out of a daze. The bleary view of wood walls slowly came into focus with the light of a solitary candle. His head throbbed, but he tried to ignore the pain and remember what happened. Frustrated, he inhaled deeply. A stab like a knife stole his wind. In short huffs, he eased his tender left side. Lying on his right shoulder, he peeked over his left to find himself in a bed covered with a wool blanket. Curious, he arched up to see what was behind, but the stab quickly poked his lungs, forcing a cough that felt like even more knives were jabbing into him. Finally, he suppressed the cough to settle the pain.

A door opening made him turn his head. Maud entered wearing a respectable dress, followed by another woman with her hair in a bun. Cole couldn't remember seeing her before. "Thank the heavens you're awake. How do you feel, darling?"

The greeting threw Cole like a mustang. Maud sat on the edge of the bed and rubbed his brow with the back of her hand. "You ain't feverish. That's a good sign. You'll be back on your feet in no time, my sweet." She turned to the other woman, who stood in the doorway. "Thanks to these kind people. If it hadn't been for them, I don't know if you'd be with us, dear." She returned her attention to Cole, leaning over him to gently kiss his forehead.

"You two, I leave," the woman chattered.

When the door shut, Cole stared Maud in the eye. "Why are you calling me them things?"

"Because that's what married people call each other."

"Married!"

Maud put her palm over his mouth and a finger across hers. "Yes, that's what I said. Don't spoil it."

"What you mean, married? How long have I been here?"

"Near a week. I had to tell them folks that you were my husband. I didn't think they'd look at it proper for me to be in here while you were without clothes."

Her words explained the rough feel of wool in places he didn't expect it. Slowly, he lifted the edge of the blanket. When he saw only what he was born with, he pulled the blanket tighter over his bare chest. "You took my clothes off?"

"Well, who else was gonna? I couldn't ask that woman, and didn't think it was her man's duty when

I said I was your wife. We had to get at the hole in you. You're lucky the bullet went clean through without blowing much apart. I had to clean the wound with that liquor you had. I made you drink the rest to get you to sleep." She paused to run her eyes over his blanket-covered body. "Besides, you've got nothing to be ashamed about. Take it from me."

Now he knew why his head hurt so bad. He never was one to handle corn whiskey. "What happened?" he said, rubbing his throbbing head.

"You got shot while we were up in the cliffs. I think it was by a bounty hunter name of Bill Wheeler. I took your pistol and fired back. I might have hit him, I don't know. There was one more shot. But it came further up the cliff. Once he was gone. That's when I spotted this house. I couldn't get you on the horse, so I rode here and told them you were my husband and you got shot. The man, he and I rode back and put you on your horse. You lost a lot of blood between here and there."

Not all that was said filtered through the throbbing, and one thing remained unknown to him. "Where's Little Bear?"

Her face turned somber. She shook her head. "I don't know. I never found the gelding."

Cole's heart sank, taking his breath. "How long did you say I was here? A week?" He threw off the covers. "Where's my clothes?" A stab slowed him, but he continued to roll out of the bed until Maud pushed him back. He didn't have the strength to push her off.

"Oh no, you don't. It took us a day to stitch you

up. I ain't going to have you rip them out over another foolish trip."

"She'll die out there," he gritted. "She can't survive out there on her own."

She stared him in the eye. "She's already gone."

The idea scared him. He refused to believe it. "No. Not if I hurry."

"Listen to me," she said, gripping his shoulders to keep from moving. "It's freezing out there. Below freezing. There's no way she can be alive. I wish it were true, but it can't be."

He slumped back onto the pillow. Her words carried too much truth for him to deny. "So you just left her out there?"

"What was I to do? You were bleeding and I was freezing, myself. It was all I could do to catch your horse."

"You could've looked. If there is a man around here, he could have looked for her."

Maud twisted away from him and rose from the bed. "Is this the thanks I get? I couldn't risk it, Clay. Some folks might throw me and you out if I was to tell them we were carting an Indian child. There's people here that would just as soon all them Injuns were dead, and here I would be asking them to risk their lives to search for one while giving up their bed for you?"

The thought sickened him. "She's just a little girl."

"She's an Indian girl, Clay. There's a difference."

It wasn't a stab that took his breath this time. "Are you one of them that thinks that way?" She faced away from him and didn't answer. "I'll be damned. How can you think that?"

She looked at him over her shoulder with glistening eyes. "I don't. But I know people who do. I couldn't risk it."

"Did you ask them? Are these some of them folks?"

"I just told you. I couldn't risk it."

Again, he peeled the blanket from over him. "Well, then I'm going to ask." When he stood, he saw her notice him from head to toe.

"You going out that door like that?"

She smirked, and he snatched the blanket from the bed and covered his front.

"Ain't like I haven't seen it before. Though I can't say I mind looking."

As her smirk grew, the throb beating his head made him wonder. "When I was drunk asleep, you didn't . . . we didn't . . ." He paused, pointing at the bed. "We ain't really married, are we?"

She shook her head, turning around and lifting his cleaned clothes from a chair to hand them to him over her shoulder. "Don't worry. I didn't take advantage of your virtue."

Satisfied with her answer, he sat on the bed and stepped into his pants. When he slipped on his shirt, he noticed the holes that had been darned closed in the front and back just below his ribs. He inhaled easily, thinking about the black coat he'd be dressed in if the shot had been a mite higher. Once he buttoned the shirt, he stood, still a bit wobbly, but steady enough to follow Maud out of the room.

When he entered the den, only the fire from the

hearth lit the room. The woman of the house wiped her hands on an apron as he limped in. A man in a collared white shirt and brown dirty pants with suspenders, and whose dark beard didn't cover his upper lip, rose from a chair and extended his hand with a smile.

"It is good you are well," he said with a chopped slur in his voice. Cole accepted the hand gently, not able to grip as firmly as usual. "I am Yasha Kopelski. This is Sofia, my wife."

Cole nodded to her with respect. "Call me Clay. According to my wife," he said, glancing at Maud, "I'm beholden to both of you."

"I am happy we could help you." Yasha pointed to the table. "We will eat soon, but first my wife and I must speak our custom."

Cole and Maud moved to the side of the table, while Sofia took a candle holder from off the wooden mantel. As she finished putting candles in each of the nine holes all abreast, Yasha took a matchstick, ignited it from the fire, then lit the middle candle. Both of them spoke in a tongue Cole had never heard.

"Ba-ruch A-tah Ado-nai E-lo-hei-nu Me-lech Ha-olam A-sher Ki-de-sha-nu Be-mitz-vo-tav Ve-tzi-va-nu Le-had-lik Neir Cha-nu-kah."

They joined their hands and took the middle candle, spreading the flame to the wicks of the other eight, all the while saying words that sounded like both of them were clearing their throats. When they finished, they replaced the middle candle. Yasha faced both of them. "Now we will eat."

"They do this every night," Maud muttered. "But she's a hell of a cook."

"Watch your mouth," Cole admonished. "Looks like God-fearing people to me." He and Maud found their places at the table. Sofia took the candleholder and put it back on the mantel, then went to the stove. Not one to nose into others' beliefs, he thought it best to know whose house he had been placed in for fear of saying something that shouldn't be said. "Are you all Mormons?"

The man's face broke into a smile. He shook his head. "No. We are not Mormons." When he peeked up at Cole, he must have read the confusion. "We are Jews." Unsure of the difference, Cole glanced up at the nine burning candles. "It is the season for the light festival. Tonight is the eighth night. If you like, I can tell you the story of the miracle."

Cole shook his head. "Don't trouble yourself," he said, not wanting to hear another history lesson. The last one he listened to brought him a thousand miles out of his way to this spot. "Maybe another time."

Sofia put plates of meat chops and carrots in front of them. Cole took a whiff, and the scent reminded him of his days in the troopers. "Mutton?"

Yasha nodded. When Sofia sat at the table, Cole picked up his fork. A glance to the side told him Maud hadn't heard of the custom of waiting on the hostess before filling her mouth. Noticing Cole's stare, she paused for an instant, only to shrug, then continued.

Cole cut the meat and took the bite. The meat was

tender and thoroughly cooked. It wasn't the taste that concerned him. "You sheep herders?"

"Yes," Yasha answered as if accused of a crime. He looked to his wife, who seemed to cower. "It is the trade of my family."

Cole took another bite, knowing the questions were making his hosts nervous. Yet he also realized the consequences of sheep farming in the West. While in Texas, he had heard stories of the Navajo having inherited the practice in New Mexico from the Spanish. When other tribes and even white easterners attempted to spread into Texas cattle country, bloodshed from shootings and hangings chased the invaders back across the borders. Not since the question of loyalty to North or South had a division split westerners so wide. Cole didn't care to take a side. He took another bite and gobbled the carrots.

His eyes drifted to a tintype featuring the husband and wife and a girl and boy. Anxious to change the subject, he blurted another question. "You two got kids?" An instant later, he realized he hadn't seen either of them. A glance at Maud's soured lips confirmed the foolishness of the inquiry. When he saw Sofia's eyes well up, he felt like a fool. "I didn't mean no harm."

The man raised his hand. "No harm." Yasha touched the hand of his wife. "We do have two beautiful children. But they have gone on without us."

Sofia wiped a tear from her eye, then rose from her chair and returned to the stove. Cole felt like joining the sheep outside.

"When we were crossing the land from St. Louis

on our way here, my children were weak and not able to deal with the heat and the cold. Soon, they have fever. The doctors in Cheyenne said it was cholera. Maybe they got it on their own. Some said it was from other sick persons. This I don't know. But my children are gone. Sofia and I agreed to come here, and although they don't live in this house, they are with us. This land is their home, too."

Cole put down his fork. Though the meal was tasty, his appetite had left him. If it weren't for his blunder, he was sure he would've enjoyed it more. Maud seemed equally ill at ease, though she nearly finished her plate. Yasha continued his meal despite his wife's absence. Cole knew it was he that kept her from the table. That thought, and the return of pain to his side, convinced him he needed to leave the room.

"My back is aching. I think, if you don't mind, I'll turn in. Might feel better in the morning. Got something I need to look for."

Surprise showed on Maud's face. Whether she thought of her wifely duty or she felt the same ache, she rose from the table and wiped her mouth. "Thank you for a nice supper," she said. Yasha stood and bid her good night.

She reached for Cole to take her hand. With the man and woman looking, he didn't think it smart to refuse. He took her hand, and she wrapped her arm under his in a show of support for his limp. They crept one step at a time into the bedroom.

"Why didn't you ask?"

"I didn't have the heart after making them think of their own dead kids."

245

The more he limped, the more twist he put on the stitches in his side. He eased down on the side of the bed. The rustle of clothes drew his attention from behind. The dim candlelight showed Maud in only her camisole climbing under the blanket.

"How far are we carrying this married thing?"

"I don't really care. I just want to go to sleep."

He gently turned. "In this little bed? I slept on cots bigger than this."

"What's the matter with you, Clay? You scared?"

The dare made him curious. "Of what?"

"Of sleeping with me here. The way you were back in Abilene. There was plenty of room, but you slept on the floor." He felt the stroke of her palm on his arm. "How long has it been since you bedded a lady?"

He unbuttoned his shirt while pondering her offer, then leaned and blew out the candle. In the dark he touched the soft cloth and eased his body onto the bed.

"I wouldn't want to rip out them stitches you bragged on."

Chapter Seventeen

Loud voices brought him out of his sleep. The first thing he noticed was the sharp pain in his side. Steadying his breath, Cole blinked in the morning of the dim bedroom. Maud still lay snoring on his left side. Her weight pinned on his shoulder. Once free, he eased from under her, squeezing his hand to pump blood back into his starved muscles. He rose to sit on the edge of the bed. The frantic woman's voice drew his attention. Quickly, he stepped into his pants and slipped on his shirt. As he went to the door, he glanced at the Colt, unsure if it was needed. Not wanting to further alarm his hosts, he left it, opened the door, and entered the den.

When the husband and wife saw him, they instantly ceased talking. The man stood by the window, then took a step back from it like a thief who has spotted a badge. "Good morning."

"Morning," Cole said with a respectful nod to the woman. "Is there trouble?"

Yasha shook his head. "No. Not trouble." He peeked between the drapes at the sunlit snow outside. He faced his wife. "They are coming."

Sofia scurried back to the kitchen, uttering words Cole didn't understand. Yasha's eyes showed their concern. "You stay in here. It is good for you," he told Cole. As he went to the door, Cole crept to the window. A glance back saw Sofia with arms clutched together. He returned his attention to the window. Four riders approached from the south.

When they reined in, their chaps and lariats identified their line. Their side arms, in plain view, made clear their purpose for the visit. Cole concentrated on the leader. A white beard with hair lapping his collar, he wore a black hat with a loose drawstring. His duster was open, showing black suspenders, a faded purple bandanna, and a white shirt dotted with a diamond pattern.

An ear near the glass allowed Cole to hear the conversation.

"I see you're still here," said the leader.

"This is my home," Yasha replied.

A wry smile broke the leader's face. He turned around to one of his cowhands and motioned. The hand rode off toward the small barn.

Cole recognized the sign. It wasn't a neighborly gesture. He retreated to the bedroom. Wincing from his hurried walk, he drew the Colt. A flick of his thumb opened the chamber gate. He spun the cylinders. Six spent shells were quickly ejected. The noise of them spilling on the wood floor stirred Maud from her sleep. Without a word, Cole held up a single finger. Her answer was still silence. Popping loaded cartridges from the gunbelt loops, Cole slid a fresh shell into an empty cylinder, clicking the chamber round until all were filled. Slapping the chamber gate closed, he returned to the den.

When Sofia saw the pistol, she put her back to the wall. "No, you will make them mad."

Cole held out his hand. "You stay here. I'm not going to use this unless they make me." His grip of the butt was still weak, but a deep breath later, he opened the door and walked outside. Trying not to shiver from the frigid breeze, Cole came to stand next to Yasha. Towering over the smaller man, he kept his eyes front as he spoke.

"These friends of yours?"

"Well," said the leader, his eyes darting to the revolver that Cole drooped in his right hand. "Who might you be?"

"A guest of the owner."

The leader chortled. "That'd be me, friend. Cauley is my name. Heb Cauley. My family owns everything you're looking at."

"This is my land," Yasha proclaimed. "I have the deed. From the government."

Cauley's wry smile was gone. "Government don't own this land. Never have. I've told you before, it was my family that settled this territory near sixty years ago. Weren't nothing here but a bunch of savages, wolves, grass, and snow. It was my grandpa that came here from Tennessee to scratch a reasonable living for the white folks that were meant to live out here. When miners came, they wanted beef, and we were the only ones that had the guts to stay here and give it to them. Didn't have no army back then to protect them. Nobody to build the houses, round up the steers, chase off the Indians that stole the stock and kill the varmints that ate them. It weren't up to no *government* that didn't have nothing to do with claiming the territory. They had no say."

"Not what the judge say," Yasha defiantly said. "This is my home."

The wry smile returned. "We'll see about that." All heads turned at the baying of a lamb. The cowhand had thrown a lariat over its neck and drug it from the barn to the front of the house. "Hell, not only are you a squatter, a foreigner, and a heathen," Cauley said, returning his attention to Yasha, "you're a damn sheeper. You don't mind if we take this one, do you? Maybe the boys might develop a taste for it. We'll let you know if they like it. Or if they don't." He looked directly at Cole. "I don't know who you are, friend, but you chose the wrong side. If you don't want part of this, I suggest you clear out. Or you may get in the way of something you don't want to be." He swung his horse around.

"Wait!" Cole's shout stopped everyone's horse. "You're going to pay for that lamb."

Cauley laughed, and his merriment quickly spread to the rest of his gang. "You got sand, mister. I'll give you that. Whoever you are. What if I don't?"

"Then you'd be a thief. What do they do to thieves around here?"

The smile faded slightly. "You calling me a thief? I don't know if I cotton to being called that."

"Pay for it and you won't be."

The dare simmered in the air. Cauley's eyes darted to his men, who looked to him for a signal. Cole kept the Colt at his side. Scanning the riders, he watched for any twitch. The young hand with the lariat switched the rope from his left palm to his right.

"Tell your boy if he don't fill his gun hand back with that rope, I'll shoot him right in the gut and out of that saddle. It'll take him three days to die." When Cole locked eyes with the young hand, he wrapped his thumb around the Colt's hammer. "What's the price, Yasha?"

"Two dollars" was the stammered answer.

Cauley grinned. "Hell, pay the man, Daniel. Better than getting shot as a sheep thief." With the orders understood, young Daniel drew two coins from his vest pocket, spat on them, and dropped them in the mud. "Bill paid," Cauley stated, then pulled his revolver and fired, killing the lamb. He turned his horse back to the south. "Be seeing you."

When the riders passed the fence, Cole turned to Yasha. "Let's get inside. It's too damn cold out here." They entered the house. Yasha came to the center of the room. Sofia, after a momentary pause, ran into her husband's arms. They embraced as if they had not seen each other in years. Maud stood in the bedroom doorway in her own dress. "Who were they?" she asked.

"They are the robbers who try to scare us away," said Yasha. "He says all of this land is his."

"And he'll be back," Cole said. "You can bet on it. I've seen his kind before. They don't take to being told what to do by nobody. Especially those they think have no call to do so. Could be you might heed what he's telling you. Or you might have more trouble than you care for."

"This my land. I have the deed to prove it."

"Do you have a gun, too?"

Yasha shook his head.

"Then if you want to keep it, that and them sheep out there, you'd better get one."

Sofia's glistening eyes stared at Cole. She pointed at him. "You stay?"

The request made him ponder for a moment, but there was still a needle stuck in his craw. "No," Cole replied. "I am beholden to you. May take me another day to get on a horse." He paused to glance at Maud. "But there's something I lost I got to find."

Heb Cauley rode ahead of his men to the front of the ranch house. He swung his leg off and threw the reins at the hitch post. Stomping up the steps, he flipped the lever up and kicked open the door. Bess and Herbert Jr. sat at the table eating supper. He waved his wife and son from the room. "I need to talk to the boys."

Both of them obeyed the order and went upstairs. Heb shrugged the duster from his shoulders and flung it and his hat to the couch and yanked the gloves off his hands. As his men filed inside, he went to the bar. He pulled a bottle of whiskey and four shot glasses from the cabinet. He slid a glass in front of each man as they all sat at the table. Heb poured himself a shot and raised it in toast. "So, gentlemen, what are we going to do about this feisty Jew who's still on my property?" He slugged down the drink.

None of the others touched his glass.

"Drink up, drink up. We've got a lot of thinking to do," he said jovially. "We can have a party." He poured and threw another shot down his throat. "We can celebrate that we rode ten miles this morning just to ride ten miles back to this house because of one man holding a pistol pointed at the dirt!" He rose and slung the glass, shattering it against the wall. "What the hell is wrong with you!"

"We thought that's what you wanted, Mr. Cauley," said young Daniel.

"What I want is that man and his woman off my property. I don't think I should have to tell you how to do it." Marching around the table, he continued. "If I let them stay there, then the whole valley will fill up with them people living next to your women and kids."

A knock at the door interrupted his tirade. Ben Fuller entered. "Boss, there's a stranger says he wants to see you."

"Who is he?"

"Says he's a bounty hunter from Texas. Says he knows who's at the Jew's place."

"Bring him in," Heb answered with a wave. A moment later, a portly man in a leather waistcoat and pale brown hat stepped into the house. "Howdy, friend. Name's Heb Cauley. Who the hell are you?"

"Bill Wheeler."

"Pleased to meet you, Bill. Come on in. Sit down. Have a drink."

"Don't mind to have a seat. No thanks on the drink." Wheeler cautiously entered with all eyes watching every step. He sat in Heb's chair.

"So, who is this man?"

"He's a man I've been chasing since I left Texas going on four months. I ain't sure of his rightful name, but I heard he goes by the name of Clay Hayes. The law and the military know him as the Rainmaker."

"The what?"

"Rainmaker," Ben Fuller said. "I've heard of him, boss. I heard he shot Will Benson and his brothers."

"Them boys who tried robbing that train?"

"He's the one," Wheeler said. "He ain't a man you want to face with a gun in his hand."

"See, Daniel?" Heb said with a smile. "I guess it was a good thing you didn't press your luck with this fellow."

"I could have got him," young Daniel replied.

"He would have killed you, son," Wheeler said, staring the young man straight in the eye. "He would have killed you, and been ready to kill the next of you. A week ago I put a slug in his back. I'd had him, too. But another shooter was after him as well and took a shot at me. I didn't have the cover I wanted, so I moved. Dark set in. The wind started blowing and nearly took me off that mountain. By the time it was light, he was gone. I tracked him back to the house that I saw you at this morning."

"That a fact?" Heb said, a bit amazed. "What's

your stake in this? Why you after him?"

"There's five thousand on his head."

"Quite a sum. Why?"

Wheeler looked to the others as if reluctant to reveal the purpose. "The army says he's a traitor. They've been chasing him since Custer was slaughtered by the Sioux. Seems they think he had something to do with that."

"I'll be damned. What'd he do?"

Wheeler shook his head. "Can't say. Ain't my business. All I know is his name's on a poster with five thousand dollars above it. It's the only reason I'd come this far."

Heb turned his back on the others for a only a moment, then faced Wheeler. "So. What are you waiting for? Why are you here?"

"Even if he's hurt, he's still a crack shot. As long as he's holed up in that house, I don't have much of a shot at him."

"Hell, we'll help you. We'll burn him out," Heb said, not able to keep from smiling at that thought.

Wheeler shook his head. "Ain't my way. Not when there are innocent folks who don't have no play in the matter. No. There's another way. As long as I've been tracking him, he's been traveling with a child. An Indian child. I've been told it's his plan to take it into Oregon."

"A damn Indian lover. Hell, there ain't no worse man born. The man should be horse-whipped."

"The thing of it is, when I shot him, that child was roped to a horse that ran. He's lost it. And I'd bet he'd be interested in getting it back."

"You got it?" Heb asked, then took a full glass from the table and swigged it.

Wheeler again shook his head. "That horse might be halfway to Kansas by now. Anyway, I don't think that baby survived the night. I don't know where it is. But he don't know that. I think it worth the try to make him think you have it. That'll get him out of that house. Once he's on his own, I'll take care of the rest."

Heb took another glass. "And why should we do that?"

"You want him out of that house. What you do when he's gone isn't my business. I'll leave you to do what you want. I'll have no part in it."

The plan seemed simple enough, and the result gave Heb a laugh. "Boy, Bill, I like how you think. So we just ride out there and tell this Rainmaker that his little Indian bastard is at our line shack and he'll ride headlong to get it back. Once he's in the open, you'll have your clean shot at him. Hell, we'll have a turkey shoot."

"I'd rather take him alive," Wheeler said. "But I'll take him any way I can get him. But beware, this man is a killer. You can't get liquored up and go shooting at him. You'll likely lose a man or two if you do."

"Don't you worry, Bill," said Heb as he picked up the last glass on the table. "Ain't the first time we've had to do some shooting."

As the sunlight dimmed in the west, Cole and Maud sat down for the evening meal with their hosts. Without words, each began eating. Cole knew the events of the morning still hung over the table like low clouds. Mentioning the conflict would only stir it into a storm. He owed these people more than to bring them more trouble. He kept his mouth closed to chew and to let peace settle.

"Rainmaker!"

The shout came from the front of the house. The husband and wife had puzzled faces, but the puzzlement gave way to fear. Cole rose from his chair and went to the window. The lone young rider who had roped the lamb sat in the saddle. Cole knew he had little to fear from a single man, but he also knew others were watching. He went to the bedroom and returned to the den with the Colt in his hand. He flicked open the chamber gate to be sure of a full load. When he gripped the lever to open the door, Maud clutched his hand. She didn't have to speak her warning. Her eyes told him what her mouth couldn't say. Cole nodded to her and the husband and wife to stay inside. He opened the door and stepped onto the porch.

Cole watched the young man's hands. Both were filled with the reins. "What do you want?"

"That be you?" The kid's tone was full of sass.

Not knowing how the name he'd been given as an infant had found its way onto this man's tongue, Cole concentrated on the purpose of the intrusion. "Just speak your piece."

"I heard you lost something. Up on the mountain. What say I told you I know where it is?"

The news made Cole's heart skip a beat. "How you

know that?" A wry smile like that of his boss crept across the kid's face.

"Word is a fellow like yourself shot some men trying to rob a train. Had a baby with him. An Indian baby. I know where it is. Are you interested?"

No trap ever had a greater stench. However, it was the first glimmer of hope he had had since he had lost Little Bear. He couldn't help being interested. "Go on."

"There's a line shack about six miles from here on the other side them hills that lead to the next range," the kid said as he pointed. "The baby is there. You better hurry, though. She's got a cough. Wouldn't want you to be late and have her die on you." The kid's grin grew to a smile as he turned his horse. "Hurry, now, you hear?" He kicked his mount and rode at a gallop.

Cole went inside. Maud was first to come next to him. "What did he want?"

He stared at her for a moment. It took an instant for her curiosity to settle into knowledge. He nodded once he was sure she understood. He looked to Yasha and Sofia. "I'll need to be leaving." He walked directly into the bedroom, followed closely by Maud. She closed the door behind her.

"What are you planning?"

"He said they have her in a line shack six miles from here." Cole looked at her, wincing with each strain he felt as he buckled the gunbelt. "I know they'll be waiting on me for sure." He peered into Maud's eyes. "But I've got to go. I got to know."

"Are you a fool? They'll kill you as soon as you show."

He nodded. "Most likely."

"Do you want to get killed?" She came to stand in front of him. "You won't do her no good if you're dead."

"Don't you think I know that?" he shouted. She covered his mouth to keep his voice from booming throughout the house. He pushed her hand away gently. "More than likely they'll wait for me at the shack. They know it and I don't. I'll take care once I get there. Can't say how it will come out, but I got to see it through."

Maud folded her arms. "How do you know she's even there?"

The question made him think. There was no clear answer. "What if she is?"

He stepped aside and headed for the door. She clutched his arm. "I'll go with you."

"What? Won't be a place for you out there with a bunch of lead flying."

"I can do something you can't. Seein' it was me that got that bullet plugged in you, I'm the one that should help you out of this. I can get her back."

"How so?"

"You said she's at some shack. I'm sure there's a bunch of men there, and probably no women if they think there'll be shooting." She cupped her palms under her bosom and straightened her blouse. "There's another way of dealing with men besides having to shoot them."

Cole felt a smirk crawl over his mouth. "So you

think you can sneak in there and get her out?"

"Well, you're going to help me. When I get them fellows how I want them, I'll grab the girl and get outside. That's where you can keep them from coming out of the shack after us."

He shook his head. Although more could go wrong with her idea than right, he didn't have a better one in mind. "If I let you go, you'll do everything I say?"

She smiled. "Don't I always?"

Chapter Eighteen

Maud peeked at the sky. With the full moon up in the east, the clear night allowed light to guide them. The snowcaps gleamed in the moonlight. Her hands around his waist, she huddled her shoulders into his coat to hide her face from the frigid air. "How long before we're there?"

"Don't know for sure," he whispered. "Ain't been there before."

His snide reply was no comfort. "Clay. Why are we doing this?" She waited for his answer. It took longer than she expected.

"I don't know," he muttered. "I guess there are just some things that you got to do that you know is the right thing to do."

"This is the last thing I ever thought I'd be doing for that reason," she chattered through her teeth. "I didn't think someone like you would. I thought you looked like a man smarter than that, Clay." She heard his huffed laugh through his coat.

"You ain't the only one. Been asking myself that before I left the Indian territory. But you know there are some things that after a while, when you're sure you ain't going to make it, that the closer you get to finishing, you tell yourself, you come this far, damn might as well finish and be done with it."

"That's the most foolish reason I could think of having to be out here."

"Then why are you?"

"Because," she said, her jaw quivering. "I'm as big a damn fool as you are. Got nothing else to do." She was about to laugh at herself, but the amusement flew from her head when she felt Cole rein in the horse. She peeked over his shoulder and a flickering light came through a row of trees. "Is this it?" she hissed.

"Would seem so," he answered, scanning left and right. At his tap, she slid from the saddle with the support of his arm. Cole dismounted and slowly led the palomino to the trees. Tethering the reins, he crouched at an angle so as to peek through the branches. Maud came to kneel by his side.

"What do you want me to do?" The words came from her mouth before she thought to speak them. Her heart beat through her blouse. She had never been scared to enter the company of men, but these she didn't have control over. The questions she had asked moments before pounded in her head. The single answer that he had put into words stood clear.

"I want you to be damn careful. Don't try to sneak

up on them. Make it known that you're there. When they call, you answer and don't make any quick moves. When you get there, they'll probably search your clothes for weapons."

"Ain't the first time men have put their paws on these clothes."

He drew the pistol from the holster. "Just the same, you let them do as they please. Snoop around and see if the girl is there. Once you see her, if she's alive, take your time with them. Don't make it known I'm out here."

She was stumped. "What should I say where you're at?"

He looked her in the eye. "Tell them I run scared."

"They won't believe me."

He raised his eyebrows. "Here you're bragging on how you can make men do what you want. You can't convince them that they had me turn tail?"

The challenge couldn't go unaccepted. "You just watch. I'll be having them boys eating out of my hand like critters." She sucked in a deep wind and blew it out. Bending to avoid the low limbs, she crept through the brush, peeking over her shoulder to be sure she wouldn't be left alone. She pushed the final branches from her path and climbed up the small incline toward the small shack. A lantern hung near the door, and the single window was draped by a red cloth. With a shaky balance on the icy ground, she finally stepped onto the front landing. Another deep breath was needed, just enough to maintain her spit, then she claimed the top step and wrapped the wood with her knuckles.

As the door creaked open, a young man, hair slicked against the sides of his head, peeked around the edge. "Going to let me in, hon? Cold out here." The door opened wider, revealing a room full of cowhands. The brisk breeze pushed her inside. A single lantern sat on a table, with four cowhands clutching rifles seated around it. With the door closing behind her, she knew she was in a den of snakes. As long as she kept her mind on her business and didn't let on her true purpose, she may keep from getting bit.

She pulled the shawl from her head. The white-bearded leader came out from the corner shadows. "Where's the Rainmaker?"

Cole crouched behind the branches. After a moment, he crept from limb to trunk to get a better look, but all he could see was the red-shrouded window. The Colt firm in his hand, he waited for a sign or signal that the plan had gone wrong. Second thoughts nagged him. It was he who should have faced these cowhands, not Maud. He chided himself for letting himself be talked into this by her. Yet she had a feisty nature about her. Perhaps she could convince them to give her the child without a shot fired—if the child was there, alive. Images of the defenseless girl wrapped in the blanket as lifeless as a stillborn flashed in his mind. He shook his head to clear his thoughts and concentrate on the line shack. An occasional voice filtered through the light breeze. He snuck closer into the tangled brush to hear the words. Moments went by and not another sound drifted his way. The bitter cold argued that an hour had gone by, but his better sense reassured him that only a minute at best had passed since the door closed.

Having heard the conversation, he was ready for the emergence of men in search of him. If he shot at them while they stood on the porch, it would endanger Maud and give what mite-size chance Little Bear was alive its final coffin nail. He had to wait. Patience wasn't what he prided himself on most. The notion of sneaking up to the shack didn't seem a poor one. If he could get by what scouts might be around, he could listen to what went on inside and be ready if Maud needed him.

Sold on the idea, he slowly inched back out of the brush. Snapping twigs paralyzed him in his retreat. He held the pistol up and ready to fire. He stayed motionless until he was sure no ears around had heard the noise. Resuming the crouched back step, he ducked his head around a low limb. It scraped the hat from his head, and the cold air felt like a bucket of spring water had been dumped on his scalp. He leaned forward and retrieved the hat. A single crunch in the snow turned his head. Hard steel glimmered in the moonlight, then crashed against his skull.

Maud stared at the white-bearded leader. "He was yellow. It was me that was taking care of the baby, and he lost it. When he didn't have the guts, I came in his stead." She looked around the room at the four others. A sly grin creased her cheeks. "I thought I could talk some sense into you fellows."

"Is that right? You wouldn't be lying to old Heb, would you?"

The only way to sell a lie was to answer the question with one. "Why would I? He ain't here, is he?"

"Well, we're going to find out." Heb waved one of the men outside. Maud watched the hand leave, then decided to use her best talent. "You mind if I make myself a little more comfortable?" she said, removed the shawl from her shoulders, then pulled the scarf from around her neck. When she had decided to wear her own flimsy dress on such a cold night it was intended to show her bare cleavage and warm the hearts of her marks. By their raised brows, she knew her suffering during the cold night ride had been worth it.

She sat on the vacated chair and rubbed her behind on the warmed seat. The action served a dual purpose. She knew she would soon have all their attention. The distraction would allow her time to win over their loyalty and learn more about the child. "What do you boys do for fun?"

"Oh, they like to have fun," Heb answered. His happy smile appeared to be one to welcome long-unseen family. She knew it to be a facade. "After long days on this range, they get kinda antsy. Once they trade each other's wages over cards, I have to take them fifty miles to take care of the wild nature building up in them. Sometimes they call on pretty girls that stay at the saloons, and they have a fine time with them ladies."

"Really?" Maud said in obvious jest. "You'll have to share with me what they appreciate most in a lady."

"Oh, I'm sure they'd like to show you. Why'd you

come out here over an Indian? A baby, at that? You take to their kind?" His friendly tone faded with the utterance of each word. Maud couldn't let the inquiry dissolve her mood, or her plan. "If you have to know the truth, Heb, the young'un is mine. Had her when I was back in Kansas. I don't like to admit such a tryst, especially with a Indian, but, well, he was a drover from Texas, a half-breed, and, well, when the night gets a little nippy, and a girl has to find a place to stay, I met this one, and we agreed to share more than the bed. Wouldn't you know it. Nine months later, I was swelled with a papoose, and I had her in a barn—yes, a barn. Just like they say where the Lord was born." The attempt to sway their opinions wasn't working, as reflected on their stern faces.

Especially Heb. "You had a savage's baby?"

She didn't have a quick answer.

"What kind of white woman are you? Hell, that's worse than them making their own. That's the only thing they can do. But I would expect a white woman, even a whore, to have more pride."

His shaming never got inside her; she had heard those words and worse for ten years. But the dim mood he cast over the room rivaled the light of the single lantern. She needed to turn it in her favor. As she scrambled for a suitable reply, one that wouldn't rile Heb further, the door swung open. In stepped the hand that had left, and behind him trailed another portly figure.

She couldn't help but stand. After a minor breath, she greeted the newcomer. "Howdy, Bill."

Bill Wheeler stared her in the eye. "Maud," he acknowledged.

Once the door closed, the hand looked to Heb and shook his head. "We didn't find nobody. Not even a horse. I don't know how she got here."

"I walked," she foolishly blurted.

"Six miles. At night. In the snow. Stop with your lies, woman." Heb's shout forced her back in the chair. His eyes focused on Wheeler. "Is that true?"

Wheeler nodded. "No sign of him. There's some tracks in the snow, but it's too dark to see where they lead. Appears two men were out there once, but we didn't see any other sign. Hoofprints show two horses heading the other way." He looked to Maud. "She didn't come by herself, but it appears she's been left on her own."

The news made her heart pound. She didn't believe it. Clay had to be out there. She had a silent confidence that he had tricked them and was waiting on her for a sign. However, first she had to gloat. "I told you."

"I guess you were right. He is a yellow coward," Heb admitted.

"No," Wheeler said. "That ain't like him. A man that stands alone against train robbers ain't the kind to shy from a gunfight. He's out there somewhere. I can't say where. But I know it in my bones."

"Hell," Heb said, stepping to the door. "No sense staying here. If he ain't around, then you lost your chance. I'm going to get what I come for."

"Wait," Maud said. "When do I get what I come for?"

Heb looked back at her. "What? Your child?"

"Child?" Wheeler questioned.

"Yeah. She says that's her baby."

Wheeler huffed in disgust. "That's what she told you." His scorn-filled face turned to Maud. "I found this woman in a Kansas brothel. After I had told her about the bounty, she went out and found the Rainmaker to keep it for herself, but she got scared and left him. I was going to give her a thousand dollars to point him out to me, but she give out on me, and I had to tend to my business. I picked up her tracks two days later and found she had met up with him again. That's how I knew it was him and what he looked like. But she never tried to find me. I guess she wanted all the reward herself." He paused. "That baby belongs to a squaw in Indian territory that the Rainmaker shot dead in the back. An army colonel stuck him with that child and told him to bring it back to Oregon. She told you it was hers, huh?"

Maud felt as if she were again falling off that mountain. "That ain't true. Not a word," she warned.

"She's nothing but a lying whore," Wheeler said in a monotone. He walked out the door.

Maud stood. "What about that baby!?"

Heb looked to her and shrugged. "I guess it's food for some poor coyote. I don't know. It sure ain't here." His laugh rattled her mind. She couldn't think of the proper insult to shoot back before Heb opened his mouth again. "But I guess you shouldn't let that get in the way of what you come for. Have at her, boys." The laugh continued as the door shut.

Surrounded by the vipers, Maud eased back in the

chair. A moment went by before the first one stood and tossed off his hat. "I know what I want." Another one agreed and did the same. Quickly all of them began unbuckling their gunbelts, pulling the chaps free from their legs. The thought of escaping through the door disappeared when she saw that the young rider who had roped the lamb stood in front of it. Hands grabbed at her shoulders. Fingers slipped down her blouse. Whiskers scraped her cheeks, then spit wiped her lips. She would have to trade for her life, as she always had.

She pushed the first one off. "Easy, cowboy. I'm not some steer. There's plenty for all of you."

She couldn't see the one grabbing at her chest. "I like being first." Two of them lifted her from the chair and pulled her to the lower bunk.

Again she pushed. "Only room for one at a time, boys."

Her minor resistance seemed to fuel their lust. The first one was only in his long handles, but his hat was still on. He mashed his lips onto hers while his hands groped the top of her blouse. He pulled apart the top, buttons popping like the embers of a fire. She couldn't see who had had grabbed her legs, and despite her best effort to kick them free, the grip was too firm.

"She's got fire." It came as a hooted call.

The bottom of the upper bunk was her only view. An instant later, the hem of her dress was pushed above her waist. More faces slobbered and bit at her cheeks and lips. She couldn't see where they all were, but when cool air enveloped her bare flesh, she knew what they were eyeing.

"I'm first."

"Not in my life."

"Hurry up, then. We haven't got the whole night."

Maud didn't want to cry, but tears dripped into her mouth. This had happened before. The memory flew in and out of her head. The humiliation from the first time had worn away, and she realized that the more she fought the more she would be hurt.

Fingers scratched her inner thighs. She winced from the prodding. "It ain't a saddle. Be done with it," she choked out.

"Wait" was yelled. She thought she had been reprieved for only an instant. "Daniel still has his cherry. Come on, son. Give it to this lady."

Loud laughter was all she could hear until the crumple of clothes hit the ground. "You can't get at it with this bunk." Maud felt her shoulders turned. Her face was full of the dusty sheet as her bottom hung over the edge of the bunk. An instant later, the harsh intrusion of a man sent a sharp sting through her body and her soul. As the pace of the thrusts quickened, she knew it would soon conclude. As the pain grew, she allowed herself one loud cry. "Clay!"

At first, sunlight seeped through his eyelids. When he saw that it was day, the back of his skull throbbed. Instinct made him try to rub, but both arms were bound behind him. His own pulse pounded out the beats like strokes from a hammer. Lying on his face, he rolled onto his shoulder. He lay in a tight circle of boulders. Despite his watery vision, he slowly focused on a black man sitting atop a rock with a Winchester cradled between his knees.

"You the one that whipped that pistol across my head?"

In his bleary view he saw the black man just sit and stare away.

"Who are you?" asked Cole.

The captor still said nothing and took a bite from an apple.

"I said, who the hell are you?"

"If you don't hush up, they'll find us."

"Who will? Who's looking for us? And what is your name?"

Like a parent frowning at children, the black man chewed the apple with a disparaging glare. Finally, after swallowing and grunting his throat clear, he said, "If I tell you, you shut your mouth?"

Cole nodded. "Deal."

"I'm called Choate." He took another bite from the apple.

The name sounded familiar. Cole relaxed his head to the dirt, trying to recall where he had heard it. Finally, the vision of an older colored man he had ridden with years before slammed into his head. "You're Jenks's boy."

"I nobody's boy. You said you'd shut up."

"I knew your pa."

Choate spat a seed. "My pa is dead and buried on a reservation. You going to close your mouth, or do I have to plug it closed?"

Cole heeded the warning only long enough to eye the rifle. It and his bound hands showed him the reason the two men were together. "You're a bounty hunter."

Choate took a final bite, then tossed the core into the brush, wiped his hands on his pants, and nodded. "That be true." As he spoke, bits of the apple dribbled from his mouth. He wiped his sleeve across his mouth.

"How long you been after me?"

Choate kept his eyes away. "Nearly four months. A little longer. I don't know for sure."

As the throbbing in his head subsided, Cole's mind turned to Maud. "Where's the woman I was with?"

Choate pointed as if to a spot below. The circle of boulders kept Cole from seeing exactly where. "Down in the shack, most probably. I ain't seen her come out, but riders left out there before daybreak," he said in a calm tone.

"Then where are we?"

"About a mile from it."

Cole recalled that it was dark when last he saw her, and the morning frost on the rocks made him fear the worst. He tugged against the rope. The tight knot wouldn't loosen despite his discreet efforts. He wouldn't get his freedom from force. "I left her down there. By herself. You got to let me go. Just long enough to see if she's all right."

Choate turned to him with a puzzled look. "Think not."

"Damn it. She was alone with them. I was supposed to keep her from trouble. Let me go. She has no part of this."

"If'n I let you go, I'd have to go. Don't care to face

any more guns than need be. And that don't need be."

Cole couldn't argue. He knew he would act the same way. The only difference would be the fate of the child. "There's an Indian girl down there somewhere." Choate shook his head. "Yes, there is. We come for it last night. Now, you listen. I know you. I knew your pa. Your real pa. He told me all about you. His name was Lucious Jenkins. He had a wife, a Crow squaw that had a baby. He called the son Choate, after a trapper friend of his. A Frenchman from Canada." As Cole spoke, Choate faced away, appearing to stare at something below. "Your ma didn't tell you all the stories, did she? Why you're blacker than the rest of your tribe. He left you there because he knew that he never could care for you the way her tribe could. You're part Crow, and a Nez Perce girl is down there somewhere. The white woman and I were trying to find it. Them cowboys said they had it, so we went looking and you took me from it. Whatever your plans, I'll go along with them. I was headed to Chicago city when I got stuck with the child. I only wanted to set it free in its home territory. With its own people. Are you going to help me?"

Unsure what to say next, Cole watched Choate rise and walk behind the rocks. The black man peered down, but Cole couldn't see at what. Then Choate stared at Cole and shook his head. "Ain't no child lost there." He bent for a moment, then stood, holding the sleeping Little Bear in his arms.

Cole's heart skipped. His breath was squeezed

from his chest at the sight. The lancing pain in his side made him cough, but he sucked in enough air to speak. "Where? How?"

"If Bill Wheeler hadn't a shot you on that bluff, I would of." He returned the child to her rest. "I shot at him until he run. I saw the horse and tracked it. Took the girl and returned to you. That's when that woman bring another man. So I watch them take you to the house. I waited on Wheeler, but he never came back. So I waited on you. Followed you from the house last night and brought you here."

"Then you know that woman is still down there."

Choate nodded in his casual manner. "Like you said, she's not part of this."

"Damn you, cut me loose. Let me go. I said I'd go with you. I give my word on it."

"You gave your word you'd close your mouth."

"Well, I'm taking that one back. And I'll keep talking until you set me free." The threat only made Choate pick up a bandanna. Cole knew it was meant to be stuffed in his mouth. "Wait." He didn't have any further ploy to offer except the truth. "I was on my way to turn myself in. To tell my side of the story. Of what I knew about Custer and the Little Bighorn. But fate stepped in and put me with that child. I didn't have plans to keep it, but the closer I got to getting rid of it, the nearer I was to doing what I was asked to do. The woman helped me. Like it or not, I have to say that." The speech didn't appear to cut much with Choate. "You saw what she did. She pulled me off that mountain. I'm beholden to her. I can't leave her there. Now you want to take me back.

It'll be a lot easier if you let me go down there. After that I won't give you no trouble."

Choate turned to him, the glowering stare still in place. "You're wanted alive or dead."

The reply gave Cole only a glimmer of hope that the half-breed was interested. "That may be true. But I sure would be rank by the time you got me to Montana." The humor did the trick. Choate's nostrils flared and the ends of his mouth turned up a bit. He drew a folding knife from his pocket and came to Cole.

"I'll shoot you dead you run."

Once the blade sliced through the ropes, Cole stood and Choate kept a hand on the butt of his revolver. "Where's my horse?" Choate pointed to a row of firs. Cole spotted the palomino. When he took a step, another welcome sight caught the corner of his eye. Little Bear lay on a blanket. He went to her, knelt, and looked at her sleeping face. "How is she?"

"The same she was before. She cries, sleeps, wants food all the time, everything her hands are on she puts in her mouth."

Cole looked to him with a grin. At least it wasn't just him. Maud came into his head. He stood and walked to the palomino. His hat sat on the horn, but he was lighter on his right side. He faced Choate. "Where's my pistol?"

Choate shook his head.

"You can at least ride down there with me."

"Oh, I will," he said, pointing at the child. "Got to get her up on the horse."

Cole knew the time it would take. He turned

around and stepped into the stirrup. "Be along quick," he said, turning the palomino toward the valley. He kicked the flanks.

Slapping the reins against the flanks, he drove the horse down the hill, dodging limbs, knifing between the trees. Even at that speed, more time than he cared to lose passed. Once he was on level ground, he kept the palomino at a gallop. Despite the cool breeze, lather seeped from its hide. Through the snow the horse ran. Powder flew behind him. When he was at a crest, the wooden shack gleamed in the morning's light.

Two horses were tethered to the side of the structure. With no pistol and an empty scabbard, he couldn't defend himself if there were shooting. However, the ride had filled his blood. Caution gave way. He charged up the hill, through the trees and leapt to the porch. A boot heel splintered the latch open. The door swung wide.

A young cowhand reached for his side arm in surprise. Reflex made Cole thrust the toe of his boot at the gut, doubling the hand over. Cole snatched the pistol from the holster while another cowhand went for his own. Cole wrapped his thumb around the hammer, cocked the revolver, and fired. The shot pierced the hand's chest, slamming the other shooter against the wall to drop like an empty sack. Cole quickly pulled the hammer again and aimed it at the young man.

"Don't shoot, please," the hand yelled, his empty palms raised. "I'm only nineteen and I never shot nobody."

The plea made Cole ease the hammer to rest. When he was sure he could turn his back, he looked to the bunk. Maud lay on the lower. Her tattered dress hung in shreds. A blanket with a red stain was draped around her waist, but her bare leg dangling from the bed told him what had happened.

He went to her side. Her cheeks and brow puffed with red whelps. His own breath squeezed from his tight chest, he knelt beside her and brushed the tangled hair from her face. "Maud?" he whispered.

Her eyelids flickered. When she opened them, she attempted a smile. He couldn't manage one. "Howdy, Clay."

"Oh, Maudy. I'm sorry." He turned to the young man, who rubbed his aching belly. "What happened? What did they do to her?" he growled.

"Boss Cauley told the boys they could have fun with her. Daniel was first, then Leroy and the others." The young man paused and dipped his head. "Once some were done, she began calling them names. Some I never heard before, but the other fellows had, and they didn't take kindly to be called names by no whore. Then things got wild. Leroy, he said he would teach her a lesson, so he commenced to have his way again. But he took to slapping at her, then them others, they took to slapping at Leroy. Leroy pulled his knife. When they punched him, he fell on her. And so did the knife."

The words stopped Cole's heart for an instant. He turned back to Maud and gently lifted the blanket. The dress was soaked with blood. "Oh, Maud. No."

The young man continued. "We was told to stay

behind. Make sure she was buried. Whenever it happened."

Cole took Maud's hand. He rubbed her bloody fingers. "What's your name, boy?"

"Kenneth Harold Crump."

"Where's this Leroy?" asked Cole, still staring at Maud.

The hand's hesitation made Cole peer over his shoulder. Kenneth pointed to the other cowhand, slumped against the wall. "That was Leroy."

Cole looked again to Maud. Her strained breath wheezed and her hand quivered. Her eyelids flickered again, but she focused on Cole. "So. I guess I got myself in a mess I can't get out of."

"Be quiet. Don't talk. Save your breath. I'll get you to that sheepherder's wife. She'll doctor your wounds and have you back on your feet in no time."

She shook her head. "I'm bleeding too bad. I know it." She gulped a breath. "You'll have to go on without me."

"No. I'm not leaving you here."

"You got to get that girl home. You can't stay here. Remember, that's why we did this. Make sure you get her home. To a good family. Don't let her grow up to be nothing like me."

He clutched her hand tighter. "Maud, you listen to me. You're going to make it. I've seen worse. Why, that bullet would have had me a goner, but you pulled me through it. Got me off that mountain and into a warm bed. We can stitch you up. Fix you for that ride west."

She weakly nodded. "You think so?"

"I know it."

A grin cracked her mouth. "Will you buy me a pretty dress in San Francisco?"

Heartened by her smile, he grinned too. "The prettiest they got."

"All right," she stammered. "I'll try. But first I want to ask you something."

"I'll tell you whatever you need."

She swallowed hard. "When we was in the snow. And you kissed me. Was that truly just to see if I was breathing?"

Cole knew the answer, but it was no time for the truth. He shook his head. "No. I just wanted to know what those sweet lips tasted like."

She huffed a laugh and coughed. Then she held her breath steady. "That's what I thought." She looked deep into his eyes. "Kiss me again, Clay."

Although the act might set her off into another convulsion, he didn't consider refusing the offer. He leaned closer and touched his lips to hers. Careful not to disturb her head, he gently pressed, concluded, then leaned back.

"Still sweet?" she asked.

"Sweet as ever," he replied. "Now, we got to get you where we can get you to that sheep herder."

She touched his hand, which stopped his mind from concentrating on the task. "Let me rest awhile, Clay. I'll go with you. But first, all I need is a little sleep." She closed her eyes. This time she was more relaxed. The tension she had held his hand with faded. Her breath wheezed more quietly with each rise and fall of her chest. As her fingers drifted from his palm, he closed his eyes. It took a moment for the wheeze to stop. A glance at the blanket showed it was still. Not wanting to admit to what he knew, he inhaled deeply, then tenderly put his fingers on her eyelids to close them for the final time.

Death is never kind, no matter who it claims. For Maud, the pain she must have endured for the last hours must have been akin to what she had been through her whole life. He had to think she deserved better. He said what little prayer he knew. From what she had told him, he was likely the only one who would.

Cole rose and stood. Kenneth eyed her with a somber face. "Do I bury her now?"

Enraged over the remark, Cole swung the pistol against the kid's head, knocking him to the floor. Cole pointed it at him and cocked the hammer. "Where are they? The ones that did this."

"They went to the Jew's house," Kenneth stuttered.

Upon hearing the news, Cole strode to the door, stopping only to turn. "Don't you touch her until I get back," he said, then pointed at Leroy's corpse. "But you can burn his or give it to the varmints to gnaw on. Either way, I don't want to see it when I get back."

"Yes, sir," Kenneth said with the sincerity a private shows an officer.

Cole marched out the door. Choate sat in the saddle, holding the reins to the palomino and gelding. Little Bear sat in front of him. As he approached the horse, Cole gritted at the half-breed. "Where's my guns?"

"What you got planned?"

"I said give me guns. Or shoot me down. I ain't going to let this stand."

After a moment, Choate drew the Colt and the Mouton rifle. As he handed them to Cole, he grunted. "You go off and get shot, going to cost me a lotta money."

Cole took the weapons, shoving the rifle into the scabbard and checking the load of the pistol. "Then go with me." He mounted the palomino and turned to the north. He kicked the flanks and held the reins tight.

Afternoon glare off the snow faded. Cole whipped the reins across the horse's rump. The horse reached a gallop, but it wasn't fast enough for Cole. Maud's bruised face haunted him with each stride. Fire churned his guts.

Over each rise, the blotches of white sank away into the mud. Reining in only long enough to eye the tracks, he counted the prints of six horses. The short distance between the prints showed that the riders had taken their time. The air grew cooler as the sun dipped in the west. Clouds erupted in the eastern sky, white at the top, orange in the middle, and dark blue on the bottom. Sunlight dimmed into a shroud of gray like that of a shade over a lantern.

He spurred the horse again. There had been times before when he drove the palomino and was sure it would drop. Through trees and plain he rode, but the animal continued without breaking stride. If it did, the burning in his insides would force him to run the rest of the way.

He crested a hill. Three riders sat in saddles at the bottom of the slope. A jolt on the reins stopped the palomino, forcing it to rear on its hind legs. Once his mount was on all fours, Cole slid off the saddle and drew the Mouton rifle. The act made the riders draw their rifles. Snatching a loaded magazine from the saddlebag, he ignored the whir of lead passing. Confident their short carbines weren't accurate at this distance, he levered a cartridge into the chamber and took aim at the closest rider. When he had the man sighted, he squeezed the trigger.

Fire spat from the muzzle. When he opened both eyes, his target was off the saddle and in the mud. The remaining two returned fire. Cole pumped the action, ejecting the smoking shell, calmly sighted another victim, and fired.

With two down in the mud, he pumped a fresh cartridge into the chamber, but the last one turned his horse about and fled back to the north. Cole snugged the stock against his shoulder and squinted his left eye, concentrating on the fleeing target. Sure of the shot, he squeezed the trigger. The blast jerked the barrel up, but when he focused in the dim light, he saw the riderless horse still at a gallop.

He mounted and rode to where the bodies lay. Slowing the palomino only enough to be sure the cowhands weren't able to shoot, he took comfort when he saw the bullet holes in their chests leaking blood. Arriving at the last one, he noticed the strong stench of kerosene. He caught up with the riderless horse and saw two drums strapped to the saddles. It likely was the reason for the horse's slow gait. The purpose of the fuel was easy to determine.

He kicked the palomino's flanks again to hurry through the forest. Dodging limbs and swiping others from his path, he emerged from the bank of trees. Rain fell like the heavens were pouring an entire river on the land. The snow washed into the mud. Cole slowed his horse. Unable to pump the action and hold the reins, he drew the Colt and ambled down the slope in front of the house. Lightning streamed across the sky, illuminating the house and three men in front of it. Darkness lasted only instants between the charges, but it was enough for him to see the husband and wife on their knees.

Cole brought the palomino to stand just yards from the house. Lightning lit up the night. Rain glistened in the air. The bolt flew jaggedly behind him but didn't expire before he noticed all eyes looking his way.

"Leave them be and I'll let you live."

The announcement brought laughter. "You think you're going to shoot us?" Heb Cauley asked. "Before the three of us shoot you?" He motioned to a cowhand, who raised a Winchester. Cole cocked the hammer, aimed at arm's length at the shooter, and fired. The breeze and rain dispersed the smoke as quickly as the shooter fell.

Cole recocked the hammer. "Now there's two of you."

Heb drew his pistol. The remaining hand scrambled for his.

"Don't do it, boy," Cole ordered, pointing to the Colt.

Heb looked to the man. "Daniel, do as I say."

"You do and you'll be just as dead as the others," Cole shouted.

"Others?" was Daniel's hesitant reply.

"Three men toting kerosene you're expecting. They're late. Forever. Appears the lack of it and this rain will cancel that pretty fire you had planned. Them, that one in the mud, and not to forget Leroy and Kenneth you left in the line shack."

"You killed that boy Kenneth?" Heb shouted. "He was only nineteen."

"He'll see twenty if he does what I told him. But there is another dead body in that shack. One you left them to bury. A friend of mine, and as far as I'm concerned you're the one that left her there to die."

"Now, hold on. I never meant for that to happen. The boys only meant to have fun with her. I heard it was an accident."

"That's right," Daniel added. "It was."

Their innocent acceptance of Maud's death fired his belly. "Just like this one?" Cole said, sighting the Colt.

Heb cocked his revolver and put it to Yasha's head. "See here. If you shoot, I'm certain my finger will have enough life to pull this trigger."

The threat eased Cole's finger. "What kind of a man shoots an unarmed man in the back of the head? Are you teaching Daniel there the way you want a man to act?"

"I'm teaching him the way a man has to act when

his family and property are threatened. Squatters are like thieving coyotes. If you don't run them off, more will follow. You have to do what you have to, or they take everything you got."

Cole steadied his Colt in the dark. If he fired, he couldn't keep his aim safe from the husband. Arguing the merits of the law in the cold rain wouldn't help his concentration. "Put the gun down and ride off. If you got a family, think of them. And put the gun down."

Daniel dropped his gun.

"Pick it up, boy," ordered Heb. "Don't you turn coward on me."

"I'm sorry, Heb. But I got a family. And I want to see them tomorrow."

"You yellow kid. You low-down, yellow, snotnosed kid," Heb screamed. "I'll hunt you and run you off like these people."

"Get on your horse," Cole ordered. "Get on your horse and ride and don't turn back." Daniel ran to his mount and leaped into the saddle. He swung the horse around and rode into the dark at a gallop.

"Seems he's smarter than I thought," said Cole. "Maybe he's smarter than you. Unless you follow him and leave these folks be."

Lightning flashed. Heb pointed at Cole and fired. The muzzle blast made Cole squint. Lead sang by his ear. Pulling back the reins made the palomino rear and throw him from the saddle. When he hit the ground, the Colt fired.

Heb grabbed the woman around the neck. "You

show yourself, or I'll blow her head clean from her shoulders!"

Sofia screamed. Yasha climbed to his feet, holding his palms out, pleading for his wife's release. Heb pointed the pistol at him. Another flash drew away Heb's attention. He stepped back, waving the pistol from side to side. "Come out! Come out now!" Yasha tried to keep his wife from screaming. Heb pulled her back to the house, but lightning turned him and he fired a wild shot into the glass. "I'll kill her if you don't show yourself." He tucked the muzzle under her chin. Sofia ceased her scream.

"I'm telling you for the last time. I'll kill her unless you throw down your gun in front of me and show yourself."

Sofia's whimper made the rain's patter on the soil hard to hear. Her husband cried as well, continuing in the same circle that Heb was making in retreat. Finally he stopped. "I warned you."

Cole had the magazine in the rifle. The lever bolt was pulled back, and the chamber was loaded.

"I'm going to do it."

Cole sighted the Mouton rifle. To keep Heb from firing, he had to hit him in the head.

"Do you hear me?"

He wrapped his finger around the trigger.

Heb swung the woman from side to side, the pistol still propped under her chin. "RAINMAKER!"

Cole squeezed off the round.

Fire pierced the dark. Heb's knees buckled and slumped to the ground. His shoulders drooped. His head dove into the mud.

Tim McGuire

Sofia ran into Yasha's arms. As the two embraced, Cole rose from his knee from beside the house. He ejected the shell, then went to retrieve his horse. Tempted to console the couple from the horror they had endured, he took solace in the thought that they would survive the memory best without him.

Chapter Nineteen

Cole threw the last shovel of dirt atop the mound. He looked to the heavens. Surely the mild weather in the middle of winter was her doing to see she was buried proper. His eyes drifted to the snowcaps, the jagged peaks protruding over the blankets of white and rolling hills filled with the green of spruce and fir. He knelt beside the grave and put his hand on top of the dirt.

"Well, old girl. I hope I done you right. It ain't San Francisco, but I think you got a better view than there. I know we had our disagreements, but I can say I never traveled with a woman that could tell the stories you told. It made the miles go by a lot easier." He paused as he reflected. "I never been good at this. And I ain't going to try to get better at it now. But you were a lady, no matter who thought not. I always thought that, and I'll be telling all that I come across the story of how you saved me off that mountain. Even though I don't remember most of it." He patted the mound. "Good night, Maudy. Get the sleep you never got while you were down here. Rest easy."

He rose, rubbing the ache from his side, and slipped on his hat.

Horses approaching from the east made him draw his Colt. Two riders came over the hill. In the distance, he saw the dark skin of Choate, but the other rider was white. Cole glanced at Little Bear looped to the palomino. The reins were firmly tethered to a dormant cottonwood.

Still with the Colt drawn, he watched closely as the riders both slowed their horses. Choate had his pistol drawn, but the white man's hands and holster were empty.

"Thought you might want to meet the man who shot you," said Choate. "This here is Bill Wheeler."

Cole eyed the small man from head to toe while scratching his long whiskers. "You a bounty hunter, too?"

Wheeler nodded. "Yes, sir. That's my job."

"I caught him up in them rocks." Choate pulled a rifle and pistol from behind him and tossed them to the ground. "He was watching you digging. I guess he had one more try to take you with him."

"I was just doing my job," Wheeler said calmly. "You a wanted man, Mr. *Rainmaker*. The law wants you, and that's what me and this fellow do for a living."

"Yeah," Cole said. "But your living is my killing. I

don't take kindly to it being someone's *job*. Especially when they use it as an excuse for murder. Climb down off that horse."

After a glance at Choate, Wheeler slid off the saddle. Cole approached him, looking down on the shorter man. "He tells me you knew this woman," Cole said, pointing first at Choate, then at the grave.

"I did," Wheeler answered as if asked by a lawyer.

"You the one I heard gave her to them cowboys to do their will with her?"

"I had nothing to do with it. She came to the shack. I didn't force her there."

"No. But you damn sure left her."

"That wasn't my business."

Cole backslapped him. "Was it your business to put a bullet in my back? So she could claw her way down that mountain and drag me back?"

"She was working with me to catch you. I offered her a thousand dollars to find you so I could . . . I could . . ."

"What?"

"So I could shoot you. That's what she was, a spy for me. Why she drug you off that mountain, I don't know why. Maybe she had a heart for you. But she came that far for the thousand dollars."

The words clenched Cole's jaw. "I don't believe it."

"It's the truth. Whether you do or not, it is."

The man's sass fueled Cole's rage, which he thought he had put to rest. He stepped back and raised the Colt.

"I'm unarmed," Wheeler said, holding out his palms. "I heard you killed men, but not ones without a gun." Cole looked to the fallen pistol. Wheeler noticed Cole's attention to it and shook his head. "I got a family. A wife and daughter back in Texas. I've been gone from them for four months. And now I've got to return to them without any money made from this trip. I sure as blazes ain't going to pick a pistol and duel with a man the likes of you."

Cole lowered the Colt. Although he still had fire enough to shoot, he had to admire a man who, with a gun pointed at him, could still think straight. "Get on you horse."

Wheeler took the reins and mounted. When he sat in the saddle, he looked to Choate, then Cole. "You're going to let me go in peace. That right?"

"You going to let me live in peace?" asked Cole.

The question hung in the air before it was answered. "I got a job to do. If I have the chance, I can't let you pass."

Cole aimed and fired. The shot grazed Wheeler's leg at the knee, tearing the pants. Blood spewed, and Wheeler screamed the ache.

"That's so I hear you come up behind me." Wheeler swung his horse around and slapped its rear. Cole watched the Texas bounty hunter gallop south, then looked to Choate, who appeared to have a slight grin. "You ain't much better." The remark wiped off the grin, and Choate steered the revolver at Cole. "No need for that. I gave you my word," said Cole as he tucked the Colt into the holster.

He went to the palomino and stepped into the stirrup. "But I got to finish this, as I said. Remember, you promised I could."

"That was before I saw you handle that gun so easy."

Cole looked to the mountains in the west. "Won't do me much good up there." He pulled himself into the saddle, ever careful not to jostle the girl. "You going to follow me?"

Choate nodded. "Can't afford not." The two laughed, and nudged their mounts.

The afternoon became night. The men sat around the fire, but they said little except to correct each other's handling of the child. Cole showed Choate how Little Bear would eat meat. Choate told him she was too young to chew the thick chunks. However, when she finished each one, Cole took pride. Later in the night, he was the one up with her when she choked and coughed. When she breathed easy again, Cole got what little shut-eye he could before the next dawn.

The following day was clear. The farther past the tree line they traversed, the colder the wind blew. Choate warned that it was nature's warning not to trespass. Cole agreed, but the journey over the mountain was the shortest. Another six weeks would be needed to go around the peaks. Rivers would be full from spring runoff and impossible to cross. The cold actually made for easier passage until they reached the summit still days away.

The men's third morning together, Cole was tightening the cinch when a thought occurred to him as he stared at the near apex. "Do you know where this 'Wind in the River' is?"

"Ain't never heard of such a place. Why?"

"That's where the elder of the tribe said she's from."

"You said it was the Wallowa Valley." Choate's tone grew loud.

"That's where I thought he said. A valley where the wind is in the river."

Choate stood stern-faced. Then a grin broke over his face. "I thought you sounded wrong when you mumbled the words," he said as he mounted.

Cole did the same. "What are you talking about?"

"The way that squaw said the words to you. It wasn't about no place. It was that girl's name. 'Wind in the River.' "

Startled by the thought, Cole looked around to Choate. "No. Can't be."

"My tribe's been living next to the Nez Perce since the days long before any white man set foot on these hills. I lived all about these peoples. There is no place named that. It must be the name the girl was given by her mother. Most tribes wait until the child is old enough to understand what a name is supposed to mean. I guess, when she was dying, she spoke the name she had chose for her baby."

Cole peered down at Little Bear. She, in turn, looked up at him. Those brown eyes that focused on him in wonder were now a bit nearer to his than when he first started the journey. The idea that he had been looking for a land that didn't exist for five months rubbed him raw. No matter what Choate said, the name he'd repeated in his head during that time was his name for the girl. He wasn't about to try to get used to another.

The daylight dimmed as they continued up the slope. Wind drove the snow into their faces. Cole had slipped Little Bear into the sack next to his chest for warmth, but the snow's bite still wore away at his cheeks and nose worse than any sandstorm. They rode at an angle to the incline. They found a pass, but once through, they saw the next snow-covered valley waiting on them.

By the end of the week, Cole had a cough. Each wheeze felt like a stab in the back. He kept his coat wrapped tightly around his neck. The scarf would keep the freeze from getting to Little Bear, as well as the cough he feared he would spread. If a sick child in the cold didn't mean a certain death, a sick child at ten thousand feet and a hundred miles from the next house surely did.

The following day they approached the last peak. Clouds set in; at first they were thin and at the top of the sky, but as the morning passed, they became thicker and lower. The horses, too, were weak. All the oats brought for the trip were gone. The grass visible above the snow cover was sparse, and the effect on the palomino's stamina after two weeks could be felt.

The only reason Cole knew there was any air was its blasting against his face. He would inhale as deeply as possible, but what he took in didn't satisfy his lungs. When he lost his cough, Choate found it. The big man wheezed and convulsed more the higher they went. Camp was as short as they could make it. The firewood they had brought was soon exhausted. Movement meant warmth; a third straight day of clouds told them the sun couldn't be relied on. Little Bear's bones stretched the skin of her belly. Her whining gnawed at his own gut, even after he had given her all the food he could spare. When they huddled in the bedroll, he cranked the music box. The tune lasted long enough to put her to sleep. He napped, waking only to nudge her and be sure she was alive.

A sheer gale from the top put Cole afoot. One step at a time was all he managed. His coat wrapped around his neck, his scarf stuffed around his throat, and his hat snugged tight over his brow, he trudged through the thick snow. The gusts blew the powder in his face. He glanced behind. Choate and the horses were gone. The cascade of white was all he could see. He gave thought to finding him, but he knew he didn't have the strength, so he resumed the climb.

He inhaled deeply, faster and faster. The more he did, his fatigue increased. He took another step. He couldn't remember the last one he took.

Slowly his knees bent. No matter what his mind told him, his body wouldn't go on. He rationalized that it would take only minutes to rest. The strength he could muster allowed him to turn on his knees to face away from the wind. His weight sank his backside into the snow. His arms folded, he couldn't move his fingers from the coat sleeves. Frozen in place, he couldn't feel them. Likely, they were frostbit and would have to be amputated. Why did he need fingers? He'd learn to live without them.

Without thought, he sagged on his side. His nose was numb to the cold. It was welcome relief. As

Maud had complained, there was never enough sleep to be gained. He would wait out the blizzard. His eyelids flickered. His conscience screamed for action, to leave, to move, but his will was frozen. The white faded darker and became black.

Green grass surrounded him. Birds flew overhead in pairs, carrying twigs for a spring nest. His ma's call for breakfast had to be heeded. He ran barefoot through the grass, past the fence and up the porch. When he arrived, his pa told him she was dead and that he had to come with him off to the war. Burnt powder seared its stench into his nostrils. Drill, drill, every day. Shot and shell bursts. Blood stained the grass. Bodies lay in the field. Some with blue, some with gray. He took a shot at a reb. His father fell from the saddle. An officer removed his hat, sternly peering down, speaking the words, "You killed him."

The sergeant yelled his name. He fell into ranks. More renegades needed to be shot. Charges and retreats. More blood on the field. Resignation. A new, different life. Jenks. Hickok. Cattle bawling all during the night. Polly. Soft white skin, long brown hair, supple bosom. Living like man and wife. They would be married. His baby will swell her belly. Fire. Flames. House ablaze. Mourners pass in the rain. Whiskey. Whiskey. Whiskey.

Saloons. Whores. Fights and shooting. Fast with the draw. Men dead in the street. "It was self-defense, but leave town." Troopers. George Armstrong Custer. A new pistol. A .45 Colt with smooth action and good balance. More renegades. Sitting Bull. Lakota and Cheyenne. Sam Grant sent a mes-

sage; stop the carnage, talk to Sitting Bull. Capture at night. Tied to a tree. Custer charges in the morning. Troopers slaughtered in retreat. "The Rainmaker is a traitor."

Colorado summer. Fair white woman with coal-black hair. Mrs. Rhodes. Claire. Ambush. Danger Ridge. Ann Hayes. Noah's tears. "I'll never be alone." Texas. Red hair and hot sand. Gold. Comanches. Mexicans. A blast and a cave collapses into dust. Miles Perry bleeding from gunshots. It's time to end it. Head north, through Indian territory to Chicago city. Geese flying.

His eyes flickered. A bleary view of white. He blinked again. Half the white turned blue. He blinked once more. Blue of the sky filtered into his view. The white peak above him showed blue. The storm had passed. Sunlight glistened off the snow. One more blink to keep from dreaming, but it was still there. The vision drew him, pumping blood into his limbs. He rose from his side and took a staggered step. Claiming a wobbly balance, he slogged through the powder. He inhaled through his nose, the air now filling his lungs. As the apex neared, he ran, lifting his knees as high as possible. With each stride more blue stretched farther behind the peak. The hat flew off from the breeze shooting over the edge. He stopped and gazed at the valley below.

A river wound around sheer mountains sloped to its edge. It cascaded through the center of the valley surrounded by green trees and lush grasses. He scanned to the left and right. Mountains lined one after another as if in parade. All of them guided the wind, which centered on this valley.

He sank to his knees and opened his mouth, gulping the air. "Do you see it?" he asked in the breeze. "Do you see it?" He peeked at his buttoned coat. His gnarled fingers bobbed at the heavy buttons, pushing one by one through the holes. The white sack sat with the lip closed. He split the crease and opened the sack wide. Little Bear's purple cheeks and closed eyes didn't stop him from asking again, "Don't you see it?" He laced another button free, opening his coat and pulling the sack agape, but the child didn't move.

He stopped breathing. His numb fingers against her skin told him nothing. He lifted her from the sack, but her body still conformed to the tight fit. He fingered her mouth open; it always made her cry. Her eyes stay closed.

"No," he muttered. "No. You can't be! Now that we're there. We made it!"

The little body didn't move.

"NOOO!" he screamed, the echo returning to ring in his ears. He looked to heavens. "Not her! Not now! Take me, you bastard! Not her!"

He shivered for the first time. Holding her in a shaking embrace, her clutched her to his chest and squeezed. "Why would you do this to this child?" he asked of the wind.

He sat still, holding the girl. Finally, his senses convinced him what he wouldn't admit. This child that had been so much grief the last six months of his life was all he wanted. Just to have her move and laugh, or cry. He squeezed his eyes shut and prayed. Why did this child have to die?

Slowly, he cradled her in his arms. Leaning carefully, he pressed his lips to Little Bear's. He couldn't release them. She had been through the worst of it, and she wasn't there to enjoy what she had come so far for.

Her lips moved. Another movement forced him to release the kiss. He squeezed his breath in fear, like a candle he didn't want to extinguish. The girl's eyelids flickered. Her nostrils flared. Her fingers wiggled, then her arms stretched. Her mouth opened for a yawn and a huff of breath came from her lungs. Her eyes cringed, and she wailed her beautiful cry.

He clutched her to his chest, and she struggled against his tight hold as always. He took another breath, then inhaled deeply and peeked to the heavens. Miracles weren't something he often asked for, but if one was to be granted, this was the one he would ask for. As long as he lived, he knew he was square with those above.

Hat in place, he took his time getting to his feet. After two startling discoveries, he wasn't anxious for further ones. Using gravity for energy, he simply kept his legs moving while listening to the girl's whining. There was no prettier music. He didn't comfort her. He wanted to listen to it all day.

Snow withered as he came past pine and fir. Warm air gushed in his face. With each breath, he could feel more life in his hands and arms, but his fingers still ached. At least they weren't numb. The afternoon had set in. As he neared the river's edge, he spotted tin cans strewn on the bank. He walked down the shore. He stopped upon seeing a broken wooden signpost:

Whitman's Tannery

He rubbed his hairy chin. Had he come this far to find another white man's settlement? Farther down the shore, a footbridge crossed the river. He walked across the heavy boards to the far side. When he stepped onto a grated road, it sounded like shots fired in the air. The shots of whites shooting Indians. He took the road, the sun still high in the west. As he walked, the road passed tree stumps, smooth from a saw edge. Not far from them a fence row stood, the wood an aged brown.

Wheel ruts lined a path farther up the road. He stared at the towering peaks high above. They looked like stern fathers, disgruntled at the scene children had left below. When he looked farther, other roads splintered from the one he walked. He squinted in the distance. The other roads led up to the hills. Mine shafts had been blown from the sides. He stopped to slowly gaze again, only now smoke plumes were easily seen drifting from rooftops.

The sun hid behind the mountains. He made his way to a house. A woman swept her porch. "Excuse me, ma'am. I'm needing to ask a favor." She appeared puzzled and a bit in fear. After a few moments she stepped off the porch and came within earshot. "Where is the Wallowa Valley?"

"You're here," she answered. "Standing right in the center."

Her words were a knife's edge jabbed into his heart. He didn't want to show disrespect for her kindness to answer. "I have a Nez Perce girl. I've come from . . . well . . . a long way. I was returning her to her family. Her people. Where are they?"

The question again put a puzzled look on her face. "I've heard of them. But I've never seen one," she said as she peeked at Little Bear sitting on his arm. "She's cute, though. For an Indian." The woman looked to Cole. "I think there is a reservation north of here. I can't be sure. I could ask my husband. He is inside."

"Don't bother, ma'am," Cole replied, tipping his hat. "You've told me what I needed to know. I thank you for your kindness." He turned away and viewed the mountains he was atop at the beginning of the day. He agreed then that he wouldn't ask for further miracles. But he needed a favor. "One more thing, if you don't mind me asking. How can a fellow get a meal for himself and a child? And maybe passage back across them mountains?"

She smiled and opened her gate. "You look like a Christian. I have supper cooking. Don't mind setting another plate for a weary traveler. There's a train brings supplies to the mine. You might find passage on it, Mr. . . . ?"

"Call me Clay, ma'am," he said as he tipped his hat and stepped past the gate. "My name is Clay. And this one, she's just a little bear. Call her . . .

Chapter Twenty

When he put her in the loop, Little Bear turned to Cole. Those brown eyes stabbed into his heart. He darted his away from them. Although he knew better, the notion of watching her grow a little more had appealed to him as their trip continued. The time had come.

Choate had loaded supplies onto his roan. Cole kept watching him until their eyes met. Choate paused, his eyes glancing at the child, then back at Cole.

"Are you going to do it?"

With a lick of his lips, Cole nodded. "Yeah. I've let this go on too long. It ain't good for her, and it sure as hell ain't doing me any favors."

"Have you thought how?"

"Oh, I thought about it, but it ain't going to easy any way I go about it."

Choate finished tying the last hank, then stepped around the horse. "How long?"

"It'll take me the day." Cole peeked at Little Bear. "Most of it, anyway." He huffed a breath. "You head back to Helena. I'll meet you there by the end of the week if I don't catch up to you first." As Choate looked him in the eye, Cole knew what was on his mind. "I ain't going back on what I said. I need you to trust me." He offered his hand. Choate peeked to the hand, slowly accepting it.

"Don't let yourself get shot."

Cole smirked and nodded. "I've tried to make that a habit."

"Didn't help you before."

"Can't help who's aiming at my back," he said as he stepped into the stirrup.

Choate watched, his face still as stiff as stone. "But you know there'll be more that will. I wouldn't like it if someone were to take you down."

As Cole settled into the saddle, he pushed back the brim of his hat. "Well, I'll be mighty careful. I'd hate to cost you that money. I know how much it means to you, it being worth my life and all."

Still without a crease on his cheeks, Choate offered his hand. The gesture surprised Cole. After a moment, he reached down and grasped the black hand.

"Do what you got to do," said Choate.

With a nod, Cole let out a long breath. It was more than just a handshake. It was a trust between the men, one Cole knew wasn't easily afforded to him.

The small gleam in the half-breed's eyes made it clear the concern wasn't all for the money. "I'm beholden to you." Cole turned the palomino's head to the south. "I'll meet you in Helena."

Once in the trees, he kept his eyes to the front. The easy excuse was that he had to be wary of hanging branches. He had never been comfortable with partings, but thinking of that was simpler than letting his head wonder whether Choate still stood, or whether there may be one more muzzle pointed at his back. The deeper into the thick growth he went without a sound from behind, the more his mind eased.

Clear of the trees, he steered the horse through the valley. Despite the green of the winter grass, snow still covered the surrounding mountains. In the afternoon, he allowed himself and the horse a rest. Removing Little Bear from the loop was the same task it had been all along. Her eyes were more fixed on the first object she saw and never paid much attention to him.

As he sat nibbling the last of the jerky, he watched her get used to her legs. Like a new foal, she charged in one direction, then the opposite, picking up a stick, a stone, occasionally giving each a lick just on the chance she had found something worth chewing. When she fell, he knew enough to allow her to regain her stance on her own. Six months had taught him not to help her too much. He had once been told that the young learned more than grown folks gave them credit for, and he realized as she grew older she would need to fend for herself. She would need that reliance.

When he glimpsed the sun, he noticed it was already heading to the west. Less than four hours of light remained. He rose, wiping his hands on his pants, and went to fetch her. However, just as before, she had other ideas. Like a chicken that has seen an ax, she scampered away from him. First to the left, then the right, he chased her with meek effort, he himself not ready to continue with the rest of the day's duties. The game of chase delighted her, giggles bubbling from her cheeks, until finally he snatched her off the grass and rolled the small body into his arms. After an instant, he realized he was giggling too.

Remounted, he nudged the palomino, resuming the ride south. As he passed by each grove of trees, he recalled the events of the journey. It had changed him just a mite, despite how much he tried to convince himself it had not. This little girl whom no one wanted, standing no higher than the top of his boot, had worn her way into his heart.

When he had first looked into the mother's eyes, he had wanted nothing to do with the child either. However, the love the mother held burned into his own soul. The same regret for his quick action with his gun, he now held for what he had soon to complete. No matter what wild idea crept into the back of his mind, the only thing to do was the right thing. With another breath and a long exhale, he pulled up on the reins. Below in the valley was the house.

He slowly steered the palomino down the slope, swiping away the low branches from his path and the little girl's head. Once clear of the forest, he approached the house. Smoke bellowed from the stovepipe propped out of the roof. The sheep complained as he drove the horse through the center of the flock. Not wanting to cause alarm, he pulled up the horse well in front of the porch. It took a few moments before the woman opened the door and stuck out her head.

"Clay?" Her voice was laced with surprise and disbelief.

He tipped his hat. "Afternoon, ma'am." Although he knew what he needed to say, the words caught in his throat. He grunted it clear and spat them out. "I come to ask for a favor."

She slowly stepped out from the door, attempting to improve her appearance for company. Her hair was fixed in a bun atop her head, her blouse was buttoned tight at the collar, her sleeves were rolled to the elbow. "What is it you need?"

With the invitation to get on with it, he dismounted and led the palomino closer. "I thought you might be able to take care of something for me." As he neared, the woman's focus crept slowly over his shoulder. He knew she had sighted the child, so he took Little Bear from the loop. For the last time, he clutched her close to his chest. However, he knew the best way to pass her on wasn't to show much affection. "Would you be willing to see to this child?" The woman's eyes widened, but he didn't see the endearing reaction to the request he had expected. It may have been too much too soon. "Just for a while? Until she could be claimed proper by the Indian Affairs folks."

Seeming a bit stunned, the woman took a step back, like a snake coiling from an intruder. Cole caught sight of a man emerging from the side of the house. He smiled and waved. "Good to see you."

"Afternoon," Cole replied.

His cheeks retracted into an expression of wondering interest. "Who have you got there?"

"An Indian stray. Likely an orphan, I figure."

"Yasha," the woman snapped. "He wants to leave it here." She sounded as if Cole held a pistol aimed at her. Although her husband approached without reservation, the woman still stood firm on the porch. If she didn't take to the idea of keeping the child, there wasn't much point in staying. Little Bear provided the needed incentive. As was the child's custom since she had learned to walk, she leaned out from Cole's grasp. In an instant, he realized that he hadn't offered one crucial thing. As the girl twisted against his chest, he didn't stop her, allowing her to slump forward with only his forearm pinned against the tiny waist to keep her from spilling to the ground. The maternal instinct he had counted on boiled in the woman's face upon sight of the child dangling headfirst.

"You can't hold a baby like a sack of flour," she shouted.

"No?" Cole's innocent accent did the trick. She scurried off the porch, arms outstretched.

"Here, give him to me," she said, quickly gripping Little Bear under each arm. The skill of a mother was quickly evident.

"Where did you find him?"

Cole smirked. "It's a she."

"A girl?" the woman replied with some relief at the news.

"Yes, ma'am. As little as I know, that much I can attest to." Cole looked to Yasha. There were still some details to provide, and just as he had through most of the ordeal, Cole found he'd have to make most of them up. "Anyway, I found her on the trail. Seems she's Nez Perce. They used to surround these parts. Likely she got separated from her ma. I thought the decent thing to do was to bring her here. At least she could have a roof over her head."

"But the mother . . . " said the woman. "This is her baby. She must be worried sick."

"Well," Cole said, trying to think of an easy answer. None came to mind. "You're probably right about that. But, knowing squaws, like I think I might have known this one's ma, I can't help think she can take comfort hoping that good folks such as yourselves would find her and take care of her until she's found." The mumbling explanation didn't even convince himself. However, he knew that every second the child was in the woman's arms, the less convincing he would have to be.

"I wonder what her name is," Yasha thought aloud.

"Oh, she don't have no name. Not a regular one, at least."

Yasha curled his lip. "How could you know that?"

Cole held his breath, ready to spit out the reason, except his tongue couldn't mold one. "I got a gut feeling about it," he answered with a nod of false confidence. Keeping his eyes away from Yasha's for fear of being accused of lying, he looked into Little Bear's.

Suddenly the reason he had taken pains to contrive came out of him as easy as breath. "I found her near a place they call 'wind in the river.' At least that's what a part Crow Indian told me. I think it's true." He then peered up at the man and woman. "Maybe you can make a name out of that."

The couple looked at the child. Occasionally, the woman bounced the child, but Little Bear, never one to show appreciation, kept her eyes on all but the two would-be parents. Finally the young one's stare fixed on Cole. An instant later, she reached out for him.

"I think she likes you," Yasha said.

"Oh, she don't mean nothing to me," Cole blurted. He had to inhale just to assume a different attitude. "She's been nothing but an orn'ry runt since I picked her up. You'd be doing her and me a big favor by taking her off my hands. The last thing I need is a baby to fend for."

"What about your wife?" asked Sofia.

"Yes," Yasha added. "Does she know you found a baby? Maybe she would like to play mama?"

Cole shook his head. "She's . . ." His pause seemed awkward, but he didn't mind. The truth wasn't pleasant. For this couple, their loss was enough. If he let all the story be known, there would likely be more questions about how he and Maud became a pair. It would further sully both of their reputations in these married folks' eyes. To fret over Maud wouldn't be fair. Yet the proposal brought to mind the soiled dove's face and his last moments with her. "She's already left for our new home. I gave her a kiss good-bye just days ago. It will likely be a long time before I see her again."

"You could take the baby with you," suggested Yasha, only to receive his wife's glaring disapproval.

"Yasha, don't say such a foolish thing. You can't take a baby a long way."

Cole couldn't help but grin. "That's the truth. I can't imagine what bigger fool I'd be if I were to try and take her across the country." He wiped the grin from his face and tried to pose as sincerely as possible. "I doubt I'd ever make it."

Little Bear grabbed Sofia's blouse, turning her head to rest on the woman's shoulder. The action relaxed Sofia's cheeks, ever easing her into the role of mother, at least in Cole's mind. The best plan was to leave them all alone and let nature take its course.

He offered his hand to Yasha, and it was quickly accepted. "I need to go. I have a lot of ground to cover. I thank you again for relieving me of this burden. I know you two will take awful good care of her. I wouldn't feel right about leaving her with any other folks except such as yourself." His babble didn't slow his feet. "I'll let it be known she is here to the Indian Affairs people at the first army post I come across, so you won't be saddled with her."

While retreating toward the palomino, he noticed the fond gaze Sofia now bestowed on the child.

"Probably needs a good bath, she does," Cole said as he turned with a wave and gripped the reins. As he was about to step up into the saddle, an unfamiliar whine broke the air. Partly stunned, he glanced over his shoulder to see Little Bear jutting from Sofia's arms, her little fingers extending toward him.

Cole's arms lost strength. He couldn't pull himself up. Never had she cried so loud. His breath shortened. Never had the girl displayed such need. With both boots on the ground, he took a step toward the child, but then his better sense nailed his feet to the dirt.

Nostrils flared, eyes watering, Little Bear lunged toward him as far as Sofia would allow her.

"I think she wants to go with you," Yasha said.

"She can't go with me," Cole answered, his resolve wavering but still in place. A presence from behind nudged his instinct. "I know what she wants." He turned and went to the saddlebag, he drew the brass music box, and went back to the child. He cranked the lever, and the tune spilled fast out of the box; it stopped the child's wailing and distracted her attention to the object. "She likes to hear it at night. Puts her to sleep quick."

He held the box out. Little Bear took it, giving him a last look before fixing her eyes on the box. Within moments, the child balled her hand and rubbed her eyes.

"You are right," said Yasha. "She seems sleepy now."

"Told you so," said Cole in a hushed breath. "It always does the trick." While the girl focused on the music box, Cole stepped backward, then twisted about as if he were a thief. He headed for the palomino. Again, preparing to mount, he was stopped by Yasha's words.

"I will tell her about you."

Once more, Cole faced him. He read in the man's face the whole truth. It was as if all the storying had been for only Cole's benefit. He saw in Yasha's eyes a contented grin.

"I'd like that."

Cole put his boot through the stirrup and pulled himself atop the horse. A glimpse of Little Bear still peering at the music box was all he could afford. As he swung the palomino's head, he caught sight of the husband and wife huddled together with a new hope, a new life.

Before anything could stop him, he kicked the horse's flanks, scattering the sheep in his wake. At a gallop, he quickly ducked into the seclusion of the trees. A lash against hide made the mount stride up the incline. He didn't relent on the spurs until he was confident he was out of sight.

At the crest of the hill, he slowed the horse, in part for its benefit. Although Helena awaited him, he was in no hurry to arrive.

He had never liked farewells, and looking back only made it worse. Still he kept the reins slackened, kept the spurs at rest, and the palomino's amble became a slow walk. Six months he had given to that child. He pulled the reins to stop the palomino. A beckoning cry came from over his shoulder. Pride be damned.

Smoke plumed from the stovepipe. The two figures walked into their home. His eyes drifted to the west. Orange sky meant peace. A hopeful omen for them that needed it in the land with the wind in the river.

GOLD
OF
CORTES
TIM McGUIRE

Amid the dust and desolation of southwest Texas lies a secret that has lasted for centuries—the hidden treasure of Aztec artifacts hoarded by Hernan Cortes. When Clay Cole finds English lord Nigel Apperson and Dr. Jane Reeves wandering the Texas desert, searching for the mythical prize, he agrees to sign on as their scout. Together they confront Texas Rangers, desperadoes, and the relentless Major Miles Perry, whose driving desire is to court-martial Cole for treason at Little Big Horn—treason Cole never committed. All that stands between them and the fortune of a lifetime is a Mexican revolutionary and renegade Comanches!

___4729-2 $4.50 US/$5.50 CAN

Dorchester Publishing Co., Inc.
P.O. Box 6640
Wayne, PA 19087-8640

Please add $1.75 for shipping and handling for the first book and $.50 for each book thereafter. NY, NYC, and PA residents, please add appropriate sales tax. No cash, stamps, or C.O.D.s. All orders shipped within 6 weeks via postal service book rate. Canadian orders require $2.00 extra postage and must be paid in U.S. dollars through a U.S. banking facility.

Name_____
Address_____
City_____ State_____ Zip_____
I have enclosed $_____ in payment for the checked book(s).
Payment <u>must</u> accompany all orders. ❑ Please send a free catalog.

DANGER RIDGE
TIM McGUIRE

Clay Cole is a man with a shadowy past. Most folks know he is good with a gun, but that is all they know. Very few know the Army is out to court-martial him for something he didn't do. And even fewer know he has accepted a job to lead a young bride along a dangerous trail to meet her husband. But the men who do know it are aiming to kill him and the woman along the trail. And the easiest place to do that is the treacherous sort few men make it through—the place the Westerners call danger ridge.

___4410-2 $4.50 US/$5.50 CAN

Dorchester Publishing Co., Inc.
P.O. Box 6640
Wayne, PA 19087-8640

Please add $1.75 for shipping and handling for the first book and $.50 for each book thereafter. NY, NYC, and PA residents, please add appropriate sales tax. No cash, stamps, or C.O.D.s. All orders shipped within 6 weeks via postal service book rate. Canadian orders require $2.00 extra postage and must be paid in U.S. dollars through a U.S. banking facility.

Name_____
Address_____
City_____State_____Zip_____
I have enclosed $_____ in payment for the checked book(s).
Payment <u>must</u> accompany all orders. ❑ Please send a free catalog.
    CHECK OUT OUR WEBSITE! www.dorchesterpub.com

MIRACLE
OF THE
JACAL
ROBERT J. RANDISI

Elfego Baca is a young lawman—but he already has a reputation. He is known to be good with a gun. Very good. And he is known to never back down, especially if he is fighting for something he believes in. This reputation has spread far and wide throughout his home territory of New Mexico. Sometimes it works in his favor, sometimes it works against him. But there will come a day when his reputation will not only be tested, but expanded—a day when young Elfego will have to prove just how good with a gun he really is . . . and how brave. It will be a day when he will have to do the impossible and live through it. For a long time afterward, people will still be talking about the miracle of the *jacal*.

___4923-6 $4.99 US/$5.99 CAN

Dorchester Publishing Co., Inc.
P.O. Box 6640
Wayne, PA 19087-8640

Please add $2.50 for shipping and handling for the first book and $.75 for each book thereafter. NY and PA residents, please add appropriate sales tax. No cash, stamps, or C.O.D.s. All orders shipped within 6 weeks via postal service book rate.
Canadian orders require $2.00 extra postage and must be paid in U.S. dollars through a U.S. banking facility.

Name_____
Address_____
City_____ State_____ Zip_____
I have enclosed $_____ in payment for the checked book(s).
Payment <u>must</u> accompany all orders. ☐Please send a free catalog.
       CHECK OUT OUR WEBSITE! www.dorchesterpub.com

Graciela of the Border

John Duncklee

Jeff Collins knows horses. He works as a horse trainer on the Sierra Diablo ranch in Arizona, and he is mighty good at it. But he wants more. He's dreamed for years of having his own ranch. He sees his chance when he wins a blue roan in a high-stakes poker game. This isn't just any roan; it is carrying the foal of a great racehorse, and that foal is Jeff's ticket to his dreams. When that roan is stolen and herded along with other horses toward the Mexican border, Jeff knows where he has to go. But he doesn't know what will be waiting for him when he gets there. The border is a dangerous place, a harsh land filled with bandits and outlaws—and the woman who will change his life . . . Graciela of the border.

__4809-4 $4.99 US/$5.99 CAN

Dorchester Publishing Co., Inc.
P.O. Box 6640
Wayne, PA 19087-8640

Genevieve of TOMBSTONE

John Duncklee

Tombstone in the 1880's is the toughest town in the West, and it takes a special kind of grit just to survive there. Ask the Earps or the Clantons. But among the gunslingers and lawmen, among the ranchers and rustlers, there is Genevieve, a woman with the spirit, toughness—and heart—the town demands. Whether she is working in a fancy house or running her own cattle ranch, Genevieve will not only survive, she will triumph. She is a woman who will never surrender, never give in—and one that no reader will ever forget.

___4628-8 $4.99 US/$5.99 CAN

Dorchester Publishing Co., Inc.
P.O. Box 6640
Wayne, PA 19087-8640

Please add $1.75 for shipping and handling for the first book and $.50 for each book thereafter. NY, NYC, and PA residents, please add appropriate sales tax. No cash, stamps, or C.O.D.s. All orders shipped within 6 weeks via postal service book rate. Canadian orders require $2.00 extra postage and must be paid in U.S. dollars through a U.S. banking facility.

Name_____
Address_____
City_____State_____Zip_____
I have enclosed $_____ in payment for the checked book(s).
Payment <u>must</u> accompany all orders. ❑ Please send a free catalog.
        CHECK OUT OUR WEBSITE! www.dorchesterpub.com